Pulchra Arcanum

A DOMUM CHRONICLES NOVEL

MANDY TREMELLING

Domum Chronicles Book One

Copyright © 2025 by Mandy Tremelling

All rights reserved.

ISBN 979-8-9988380-0-2

CONTENTS

SALUS

CAMELOT

DOMUM

This story is dedicated to my own Margaret, my grandmother. She has always been one of my biggest supporters and so important in my life. In the same vein, I am also dedicating this story to my late grandmother, Nona, and my grandfathers Darwin, Richard, and Giles. Finally, my grandparents through marriage—Debbie, Donald, and Birgit. You have all touched my life and encouraged my dreams in so many ways. You led me on my journey of success. Thank you.

Playlist

"You Are My Sunshine" - Jasmine Thompson
"Warrior" - Beth Crowley
"Make Me Like You" - Tore
"Homeland" - Celtic Woman
"Never Getting Over You" - Colbie Caillat
"Don't Give Up on Me" - Andy Grammer
"Wild Horses" - Grace Power
"Love We Are We Love" - The Sea The Sea

PART I

PART 1

CHAPTER ONE

*They always say that magic comes with a price,
but they never tell you what it is; and like a fool,
like a mere human, you will think that you can
pay it.*

M EGARA WATCHED AS THE sunlight peeked through the crack in the wall next to her head. She heard Camelot begin to wake. The birds were calling out to each other, the people waking their children to begin the day's work. The cold air made her skin tingle as she stretched under the threadbare blanket. She rolled on the floor for more space to stretch her arms out above her head. Her toes brushed the dirt wall as she did so. She could smell the chamber pot in the corner and wrinkled her nose.

The greeting thud on her door told Megara that Merlin was up and meeting the day. He pounded on the cellar door once more and hissed through the crack, "Meggy! Are you awake?" He didn't dare speak too loudly. If anyone were walking past the small home, they might believe he'd finally gone mad now that he was talking to himself. That would not be good.

Megara smiled and sat up, stretching her arms above her head. "Yes, Father, I'm awake."

"Not too loud, Meggy!" Merlin was a little grumpy, as always, when he opened the door and exchanged a bag of food and a new book for the chamber pot. He returned soon after with the empty pot. His shoulder-length dark hair appeared wavy, as if he had washed it. His beard was trimmed close to his skin. Though it was early in the morning, his eyes looked tired. "I'll be home a little late tonight. Don't wait up."

"Are we not going to discuss what I've learned?" Megara was surprised. They never missed an evening together.

Merlin sighed. "All right. I'll still be home late, though. You'd better make that food last."

The cellar door closed softly, and she heard the heavy bags being moved to cover it. That was key—no one could know there was any significance to the small room. If they knew, they might come looking. And if they came looking, they might find Megara.

Megara lay back in the dirt with her bag of food, pulling apples from the sack and setting them on her blanket. She watched as ants moved through the dirt, pulling pieces of hay or grain with them as they went. She smiled at them. They worked hard to eat, like she did. If she could find something in her reading that stumped Merlin, he'd bring her some sweets from Camelot. She hadn't managed it often, but she tried every day.

For as long as she could remember, she and her father had lived in Camelot under these same rules. Megara was never allowed outside—it was too dangerous for Merlin if she were discovered. The people of Camelot did not know she existed—they did not know about the magic Merlin had Megara performing right under their noses. Her whole life, she had played her part well, though Merlin never really said it, and she knew he appreciated her efforts—aside from those few dark times when Megara was younger, when she'd made some mistakes that almost gave them away.

She remembered one time when she was eight years old. Merlin used to lock her in the cellar with an actual lock and key so she wouldn't be tempted to leave the house. One day he had forgotten to lock the door. She had left her cellar and run to the front door and thrown it open. Right outside the house, there was a cluster of men in armor. They'd seen the door open and faced her. "Hi!" Megara said. "My name is—"

Merlin had come running past them and stood beside her, gripping her shoulder and smiling at the men. "This is Morgana," he'd said. "I asked her to clean my house for me today. Isn't she a friendly thing?"

The men had all laughed. Merlin pulled Megara inside. That night, after the sun had gone down and the noises outside had quieted, Merlin had pulled Megara from the cellar. He punished her by spilling hot oil on the floor and making her scrub it clean. He spilled the dirty water three times and made her scrub the floor each time before he allowed her to eat and go to bed.

Megara rolled onto her back and gazed at the roof of the cellar. Her earliest memory was sitting on Merlin's knee by the fire. She couldn't remember how old she had been, but she had outgrown his knee around the time of the incident when she was eight. She knew it was before she learned to read because he'd been reading to her, and he hadn't done that since she had learned for herself. But in her memory, Merlin told her so many wonderful stories. Knights and dragons, saviors and villains. "Now, Meggy," he used to say, "sometimes people don't know they need saving. Just like the people of Camelot. You're going to save them, though, Meggy. When you're bigger and stronger, you're going to show them a higher way of living."

A higher way of living. He always used to say that before bed.

Megara smirked now as she watched the ants get interrupted by the mouse climbing through the crack in the wall. The mouse sniffed at the ants before taking their pieces of corn away from them and eating them himself.

A higher way of living.

Megara lost herself in her musings again. Once upon a time, she had slept with Merlin at night because the noises outside the cellar were scary. She had imagined all sorts of dangers and people calling her name. He'd chuckle and hold her close and whisper, "Don't worry, my Meggy. When you're big and strong, those people will be scared of you! They won't be able to frighten you anymore. No one will come and take you away from me."

Megara couldn't wait for the day, whenever it was, that she'd be bigger and stronger. She hoped it was soon. She hoped, with all her heart, that someday soon Merlin would think she was ready to go about the world with him, to heal the sick and offer fantastic insights to the apathetic people of Camelot.

But for now, Megara sighed and sat up on her bed, biting into one of her apples and opening the cover of her new book. Yesterday's book had been rather boring. It had been all about poultice healing and the different herbs that one could find in the forest. Why would she need that? She lived in Camelot, with Merlin of all people. She'd never need to heal herself, and when Merlin allowed her into the world, she wouldn't need herbs to heal others. She hoped today's reading would be more productive.

She opened the heavy leather cover, and the first words that caught her attention were in Latin, a language she'd been learning for at least half her life. She often used her studies of the language as a distraction from the boring studies of everything else Merlin gave her. This book was titled *Lingua Mortuorum*—"The Tongue of the Dead."

Megara almost bit her cheek and choked on her apple in her excitement. Now *this* was something worth learning! The dead always had much to say; the old people were always so wise in the stories, and the mentors who were killed to start the hero's journey were always insightful. If she could learn to speak to them after they died, what could they tell her?

Later in the day, she laid the book down after marking her spot with a piece of straw and watched the ants and bugs crawling around her. She very carefully stepped on one of the smallest ants with her bare toe, an ant she knew would not be missed too terribly. It was so small, how could it be necessary? Then, after she'd moved her foot away, she spoke the string of words the book mentioned and watched, waiting for something to happen. After a few more moments of nothing, Megara continued to read her book, searching for answers as to why she couldn't reanimate the ant she'd killed.

This spell we have learned only works on those who have died of natural causes, or those who have died with no damage to their physical and mortal bodies.

Megara felt a momentary pang of regret. She had killed the ant by breaking its delicate body—that was the only way she knew to kill the small bugs. Though she felt terrible that she'd killed the bug unnecessarily, and knowing the bug would still probably not be missed, she told herself she'd have to learn how to kill without inflicting physical damage before she could attempt the reanimation again.

Megara read the entire book before the sun was at its highest point. It was just so interesting! It wasn't at all what she'd expected it to be—no way to read the minds of the dead. It instead showed Megara how to *manipulate* the dead. She learned what it meant to actually kill something, to kill it with nothing but her mind. She learned what it meant to suspend the dead in a state of animation where they were most definitely not alive, but they weren't quite dead anymore either. However, the book hadn't told her how to go about killing, and she wasn't ready for the possibility of failure.

As the day continued on, she felt the cold breeze blow through her small cellar. She wrapped her thin blanket around her shoulders and made a mental note to ask Merlin if she could maybe receive something warmer this year, as the winter season already seemed to be upon them. Her toes were rather red by the time she decided to put her next book away and climb onto her bed of straw to protect her exposed toes from the cold. She considered continuing her reading in bed, but the sun had reached the other part of the house and she no longer had light in her room to be able to read. She chose to eat more of her food instead, realizing she'd been so caught up in her book all day that she'd forgotten to eat. This time, she pulled a piece of dried meat from the bag.

She pondered the things she had read while she chewed on the meat. Who else knew the things she had read in that book? Did Merlin know them? He didn't ever use any sort of magic in front of her, instead asking Megara to practice what she learned If they were ever attacked, if anyone ever learned of Megara's existence, would they be able to defend themselves with the ones who had already died? Megara didn't think they'd mind; after all, they'd already lived their lives. They'd succumbed to death already. Wouldn't that mean they'd be willing to defend someone else's life?

She couldn't wait to perfect how to kill without leaving a mark so she could try. Maybe she could even ask one of them if they really did mind being reanimated. *I wonder what death is like. I must ask Merlin if he knows what comes after death.*

The sun set, and Megara stayed in her bed. Her room was very cold now. She wished Merlin would come home and start a fire. Even if she hadn't been locked in the cellar she wouldn't be able to start the fire herself. If she did—well, an empty house with a fire was sure to draw attention. No, she would wait for Merlin to return home.

Megara heard Camelot begin to go quiet for the night. Children were called home, and animals were put into their corrals. Everyone seemed to sound content with their day's work. Megara tried to be patient, reminding herself Merlin *had* told her he would be home late.

She ate a piece of bread from her sack simply to pass the time. She couldn't wait to discuss what she had learned.

Finally, after what felt like an eternity, Megara heard the sounds of Merlin stumbling up the path outside their home. So, he'd been drinking—that's why he'd been out so late. Megara wondered which woman he'd spent the evening with. Was it one of the ones who'd been nice enough to walk him home before? Somehow she doubted it. Merlin didn't like to bring women to their home, and when he did, it was never someone he had brought before. Megara stood and waited by her door for him to come and open it for her. She waited and waited. She heard the sound of snores echoing from his bedroom instead.

Her stomach rumbled, and she felt a fresh chill as she realized Merlin had been too drunk to light a fire. Or give her a warm dinner. Or even acknowledge her at all. *There's always tomorrow*, she thought as she crawled into bed. *I'll see him tomorrow.* Sometimes this happened, and Merlin usually made up for it the next night with a wonderfully large dinner.

Megara's days bled into weeks that bled into years. She learned more and more every day and practiced what she could in her small cellar, but with a lack of unique items to practice on, she couldn't do much. After a while, she started trying to conjure things into her room, but those attempts typically ended poorly and she didn't enjoy the repercussions, so she didn't often attempt it. If she wasn't punished by Merlin for wasting her energy—and sometimes he would find her passed out on the floor—she would misjudge the size of the object she was trying to summon and cause damage to herself or her room.

Like every night, Megara found herself in the cellar in the darkness. It seemed most of Camelot had gone to bed, but Merlin had yet to return from the birthing he was assisting with. They'd had a scare during dinner that evening. Merlin always locked the house door at night when he let Megara out for dinner, and tonight they remembered why. Someone had slammed against the door in their effort to get in quickly. "Merlin!" the man shouted with a thick accent and his fist assaulting the wood. "Open the bloody door, ye drunk! We need ye!"

Merlin had ushered Megara into the cellar and hid her away before ushering the man into the house. "What? What is it?"

"Me wife," the man sobbed. "Somethin's wrong. Please, ye have to come quick." And just like that, Merlin had left.

Megara didn't mind this much anymore. She was a young woman and had spent so many of her years in solitude in this small cellar that, though she did not fit in it very well anymore, was quite cozy and comforting.

Megara stared at the mouse that was climbing through the hole for the night. She petted it with one finger on the head. It jumped and squeaked and ran away, but Megara didn't care much. *What does the world look like from your eyes?* she wondered silently. *Do you have a family you hide from?* She felt a bubble of anger form in her heart. How dare the mouse avoid his family?

But Meggy, you don't know if he has a family or not. She reminded herself this before lying on her bed, her arm beneath her head. She thought through the reason for her sudden anger. Her whole life it had been herself and Merlin, and more and more lately, Merlin was staying out late or not even returning until morning. *Maybe I'm just missing him.*

During dinner that evening, she had told Merlin what she had learned in her reading about control over animals. He asked her if she had tried yet, but the mouse she'd seen crawling through the cellar was the only one she'd seen.. She thought about the last time she had asked Merlin for an animal to practice on. It had been when she was studying transformation and she wanted to practice. *I wonder . . .* Meggy rolled onto her hands and knees and looked for that mouse again. Would it be possible for her to transform *herself* into a little mouse? Now she was faced with pure boredom and decided it was as good a time as any to try.

She turned to her pile of books and glanced through them, staring at the covers in the near black, looking for the correct one. It was near the bottom of the pile when she found it. She held it in her lap and tried to use the light from the moon shining through the crack in the wall to read the pages. She flipped through them quickly, searching for the correct words to use. *I know it's here somewhere.* She finally found the page she was hunting for and sat as close to the wall as she could, trying to use the light from outside to see the page.

After several minutes, Megara threw the book at her bed in anger and let out a small scream of annoyance. She couldn't see a single word anymore. How was she supposed to practice? And where was Merlin? *If Father was home, he'd allow me light to do this. He'd probably help me!* Megara thought about it for a moment before crawling to the door and testing her new idea. Had Merlin had enough time to lock her door? She jiggled the door and felt it give a little bit more than it should have had it been covered with the wheat bags. She reached her arm through the small hole, wincing as it pressed into the skin on her elbow, and felt around the bags of wheat. Merlin had secured two of them in place, not all four.

Megara concentrated very hard. This was a spell she used when she felt extremely lazy, and whenever she could in front of Merlin as an attempt to impress him. It was rather draining, though, when she did it with her books or food on the table—moving two large bags of wheat with her mind was going to be difficult, but she was determined to try.

"*Movere triticum*," she whispered. Nothing happened. She said it louder, pushing as much as she could with her arm against the door. All she was wanted to do was move the wheat bags! The most frustrating part was that she could feel the energy seeping from her body as if her spell was working, but she couldn't feel any difference in the weight of the door.

She sat on her knees in a huff, pulling her arm back and glaring at the door. *Fine. I'll just sit here, then.* She knew she wouldn't be able to stay awake for long, though, now that she'd allowed all that strength to leave her body. She lay down on her wool mattress and went to sleep, content to wait out the night until she could reread the text that would let her become a mouse.

CHAPTER TWO

T HE NEXT MORNING, MEGARA awoke to the typical knocking on her door as Merlin started his morning. He opened the door and sat on the floor next to her, leaning against the dirt wall. "I am planning on staying home today. I thought maybe we could work through some magic together, if you're interested in the help."

"Yes!" Megara sat up quickly, her head going light. "Yes, please!"

Merlin laughed lightly. "All right. Well, get up. Meet me in the main room."

Megara was up before he'd even stood from the floor and ran into the kitchen with the textbooks she wished to study. "I want to start with animals."

"Animals?" Merlin laughed heartily. "What in the world do you want animals for?"

"They could help us," Megara insisted. "Father, if we could *speak* to them, or even learn to understand the way they communicate, maybe we could use their intelligence to accomplish what we need to do. If I could transform myself into an animal and learn to communicate with them, think of how much knowledge we could obtain."

Merlin rubbed his short beard along his jaw and sighed. "I suppose you're right, Meggy child. We may as well try."

They spent hours poring over the books. Megara hadn't expected so much study. After all, hadn't she been reading these books for years? Why did they need to read more? When she asked Merlin this, he became angry. "Meggy, if you don't study the dangers as well as the benefits, how could you know what to do if something goes terribly wrong?"

Megara didn't say anything. She knew he was right. Of course he was. *Father is always right. He knows so much more than I do.*

"Enough." Merlin sat back away from the books and laced his fingers behind his head. "What is the spell?"

"*Mutare ad mus.*"

"Wrong."

Megara's eyebrows wrinkled. "But that's the spell! That's the spell to become a mouse."

Merlin leaned forward and glared. "That's not the spell I need you to know!" he shouted across the table. Megara jumped, her hands in her lap as she listened. "Meggy, what is the spell to become *human* again? The most important spell of this entire plan of yours? How will you become my Meggy again once you have accomplished your task? What have you learned?"

Megara felt her heart drop. She hadn't considered that. *Merlin must be so disappointed in me,* she thought. *I am so glad I didn't try this last night while he was away.* She looked to the books, completely at a loss. "I . . . I don't know."

Merlin pushed a page toward her and jabbed a finger at it. "*Redi ad me.* You must say this while thinking of your original form."

Megara stared at the book, unseeing. She didn't want to voice the thoughts in her mind, but she knew he'd be even more disappointed if she neglected to tell him this before she started this journey. "Father, I . . . I don't know how . . . I don't know how I would be able to imagine my original form. I have never seen my face. I don't know what to imagine if I don't know what I look like." She feared he'd be angry with her narcissism.

Merlin simply laughed once. "Oh, my girl, I do suppose that would be a problem, wouldn't it?" He stood and retrieved his small shaving mirror from his room, then handed it to her. "Here," he said. "This is what *I* see when I see you. I see a young woman, a beautiful woman, who will learn of her true strength as the time passes, but no sooner."

Megara gazed into the mirror, her eyes moving quickly as she tried to absorb all she saw. She noticed first the thin mark along her cheek under her left eye. It was faint, and for an instant she thought she could remember a blinding pain in that spot, but then it was gone. Her eyes were blue, like a stone Merlin would sharpen his knives with. They were lighter than Merlin's—his were such a dark blue, reminding Megara of the night sky. Her lips were more plump than Merlin's were. Her face was much thinner, too. Her skin was much whiter than his, nearly translucent. She looked at her eyebrows, which were the same brown as Merlin's hair, but this did not match the rest of her hair which was long and yellow and thin. Her nose was almost as thin as Merlin's but tilted up a little at the end where his continued straight. Faint freckles mottled her pale skin.

Merlin took the mirror from her fingers and put it away before returning. "Now," he said. "Would you be able to perform this skill properly? Can you picture yourself?"

Megara hesitated, trying to retain her image in her memory. "I . . . I believe I may be able to, yes, Father."

Merlin stood and moved the table and chairs out of the middle of the room. "All right, show me. Put this plan of yours into action."

Megara ran to her room, pulled a screeching mouse from under her bed, and handed it to Merlin. He took it by the tail with an expression of disgust on his face. He held it up, and she stared at it. She watched it struggle and heard its scream. She took a few moments to study it before speaking the words she knew would work.

It took Megara several tries. With each moment that passed, Merlin's face became stonier, his dark eyes angrier. Megara tried not to look at him and focused on the mouse, speaking the words quickly and quietly. All at once, Megara felt a sliver of her energy seep toward the mouse, an invisible thread that seemed to connect them. She felt it pass between them as the mouse calmed and stared at her.

As Megara continued to whisper the words, she felt her body begin to change. Her line of sight lowered, her voice raised in several octaves, and her face elongated. She dared not break eye contact to observe the fur covering her body, afraid she'd be stuck in an in-between state.

After it started, the transformation only took seconds. Megara stopped speaking the words when she felt the connection cease between her and the mouse. She tried to smile at Merlin, but her face did not stretch properly. She tried to speak but only heard high squeaking instead. Merlin knelt down and placed the real mouse on the floor beside her. It stood there shivering, staring at her.

"What?" Megara could hear the squeak, but in her mind, the word came with it.

I can understand it! But can I communicate back?

She tried to say something, but the words wouldn't reach her lips the way she normally felt they would. She stared at the mouse, wishing the connection she felt before would return. The mouse stepped closer to her and sniffed the air around her. "Speak," it squeaked at her.

I'm trying! she thought. The mouse stepped closer, and she looked up at Merlin. He was crouching next to them, staring at her. She screamed in frustration at the. She faced it head-on and screeched, *Help me!* But only a single word that made sense escaped her lips. "Help."

The mouse cocked its head. "How?"

She concentrated as hard as she could, trying to understand how she'd made it work before. She screamed, focusing all of her energy on her words. *Teach me! How do I speak to you? That's all I want.* "Teach."

Why am I speaking one word at a time?

The mouse sat on its hind legs and held its little paws in front of himself. "How?"

Megara screamed in frustration, reached forward, and smacked the mouse around the head. *I don't know how!* She squeaked many times, but apparently it was meaningless, as she felt no words escape her mouth. *If I can't speak, how can I become human again?*

She stared at Merlin, wondering if maybe the same connection would appear between them while she spoke the words. She tried to remember the words she'd learned from him before looking into the mirror. *The mirror—I can't remember what I look like!* She started to panic and squeaked loudly. Merlin's large hand lowered over her and picked her up by her tail. It hurt, as if he was grabbing her by the hair. She screeched and wriggled until he set her down on the table. His voice boomed as he spoke down to her. Megara wished she could cover her ears—it was so loud.

Redi ad me, redi ad me, redi ad me! She thought the words as hard as she could; she screeched them, though they didn't make sense to the mouse on the floor. Almost instantly, she felt energy surge out of her. It wasn't connected to Merlin, or to any being, but the invisible strand of strength left her and filled the house around her. It seeped out so quickly, Megara was afraid for her life as her vision began to dim. She screeched louder, her body writhing in pain.

Redi ad me!

As she shrieked it this last time, the words began as the mouse's squeak and ended as spoken word. Her body grew, the brown fur shrank into her arms, and her face shrank to its original size. As her body grew, the items on the table were thrown to the floor, and Megara eventually fell off the small table.

She landed on the floor, her blond hair strewn around her as she panted against the stone. "Meggy? Megara, are you all right? What happened?" Merlin was crouched next to her again, his hand on her shoulder. "What went wrong?"

Megara began to cry, an unusual sensation for her, as she didn't remember the last time she'd cried. "I couldn't speak!" she cried. "I couldn't figure it out."

"But you were making so much noise, I thought you were telling the rodent your life story."

"The only words he understood were 'help' and 'teach.' Other than that, none of the squeaks were making sense to him. I was so scared

I had lost language—I was so afraid I wouldn't be able to become human again."

"Well, now you're back, and you know there's so much more you need to study before you can try it again. On to the next task."

"No!" Megara cried and sat up, pushing away from Merlin. "I'm so tired, I can't do anything else."

"You can't grow your strength without testing it first. Come on, up you go." Merlin grabbed her arm and lifted her from the floor. He pushed her into a chair next to the table and pushed a paper toward her.

"Father, I can't. I'm so tired, I can't do anything else today."

"Stop making excuses—get to work. Read this. I have a job for you. I let you have your fun—now it is time to get to work."

Megara tried to read the parchment he put in front of her—she really tried. Her eyesight was blurry even when she wasn't crying. Her hands shook as she tried to trace the words with her finger. After a few moments of watching her, Merlin became angry and swiped the parchment from her. "Fine. Take a nap. When I return, you'd better be ready to start again."

Megara stumbled to her bed and fell upon it, tears sliding down her cheeks. It didn't take long for her body to give in to the comforting sleep she sought.

The boy ran through the forest, his breathing hard and his footsteps light. He knew the path was here somewhere—he had to find it. Merlin had told him it would be here. He had trusted the old fool, but now that Merlin was gone, Arthur had to continue the battle. He had to do what was right. He needed to avenge the death of his mentor.

"There it is," he thought as he stopped running. He could see the village border patrol through the trees, the first marker on the path. Arthur raised his fist to stop those he knew were following close behind. "This is it," he thought again. "Finally, I've found them. I'll eradicate this disease once and for all."

Megara woke with a start, her heart racing as Arthur's had been moments before. She'd never had a dream like that before—her dreams had always been very clearly her own. But this was different. She could sense this man's thoughts, feel his hatred. Know his plans. This place he'd found—it had been full of people who had killed Merlin. Megara's Merlin. She'd seen his face in her mind. *Well,* his *mind,* she thought. Her instincts were telling her she had seen something to come, but she couldn't have. No one could kill Merlin. He was too smart to be surprised and too strong to be murdered.

Megara shook herself and walked out to the kitchen, surprised that Merlin had left her door open. She sat down at the table, waiting for him to return from wherever he was, ready to run for her cellar at a moment's notice if he came with someone else.

Megara waited for what felt like hours. She was so ashamed. She shouldn't have become so upset. She shouldn't have chosen to attempt to speak to the mouse. She should have listened to Merlin. *Father is always right,* she thought. *I should have just done as he asked.*

23

Merlin did come home. He wasn't in a drunk mood as he usually was in the evenings, but he seemed to be in a better mood than earlier. "Are you ready to begin?" he asked, his voice gruff.

"I'm sorry about earlier today, Father. It won't happen again."

Merlin waved a hand pulled the parchment from a shelf behind her. "Enough, child. I understand; you exhausted yourself. It was my fault, really, I knew I had this task for you. I shouldn't have allowed you to try something new when I needed your strength."

"Father," she began as he walked to the table, thinking of the dream she'd had. "Father, what would happen . . . if you were to die?"

"I would die," Merlin said. "Why?"

"I just . . . I had a dream. What comes after death?"

"What was this dream?" Merlin put his hands behind his head and watched Megara intently.

"A man named Arthur—he was chasing someone . . . Someone who had killed you."

"Arthur?" Merlin's voice was sharp as he placed his palms on the table. "Are you sure?"

Megara nodded, eager to please him. "I believe so, yes."

Merlin seemed lost in thought for a moment.

"Father," Megara began again. "What happens after death?"

"There are many opinions," Merlin said, sounding bored. "Take your pick: a mansion of riches, endless torment, or eternity of darkness." He seemed to consider something as he watched Megara before adding, "Some say that when someone with magic dies, their souls release into the ether and become energy for the next magic user to be born."

"That all sounds terrible." Megara shook her head. "Why must we die? Why can't we remain together, here, forever?"

"That is not a concern for now, Meggy." Merlin pointed to the parchment on the table. "*This* is our concern."

Megara stared at the leather cover, then at Merlin in confusion. "Charms, Father? These are simple. I could have done this when I was a child."

"This is different." Merlin moved across the kitchen, opened a cupboard, and pulled a long broadsword from it. He dropped it on the wooden table in front of Megara with a thud before returning to his seat. "This needs to be charmed to protect someone. Unceasing, unyielding. It needs to be able to remain clean with no work, and those who possess it must not be able to lie. Do you understand that, Meggy? The user must speak the truth, whatever they believe is true. The sword should also be able to undermine any magic it is wielded against. And . . ." Merlin seemed to be thinking of other challenges for Megara. She was excited. This was her chance to make him proud and return to his good grace. "And it must not . . ."

"Must not injure its owner?" Megara offered, wondering if it was even logical. In the stories she had read the knights never allowed their sword to be used on them. The bad guys did, though, so maybe it was possible.

"Yes." Merlin's eyes flashed with excitement. "Yes. You must do this, Meggy. Do it before the sun rises."

"Tonight?" Megara stared at the window, the stars already shining.

"Tonight. Finish it by morning. I will bring you whatever you want from Camelot if you finish this task by morning."

Megara gathered the books she thought she would need. She pulled some from her cellar and some from Merlin's room, and some more from the various piles around their home. She started by reading all she could about the different charms, reading as fast as she could so as not to waste time. She folded down the corners on any page that even mentioned what she was looking for. It was a lot of work, but she'd finally found a page for each of the charms she was searching for. She studied each page, learning the words and materials needed to perform the charms. Megara assumed they'd take quite a while, as they couldn't be done at the same time.

After every spell she cast on the metal sword was completed, she glanced out the window. The moon had drifted across the sky, and she could see the morning sun beginning to creep over the horizon. She began to worry she wouldn't be done in time. Merlin had gone to bed several hours before. He knew the results would be the same whether he went to bed or not. *I've gone a little faster since he went to sleep,* Megara thought. *I'm not worrying about what he's thinking.*

At last, Megara spoke the final words of the chant for the protection against the sword itself toward the bearer. This was the addition Megara had suggested, and she wasn't quite sure how it would work. According to the words of the charm, it should protect the master of the sword from someone picking it up and using it against him, by increasing the weight exponentially when it was directed at the owner. Megara wondered, for what must have been the hundredth time, who would need a sword such as the one she was creating.

Megara yawned and sat back in her chair, exhausted from staying awake all night to perform magic, but she had done it. This sword was the luckiest sword in the entire world. Soon after, as if he had sensed her success, Merlin walked from his room, laying his hand on her shoulder. "Is it done?" he asked.

Megara nodded. "I just finished."

"Good. I have a cloak on the back of my door. Go put it on."

Megara slammed into the wall in her rush to please her father. She returned with the black cloak draped over her shoulders. It fell to the floor with a length to spare. She was much shorter than her father. "Why, Father?"

He looked at her feet, swearing under his breath. "Where are your shoes?"

"I—I haven't had shoes for years, Father," she stuttered. "The ones you brought me haven't fit me for a long time. I haven't wanted to bother you with it."

"I'll have to get you new ones, then. Go find my old boots. Put them on. You're coming with me."

Megara's heart fluttered. "Outside, Father?"

"Hurry. We're running out of time."

Megara ran back to his room, searching for the old boots. She knew they had a hole in them. She hadn't been able to mend them when he'd asked and he'd become very angry, but now she had to hurry. *Outside!* Megara was so excited. She couldn't remember the last time she'd been outside. It could have been the time Merlin had called her Maira when she was eight.

She found the boots, pulled them on, and ran, her feet thudding on the stone. The boots were too big for her by several sizes, but she wasn't about to complain. "Where are we going, Father?" she asked as he pulled the hood over her face and covered her body with the cloak.

"Bring the sword. We must hide it."

Megara was confused. "Hide the sword?" *After everything I've just done?*

"We don't want just anyone having it, now do we?" Merlin asked with a smirk. Megara supposed he was right. This was a very powerful sword.

Father must have a wonderful plan for it, Megara thought.

When Merlin was convinced Megara could not be seen, he nodded and walked to the door, waving her forward. "Quickly," he hissed as he opened the door. She moved, her feet pounding. Merlin closed the door behind them and waved her forward, leading her down the road.

Megara knew Camelot would be waking soon. *Will I get to meet someone?* she wondered. Her eyes flitted this way and that, wanting to absorb as much as she could. She saw so many animals waking up and walking around. She couldn't wait to see the other people. *Will they come and talk to us? Will they be smart, like father, or will we have to speak on their level? Will they have an understanding of magic?* Megara could barely contain her excitement.

Merlin led her out of Camelot and deep into the surrounding forest. She didn't dare say anything, but she was disappointed they were leaving. Megara could sense Camelot waking behind her, but they were leaving the city far behind.

They didn't slow until they'd gone deep into the forest, and Megara had lost all sense of direction. Merlin had led them to a large boulder in between a couple of trees. He walked right up to it and waved Megara forward when she hesitated. "What are we doing here, Father?" she asked, her mouth dry.

"I need you to seal the sword into the rock."

Megara's eyebrows wrinkled. "How?"

"Come here." He growled and pulled her forward and took the sword from her. He recited some words to her and instructed her to repeat them. "We're going to start by softening the rock. Place your hand here and speak the words."

Megara obeyed and felt her strength leave her and connect to the stone, as it had to the mouse the day before. It was much more draining, though, possibly due to the size of the stone. Megara was frightened, but she continued to speak the words while Merlin pushed the sword slowly into the rock. Megara gasped and winced, feeling a cold slice down the center of her body as well as the rock. She reached her free hand to her head, feeling for blood. Nothing was there. She continued to chant while Merlin set the sword as he wanted. "All right, Meggy. Stop the chant."

Megara stopped and felt the connection end, and as it did so, her knees gave out and she fell to the ground, panting. Merlin inspected their work, and Megara could hear the stone closing around the sword. Only after Merlin was certain the sword was in place did he kneel down next to Megara. "Can you stand?" he asked her. She tried to push herself up, but her arms shook too badly. Merlin sighed. "I figured this would happen. You weren't fully recovered from your mess yesterday. You're going to have to stay here until you recover, and I don't want you coming home in the daylight. So, wait here until I come back for you. Stay hidden—don't let anyone see you. I'll see you tonight."

And with that, Merlin stood and walked away from Megara, leaving her shivering against the dirty ground. It took a long time for Megara to feel her strength return. When she finally did, she crawled to her knees and crept toward some bushes nearby, intending to hide herself. She didn't know how far away she was from Camelot, but she did know she was too much in the open if she didn't hide. She pulled herself under the bush, using Merlin's cloak as protection and hoping it wouldn't rip.

She began getting hungry around the time the sun was at its highest point. She became anxious, thinking she heard voices nearby several times. Through the leaves, she saw a lot of wildlife. A bunny came rather close to her a couple of times. *Do other fathers leave their family unattended like this? In the woods? Away from Camelot's protection?*

It wasn't until the sun was halfway down that she had the idea of becoming an animal for the rest of the day. Other than being hungry, most of her strength had returned. *I could just become an animal until Merlin comes back. He wouldn't be angry—I had to defend myself. And no one would know I was here if I was an animal.* But she wasn't sure how to do it. *I had the mouse to focus on yesterday. I don't know what to focus on here in the forest.* She half wished a wolf or other predator would come near, but that also meant she was near a deadly animal. *Probably not the best option,* she thought. Instead, she started hunting for a mouse. She was afraid to try anything bigger than what she'd done before, just in case. She crawled out of her hiding place and started spiraling away from the boulder, being sure to keep it in her line of sight as she crawled through the underbrush.

After sometime searching Megara became desperate. She became aware of a small creature staring at her from above. Megara recognized the stoat from one of the books she'd asked Merlin to read to her when she was younger. It was a long and slim creature that crawled against the ground. Its whiskers were long and black, and its eyes were watery and moved quickly, investigating the world around itself.

Megara watched this creature for a moment longer before she decided this would be the animal she chose. It was bigger than a mouse, but it was likely the very reason she couldn't find any mice. She sat very still, hoping she wouldn't scare the animal off while she whispered the words. Her whispers caught the animal's attention and he stared at her, his nose twitching.

The connection came much easier this time, and it was a much slower drain, much easier to maintain. She felt peace as she shrunk down to the stoat's size. When she felt the connection end, she held still, realizing the teeth inside her little mouth were very sharp The creature hadn't seemed dangerous before, but would she be attacked now that she had become its size?

The stoat crept toward her. "What are you?" it asked. Its voice was richer than the mouse's had been.

Megara's heart soared. It had said more than one word. Would she be able to? She tried to mimic the sound she'd heard the creature make. "I'm a human." Her heart nearly exploded from excitement, but she tried to remain calm.

"No, that's most definitely not what you are." The creature shook its head and sat. "I watched you change. What are you really?"

"I'm a girl," Megara insisted, walking slowly toward the other stoat. It felt strange, having her body so long and low to the ground.

The stoat tilted its head. "Well, you're one weird girl."

Megara was offended but chose not to grace that insult with a response. She walked a little closer to the stoat before stopping. "What's your name?"

"Name?" he asked.

"Yes. What does your family call you?"

31

"My family?"

Megara was annoyed. "The ones who care for you. What do they call you?"

"I don't believe I have a name because no one cares for me. I hunt for myself and I defend myself."

Megara was astounded. "You don't have a family?"

"No."

Megara thought on this. "All right, I'm going to name you then."

"You aren't going to hunt for me, too are you?" he asked. "I don't believe you'd do a good job at it, since you can't even decide what you are."

Megara felt a laugh in her chest, but it didn't bubble out like it would in her human body. It sounded like more of a hum. "No, you can continue to hunt for yourself. But I think I'm going to call you . . ." Megara thought very hard on this. "Actually, I don't know what to call you quite yet. But if you stay with me for the rest of the day, I might figure it out."

The stoat was silent for a moment before it hurried to Megara. She was worried at first that he would attack her, but he ran around in a circle and lay down next to her. "All right, just because I'd like to know my name."

Chapter Three

T HE STOAT STAYED WITH Megara for many hours. They talked throughout the afternoon, discussing the things that interested them. Megara spent the evening chasing insects with the stoat. He showed her how to chase rabbits for food as well. This intrigued Megara. How could an animal so much bigger than herself be the source of food for a stoat? After they had captured the rabbit and her friend was eating it, Megara lay studying the creature. She was disgusted by the stoat eating the raw meat, but she knew it was his way of life.

"I think I've decided," she said when he'd finished eating.

"Decided what?" he asked as he licked his paws.

"I know what to call you."

"Oh?" The stoat sat up in interest, his dark eyes wide, his jaw chattering. "What is my name, strange girl?"

"Superus, I think."

"Soup- what? What the bloody rabbit does that mean?"

That humming laugh bubbled within Megara again. "It's Latin."

"Ah! So, it must mean something courageous like . . . like Gallant Knight, or . . . or something."

Megara hummed again, and his little foot faltered to the ground. His nose twitched in anticipation. "It means otherworld-ly."

"Otherworldly?" He stood up on his back legs again and bared his little teeth at her. "H-how *dare* you! I am a knight of death and destruction!"

Megara's hum was much louder now, and Superus bared his teeth at her. "I think it fits you," Megara said to him, struggling to make the noises she needed to in order to convey the message.

Superus spun around and stalked off a ways before lying down. However, Megara took heart from knowing he didn't leave her behind. Especially as the sun was beginning to set, and she felt as though she could hear voices again.

As the moments passed, Megara realized the voices were actually approaching. "Superus!" she hissed. His ear twitched. "Superus, do you hear those voices?"

"The humans?" he asked.

"Yes, the humans!" Megara hurried to his side.

"Yes, I hear them." He stood , shaking his body to dislodge the dirt. "Come on. We can hide in this bush over here."

He led Megara toward the bush where she had hidden herself that morning. His fur blended in with the shadows. Megara turned the best she could to see her own coloring for the first time. She appeared just like Superus, but she wasn't sure if that was because of the species or because she had used him as her model. She'd have to pay attention next time she did something like this.

As the voices got closer, Megara became excited. One of them was definitely Merlin! She'd know his voice anywhere. She started to move forward out of the bush until the next voice sounded. "Arthur, you don't understand. You have to learn patience with these people. One day soon, you'll be king!"

"I don't understand why you keep saying that, Merlin." The unknown voice argued as they climbed through the forest. "I'm not the crown prince! I could never be king!"

Crown prince? Arthur? King? This was all sounding too strange to Megara. The night before she'd been telling Merlin about the dream she'd had about the boy and the sword. The boy had been named Arthur. She didn't think he'd been a king, though—just someone with power chasing people who had killed Merlin.

But this boy was right. He could never be king if he wasn't the crown prince! What was Merlin saying? This wasn't making any sense to Megara, and this Arthur man sounded equally confused.

Megara saw feet enter the clearing. "Look here. What do you see?" Merlin asked.

The man scoffed in amazement. "A sword! There's a sword there, buried in the rock."

"I am going to tell Camelot of this stone. They'll bring it into the square. Look, read here."

Arthur stepped toward the stone. From her hiding spot and lowered vantage point, Megara couldn't see his face. But she could see his dirty boots, and she was rather disgusted by the sight of them. "What does this say right here?"

Megara hadn't remembered any words written anywhere near the sword. What could he be reading?

"Who. . . Whoso pull. . . pulleth . . ." Arthur stumbled over the words as if he was struggling to read them. Megara ached to run out and read them herself. "This sword. . . Merlin, I can't. Just read it for me."

Merlin sighed. "Whoso pulleth this sword from this stone is right-wise king born." Merlin waited and sighed again when he didn't get a reaction. "Don't you see?"

"No," Arthur said.

"It means, whoever is able to pull the sword from the stone is rightfully king."

Arthur laughed. "Merlin, can you see that thing? It's stuck—in a stone!"

"Laugh all you want," Merlin said. "But I know what this means. And I know, if anyone can pull this sword from the stone, it'll be you."

"You're crazy, old man."

Megara saw Arthur walk off.

"Where are you going?" Merlin called.

"You said you'll bring it to Camelot. I'll play your game when you get that bloody boulder into the center."

Merlin waited long after Arthur was gone and the sun was almost set before speaking again. "Meggy, where are you?" he called.

Megara hesitantly crawled out from underneath the bush. She could feel Superus not far behind her. Megara crawled up behind Merlin and crawled up his pant leg. Merlin jumped and started to shake her off, but Megara held on. "Meggy?" he asked. Megara nodded, and he wrapped his hand around her center and held her up. "What have you done to yourself, Meggy? Will you have enough strength to change back?"

Megara thought about this for a moment before nodding. Merlin set her on the ground, and Megara started the process of becoming human again. "*Redi ad me,*" she whispered, feeling the strength leave her body and surround her in the forest. As she sensed the energy enter the trees, she was surprised by the reciprocation from the trees. She felt energy fill her, drawing from the world around her. It was as if the life around her was rewarding her and providing its own relief to the energy drain. "*Redi ad me.*"

Within moments, Megara was kneeling on the dirt, a single line of sweat leaving her forehead. *What was that energy?* Megara wondered. She stood to meet Merlin.

"How are you feeling?" he asked her.

"I'm fine." Megara smiled. "It wasn't as hard this time."

"Why not?"

Megara shrugged, not sure how to explain what she had felt.

"All right. Well, we have to get you home before anyone notices. Pull that cloak over your head and let us get going."

When Merlin turned his back on her, Megara impulsively spun and leaned down, offering her hands to Superus. She wasn't sure if he'd understand her meaning, but it only took a second for him to rush forward and spin around between her hands. She took this as a good sign and lifted him to her chest under the cloak so as to hide him from Merlin. She ran to catch up with Merlin, feeling Superus's warm heartbeat next to her own, thrilled that she finally had a friend.

The next morning, Megara woke with a rumbling stomach. Merlin had been so wrapped up in his own thoughts, he'd forgotten to feed her dinner. *It's been more than a day since I have eaten,* she realized. *I should have eaten some of that rabbit with Superus. But it was raw! And so bloody.* For a moment Megara considered changing herself into a stoat to find some food. *Maybe I will if Merlin doesn't feed me breakfast.*

She didn't have to wait long for Merlin to knock on her door that morning. When he did, Megara threw her tattered blanket over Superus to hide him. "I'm awake," she called.

Merlin opened the door, and Megara was grateful to see he had a heaping plate waiting for her. He handed the whole plate to her, and she started digging in as soon as it was in her hands. She looked at him as she filled her mouth, not much caring that he was disgusted, though she knew at any other time she'd feel ashamed. She did not have the energy or will to be disappointed by herself in that moment. She was so hungry.

"I have to move that boulder into town today," Merlin told her. "I'll be discussing it with the people of Camelot all day. I will not be home for dinner tonight. Take a break from your studies. You deserve it." He added something else beneath his breath, and when Megara asked him about it, he shook his head. "I'll be back late. Don't wait up."

Megara finished her plate before she saw Superus begin to move. She felt sorry for not saving him anything, but tried to tell herself he wouldn't have wanted berries anyway, not if he was used to eating raw meat every day. Superus walked out from underneath the blanket and shook as if to rid himself of the last of his sleepiness.

He and Megara looked at each other. "I wonder if there's a way to communicate with you without turning into a stoat," she mused aloud, surprising herself with her daring. She glanced toward the hole in the wall, hoping no one had heard her. *I must find a way to talk with Superus without speaking aloud. Otherwise, someone will find us. Father would be so furious with me if we went all this time and just now had that disaster!*

Megara allowed Superus to lay across her shoulders while she read through her textbooks for the morning. She was trying to see if there was a way to speak with animals without sharing their form. She found several possible entries and noted them all so she could try them. Her biggest concern was the amount of energy that would seep from her if she tried. When she had tried to be a mouse, it had almost killed her. She had been lucky when it hadn't taken as much energy to become a stoat, but she still wasn't sure why that was. *Something to discover later,* she decided.

After she'd skimmed through all of her books, she looked at the hole in the wall. She could tell the sun was beginning to set. She heard the people of Camelot returning home after their day's work. *Father said he'd be home late. I have a few more hours before I should hide Superus. Maybe now is the best time to practice what I've found.*

Megara put Superus on the floor next to her book and began reciting the words she'd found. She knew which ones wouldn't work because she felt no drain on her body. She kept working through other charms, trying not to become frustrated. Superus seemed to know how hard she was trying as he sat very still and stared at her while she worked.

"*Intellege,*" Megara whispered, and as soon as the word left her mouth, she felt an indiscernible thread of energy leave her mouth and connect with Superus. She saw his ears twitch and he sat up straighter. She said the words once more with a more determined force and felt the thread connect between her and the stoat. "Can you understand me?" she asked.

Superus's ears twitched, and he seemed pleased. "Yes. It took you long enough, weird girl."

"My name is Megara," she corrected. "But you can call me Meggy. I guess you should know that if you plan to stick around. Why did you decide to come with me, anyway?"

Superus crawled into Megara's lap and curled up. "Well, you named me. And didn't you say 'family' is the reason why we have names? What was the point of me having a name if there was no one who would use it?"

Megara felt touched that this animal was so genuine and honest. "Well, I'm very glad you came, Superus."

"I was thinking about it a lot,." Superus lifted his head. "Why did you choose me? What made me the one you wanted to name?"

"Well, I wasn't looking for someone to name," Megara admitted. "I was trying to find a way to hide. And you were the first animal I saw. And I needed to see an animal in order to become that animal."

"So . . . Had I been any other animal, you still would have chosen me."

Megara laughed. "I guess so, except a mouse. Those are hard for me."

The stoat hummed his laughter. "That's because mice are obnoxious. They don't like to communicate with you. They expect you to solve all their problems for them."

"Can you speak to them?"

"I would rather not."

"Can you speak to all animals, I mean? Can you talk to other species?"

Superus stared at her. "You use strange words, Meggy. But yes, I can speak to any creature." He lay down and tucked his nose under his feet.

Will I be able to speak to any animal as well with this spell? Megara wondered. She was excited to try it but wasn't sure when she'd get the chance again. The thought formed slowly, but she expressed it to Superus anyway. "What if . . . what if tomorrow I became like you again . . . and we wandered Camelot together?"

Superus seemed excited. "You mean it? It's rather boring here in your hiding hole. I'd love to go explore the Other Peoples' land!"

Megara lay down in bed with Superus curled up next to her stomach. She didn't want to cut off the connection between them, but she was afraid the thread would draw on her strength while she slept and she wouldn't be able to wake up. She could still feel the thread's constant draw.

"I'm going to have to stop talking to you for the night, Superus. I can't keep it up for too long. Well, I don't actually know how long I *can* keep it up."

"That's okay, Meggy," Superus said. "You go to sleep. I'll keep watch that the evil man doesn't hurt you."

"Evil man?" Megara asked in surprise.

"You know, the one who brought you the berries this morning."

Megara laughed. "No, silly, that's not an evil man. That's my father."

"What's a father?"

"He's … Well, I mean, he's …" Megara wasn't sure how to explain it to him in words he would understand. She had read some of Merlin's medical books, and when she asked, he had once explained how the women he helped had babies in them. But she wasn't sure how to simplify that for the stoat. "He's one-half of the reason I'm alive, I suppose."

"And what's the other half?"

"Well, usually the other half is a mother."

"I know what a mother is," Superus said. "I have one of those."

"Well, you must have a father, too."

Superus examined Megara. "My father was not in my life, but I stand by what I said, Meggy. That man is not good for you."

"He's my father, and I won't hear one more nasty thing about him. Now, go to sleep."

As she said the words to end the connection, her mind wandered. How had she never noticed the lack of a mother in her life? Merlin was always spending his evenings with different women. Who was her mother? And why did she not know this crucial fact?

That night when Megara heard Merlin stumble in, she left Superus, motioning for him to stay when he woke up, and knocked on her door, waiting for Merlin to come to her. After a moment, she heard him stumble over. He unlocked the door and allowed her out while he sat in a chair with a half-empty bottle in hand. He gestured toward the other chair at the table with his free hand.

"Father, I have a question for you."

"Go on," he slurred.

"Who is my mother?" she asked.

Merlin began to chuckle, but it became very robust. Megara smiled at his mirth. *My mother must have been a pleasant woman to have him laugh like this!* Merlin continued laughing for quite some time.

"Father?" she asked.

Merlin took a deep swig of his drink and smacked his lips. "I thought you would reach this point a long time ago, Megara. I was certain you'd reach so many points before this." He swigged the last of his drink and threw the bottle against the wall. Megara jumped, surprised at the violence. Superus's earlier words came back to her about danger, but she didn't want to believe them.

Merlin stood from the table. He began pacing, or pacing the best he could in his debilitated state. "You, *Megara* . . ." He laughed again. "You, child, are so much less . . . Less impressive than I thought you would be." His words slurred so much that Megara had a hard time understanding him.

He doesn't know what he's saying. He's drunk.

"You were supposed to be stronger than this!" Merlin threw his chair at her, but it flew wide. Megara stood in surprise, backing away from him. "You had the potential to be the most powerful woman in the *world*. You aren't even *half* of who I thought you would become!" Merlin threw up his head and laughed like a madman, stumbling.

"I took you." His eyes were bright and clear. "I took you from your mother."

Megara held her breath. *What does that mean?*

"I took you from your mother. And when I did so, your father found me. And I killed him."

Megara's heart seemed to stop. The world seemed to still. "What?"

Merlin advanced toward her, his fists balling up. "I took you from them. Because I saw in you a power that I had never seen before. And they would have *wasted* your potential." He spat the word and threw Megara's now-unoccupied chair aside. Megara took several steps back. "But I see now how incredibly wrong I was. You are nothing, *nothing* like I thought you would be."

When Merlin's fist connected with Megara's face, she almost didn't feel it. The pain was nothing like what she was feeling inside. What was Merlin saying? What did this mean? *He's lying. He's angry and drunk. It's that boy Arthur's fault! This is because he made Merlin angry by denying him at the boulder!* She wanted to believe anything, anything that would protect her from the words she was hearing.

Merlin threw her to the floor. Megara was too in shock to move. "Your mother cried when I took you," Merlin continued, kicking at her side and stomach and head, whatever he could. "Or maybe that was because I killed those sniveling brothers of yours, and your poor father." Merlin laughed again and rested his hand on his stomach. He glared at Megara. "I was wrong. I never should have expected anything extraordinary from a farm girl."

Chapter Four

MEGARA FELT THE ASSAULT on her body pause. She heard Merlin scream, and when she lifted her arm from around her head she saw him retreating from her. She lifted her head with caution, feeling throbbing pain and seeing her blood paint the floor around her. When she looked at the man she'd called her father all her life, she saw him clutching his leg, hopping on one foot. Megara's gaze flitted down to the floor, not sure what had hurt Merlin but not knowing whether to be grateful or frightened.

She saw a flash of brown and would have gasped had her lungs obeyed. Superus was skittering around on the floor, his teeth bared as he attacked Merlin's ankles. In Merlin's drunken state, he was unable to track Superus, but Megara was afraid of what would happen if he were to come to his senses and see the creature. She knew she had to act now.

She said the first words that came to her mind, though what made her think of them, she wouldn't be able to guess. "*Ignis flammans,*" she whispered. The words ignited within her heart, and she could feel her physical pain, her emotional pain, her anger, and her fear crawling from within herself to Merlin's feet. The energy built in strength as it moved faster toward Merlin, as if being drawn to him. As the power left her, Megara pulled herself to her knees. Hatred and anger boiled deep within her as the bottom of Merlin's cloak began to smoke. Then Megara watched Merlin's cloak catch fire. Merlin screamed and threw it off, stomping on the flames.

His efforts did nothing to dim the flames. They *whooshed* from the cloak to his feet and then up his legs. His screams became piercing as he ran toward the door and threw it open. "Help me!" he screamed to the night air. "Help me! Somebody! Water!"

Megara came to her feet and followed Merlin to the street, feeling Superus catch up to her and climb up her skirt. She held him in her arms as they walked toward the man in the street. Megara felt empty as she watched Merlin struggle to breathe through the smoke. She didn't know what she was supposed to feel. Angry, because he'd told her the truth? Outraged, because of what the truth was?

Or miserable, as the only father she had ever known was now here before her, dying in the street?

Under her breath, Megara spoke the words that allowed her to communicate with Superus as the people of Camelot exited their houses and see the damage she had inflicted. Shouts for water spread with haste. Megara seemed not to have been noticed yet in the doorway of their home.

"Are you all right, Meggy?" Superus asked.

"No," Megara whispered. "We can't stay here. We have to leave."

"Where to, my friend?"

Megara's eyes filled with tears as she looked down at the stoat. She had a friend, and that was more than she felt she deserved. She looked at Merlin, burning and screaming in the road. "I don't know. But we must leave."

She returned to the house and grabbed Merlin's work bag. She knew it contained a few healing salves. She threw a couple of charm books in with the salve. Her heart was beating hard as she pulled the strap over her head. Superus crawled from her arm into the bag as well. Megara grabbed Merlin's spare cloak as she left.

Megara stayed in the shadows as she tried to avoid the crowds, but she gave in and glanced back. Her eyes locked with a young boy's gaze. They stared at each other for a moment before the child opened his mouth wide and screamed, pointing at her, "It was her! Mother, the woman! She's a dragon!"

Megara felt confused. Why was he saying these things? "Meggy, run!" Superus squeaked.

Megara held the bag steady and ran as fast as she could, her bare feet slipping on the dusty stone streets. She noticed the boulder from the forest in a conspicuous place in the town when she ran past it, but couldn't ignorethe crowd running at her heels. "What do I do now, Superus?" she asked, her voice high and scared.

"Run to the forest and become like me," he suggested. She listened and ran as fast as she could, hoping to put more distance between them and the angry crowd. When she looked again, she saw that most of the crowd had disappeared, but three angry men were staring her down. She screamed the words she'd whispered earlier that night, and she saw smoke billow at their feet. The men stopped and began screaming as the flames rushed up their trousers. A crowd surrounded them and tried to stop the flames, as they had for Merlin.

Megara reached the forest and hid behind a tree, locking eyes with Superus and stumbling over her words, begging herself to shift. Tears slipped down her cheeks as she spoke. Finally, the connection latched as cries of discovery filled the air. Within seconds, she and Superus were eye to eye. She noted that her bag of books and salves was no longer present. She was too panicked to care about them in that moment.

"Come, follow me!" Superus instructed, and together they sprinted into the darkness.

They moved through the undergrowth for hours. They got deeper and deeper into the woods until they came to a clearing. They hid beneath a bush and listened to the people scream and scare each other while searching for the Dragon Woman. "Why do they call me that?" she asked Superus.

He was quiet for a moment while they watched the smoke fill the air above the trees. It sounded as though the crowds hadn't been able to stop the flames Megara had created, and it had spread to the houses surrounding them. The townspeople were struggling to stay on top of the spread in their panic.

"I think . . ." Superus began, bringing Megara's attention to the undergrowth and the world around her. "Meggy, I couldn't tell really, but I think your eyes changed colors whenever you saw the fires. The young one must have assumed you'd started the fire with your eyes."

"But dragons spread flame with their mouths."

"Well," Superus said, "is that not what you did?"

Megara said nothing while she thought this over for the next several hours. Superus curled himself up with Megara, and she rested her chin on his back. He was soon asleep, but she couldn't bring herself to settle. She had killed the only man she knew. She had watched him suffer and cry out, and she hadn't even thought to offer him help. *Did I want him dead? Did I truly want to kill him? What will I do without him? There's nothing in the world I've wanted more than to please him. How can I do this now? I can't—my father is dead.*

Thinking those words made Megara stop. *My father is dead . . . Both of them. What should I do now? Where do I go? I cannot return to Camelot*

Megara thought about what Merlin had told her. He had said he took her—he called her a farm girl. He told her that her mother had cried over her—over her and the death of her brothers. She'd had brothers. She had once had a mother. Merlin wasn't her father. Everything she knew had been a lie. When had he taken her? Where was she from? Who was she?

Weeks went by before the men of Camelot stopped hunting for her in the woods. Megara stayed with Superus, eating like him, staying near him. She didn't know what else to do. She felt as though her life was over, that nothing would ever be good again. *Will it ever be safe for me to be human again?* She often wondered if it would be better to die as a stoat, unbeknown to anyone. There was no one to miss her anymore.

Megara's thoughts wandered again to where her mother was. *Where am I from? Can I ever find my home, my real home, again? Would I be able to live with my mother? Would my mother accept having a murderer for a daughter?*

Megara stayed near the edge of the forest, still in her stoat form. She was watching as Camelot repaired itself. The men and women worked together to repair the homes she had set ablaze. She watched as they mourned Merlin and the other men who had died. As she had sat alone these many weeks, though a solitude disrupted by her new friend, Megara had had plenty of time to think about what had happened that night.

She had not meant to kill anyone—not really. She had meant to defend herself and Superus. She still didn't know where the words had come from, the fire ones that had killed Merlin. She couldn't remember ever reading them before. She'd spoken them, and they'd provided a release for her pain. She'd allowed the flames to eat up her fear and anger. She'd been weak, but she'd proven Merlin wrong. She was not weak in magic, just in emotional strength. *He could never have expected that I would fight back. He was beating me. Had Superus not interfered, he probably would have killed me.*

Though she had not meant to kill Merlin, she no longer had to hide in a tiny cellar. She was able to breathe fresh air every day and practice magic the way she wanted to—once she was brave enough to become human again.

As she watched the people of Camelot, she'd been intrigued by the differences in their appearance and sizes. They all appeared so different, but they were all so willing to serve each other. They were willing to help in any capacity they had.

By contrast, she was here in the forest, alone with her stoat friend, waiting. Waiting for the feeling of love and security to return to her heart. Waiting to know what she was supposed to be doing now, where she was supposed to go. As much as she wished for these answers, as she sat with Superus day in and day out, she understood something she never thought she would—she understood what it meant to be free.

She understood now that this world, this large and unyielding and dangerous world, was one she had been protected from, but it was also one that had been protected from her. She understood that she *did* have potential. Merlin had been right about that. She was learning that she could feel her power within her, which had just begun to be touched. It was yet to be uncovered how much damage and pain she could inflict upon people, upon herself. She thought back to a conversation with Superus a few days into her self-banishment.

"What if I killed myself?" Megara watched the hawk in the air after Superus had told her of the danger it possessed. "What if I let a hawk eat me?"

Superus looked up at the bird and was quiet for several heartbeats before speaking. "That would be the natural way of life," he said. "But now that I have met you, Meggy, I think I would miss you if you were to die."

That was enough to convince her to stay, at least for a little longer. That night, they promised to accompany each other on this journey, wherever it might lead.

PART II

PART II

CHAPTER FIVE

L EOPOLD, HIS ARMS STRAINING, convinced the ill cow to move the last few meters toward the healer's agreed meeting point. Thankfully, the healer hadn't insisted on him bringing the cow all the way to the center of town, but she was so busy, she wished to meet him at the council house by the river. "How long has she been like this?" the healer, Stace, asked when they arrived.

"They told me a day."

Leopold studied the healer as she worked. She was young, in her late teens, but she was the second most trusted healer in the village, earning herself a place on the council. Her hair was brownish-red, like his own. She kept it loose and long, even though it kept falling in her face. She pushed it back and continued to move her hands over the cow's hide. Stace was very pretty.

The words of Leopold's older brother, Jasper, filled his mind. "*You should start looking for a girl, you know.*" But Leopold didn't see the need. He was still young, only twenty-six, and he was learning so much. Why settle down and force himself into a relationship? He would lose his position next to Adina, too.

He wiped sweat from his brow and continued to watch the healer's hands. It wasn't too warm out, the weather was finally taking a turn to autumn, but the cow had been a lot of work. Within minutes, the bovine perked up again and pulling as if wanting to go home. "What was wrong with her?" Leopold asked, straining against her weight.

The young healer looked troubled. "Poison. Has she been near anything out of the ordinary?"

Leopold shrugged, smiling apologetically. "She's not our cow. Her family wasn't able to bring her, so I offered to help."

"I will be in touch with the family, then. For now, she is healed." Then she was running toward the bridge leading into town, to her next appointment.

Leopold allowed the cow to lead him to her field. He enjoyed helping on the village farms, which was why he had offered in the first place, despite having to leave training for the day. He knew Adina would put in extra hours with him if he asked.

As he walked, Leopold waved to several neighbors. He loved Domum, his village. It was always such a peaceful place, and everyone was generally pleasant. He gazed across the river and could see one of the fields was almost ripe. He was excited for the harvest festival Domum threw every year. It was an evening of music, loud speaking, and sharing of food. It always took place before the reaping began, to give everyone excitement to gather the crop. It often worked, especially for the children harvesting for the first time.

Leo allowed the cow to enter the field shared by all the keepers of the livestock in the village, and thwacked her hide affectionately with her lead as she entered. He leaned against the fence and continued to watch the animals welcoming her back with flicks of their ears. She called to her calf and began grazing next to it.

"Leo!"

He saw one of the older women he knew with her daughter near his age walking up behind him. He waved in greeting, and they wandered over to him. He left the corral and met them. "Hello, Sarah. How is your family today?"

Sarah grinned. "We're doing fine, thank you." Leopold smiled at Sarah's daughter. When his eyes met hers, secret moments behind trees and in barns flashed through his mind. Sarah continued to speak of something Leopold had little interest in. He nodded and feigned excitement for her, however, pushing the memories of her daughter out of his mind. After several minutes, Sarah's daughter—Philipa—reminded her mother with a wince they had errands to run. *Does she think about that often?* Leopold wondered but then shrugged it off after waving goodbye to the women. Their activities had been years ago. They'd both moved on.

He loved his home, but sometimes the people were too routine. He yearned for something out of the normal—something to break up his constant training. Most people of Domum, however, were content to let life pass them by while they remained unchanged. He felt something was missing from his life, and it wasn't marriage.

Later that night, Leopold made his way to his mother's home. He walked through the door, and his younger sister greeted him from the table. She was cutting carrots for the evening's dinner and talking a mile a minute to their mother, Anora. Anora smiled at Leopold as he took off his jacket and hung it up. Emaline, Leopold's sister, was the youngest of the family. *If anyone needs to be looking for love and creating a life, it's Emaline,* Leopold thought. He knew their mother was pleased to allow them to stay in her home with her, but he also knew she had high hopes for Emaline now that she was grown.

Anora stood while encouraging Emaline to continue her story and walked toward Leopold. She kissed his cheek once and smiled at him before she continued her preparations for dinner. Emaline stood as well, her bowl of carrots chopped, and kissed his other cheek on her way past.

Emaline imitated her mother flawlessly and had done so her entire life. She had no memory of their father, so Anora had been her only parent. Anora was a short woman with a kind face. Her shoulders bowed, and Leopold suspected it was the stress of raising three sons and a daughter on her own. Her hair was a pale yellow, which contrasted from her dark-haired children. Emaline was a tall and slender young woman with her brown hair plaited like her mother's. She walked with a lasting childish optimism and was always quick to smile.

Leopold sat down at the table, knowing it would be pointless to offer to help with preparations. Anora would forbid it, and Emaline would complain about Leopold being in her way. He was content to sit and rest his legs.

Before dinner was prepared, Leopold's older brothers Aldus and Jasper came through the door. Leopold hadn't been expecting to see them, as they were both often gone for weeks at a time to patrol the borders of Domum. They tackled Leopold at the table, and the three of them moved outside to wrestle at their mother's bequest.

Leopold was the youngest of the three men and the resemblance was strong. They all had the same shade of red-brown hair and hazel eyes.

Leopold often thought Aldus looked the most like their father, from what he could remember. And he carried himself with the same confidence, which made him fit right in with the elite of the village. Jasper was quiet like their mother, but proud like their father.

When Emaline called them in for their meal they sat together and discussed the day's events. Aldus explained their presence in the home. "The council asked us to change rotations," he said.

"They don't get involved in patrol duties," Jasper added. "So we listen when they do."

"Did they tell you why they wanted the change?" Leopold asked as he shoveled food in his mouth.

Aldus shook his head. "They said the prophets needed things a certain way. Jasper and I came home and rearranged the schedule. When the prophets say the gods have a plan I tend to listen."

Leopold fought the instinct to roll his eyes. It wasn't that he didn't believe in the gods – he did. He didn't believe the prophets always got direct instruction from them. Specifically Judd, a council prophet Leopold's age. He couldn't imagine the gods talking to someone as mundane as Judd. He couldn't imagine a person his age being that important at all.

Later that evening, as they readied for sleep, Leopold asked his brothers "Do you ever feel as though there's something missing from your life?"

"You mean, like a woman?" Jasper chuckled.

Leopold glared at him. "No. I've told you—that's not something I'm ready for."

Aldus made an annoyed grunt. This was a script Leopold and Jasper went through often. "Leo, you seek adventure. Jasper, you need to find *yourself* a woman. Yours hasn't shown interest yet, and she most likely never will."

"I'll wait every sunset and every sunrise until Adina realizes her love for me," Jasper said. Leopold and Aldus would have laughed at this if they hadn't known Jasper was speaking the utmost honest truth, despite his jesting tone.

"And what of you, Aldus?" Leopold asked. "Don't you seek adventure?"

"You know my position, Leo." Aldus smiled. "My work is my one true love. I will not stop trying to provide for our mother. However, I do agree with what Jasper tells you. Find a woman, Leo. We all know that is what *you* need."

Leopold shook his head. "I don't need a woman." *I like the idea of adventure.* Adventure would be different. Leaving Domum on a quest would be new and exciting. He had spent the last dozen years training and hadn't once seen a use for it. Adventure would put him to the test.

They went to bed that night without another word. Both brothers would be gone from the home before the roosters would crow in the yard.

Leopold's brothers both chose to join the border patrol scouts. Aldus now held one of the highest positions. Jasper fancied himself the most cunning scout. When Leopold had been twelve years old, he had been handpicked by the council to train for the militia alongside Adina. It was an honor bestowed upon few to be chosen so young.

Adina, a girl of the same age as Leopold, had requested the council allow her to train at that time. The council had agreed, though tradition stated permissions like that would come in pairs. So, of all of the names submitted for consideration by their families for the honor, Leopold was chosen by the seers who sat on the council at that time.

Ever since then, Leopold woke with the crow and met with Adina and the other soldiers. Though they were young, they had been training alongside the militia for half their lives and possessed more skill than many of the new recruits. Adina was often asked to train them, and Leopold accompanied.

He woke this morning and took a slice of bread from the kitchen before making his way to the council building to meet with Adina. Today they would practice tracking with the new recruits in the woods surrounding the village.

Adina had chosen her vocation (and subsequently Leopold's) because of her skill. Her father was on the village council as a healer, Stace's counterpart. Adina's father being on the council prevented anyone else of his line to possess a seat. She had passed her challenge proving her skill in magic and opted to study with the militia.

Leopold reached the council building. There was no smoke rising from the chimney so he knew he was the first to arrive. He stepped through the doors and into the cold room. He disregarded the council meeting room and instead walked to the left, the back of the room away from the firepit, toward a door. On the other side was a storage room for the council which had been transformed into a mini library. On the far wall in this room was another door. He stepped through it and into the training yard behind the council building.

Domum was ruled by a twelve-person council. Each pairing within the council possessed powers gifted by the gods, a male and a female touched by a singular god possessing the same gifts. Every person on the council was the most proficient of their gifts. Every position could be challenged by someone who believed their skills to be more advanced than the representative on the council of the same gender. The council were fair rulers, imposing laws and providing leadership when necessary. Leopold liked this system of ruling very much and didn't understand why larger populations did not do the same.

Leopold was collecting supplies and placing them in a pile near the wall when Adina arrived through the same door. She was tall and beautiful with long blond hair she often kept plaited so as to hide it away in her knight's helm. Her eyes had always been a piercing gray, but as she had gotten older, they had become more understanding and discerning – an echo of her father's. Leopold was surprised this morning to see Adina followed by her mother.

Adina's mother She had the same face as Adina, though she was shorter and already possessed a head full of white hair. "Leo! How are you this morning?" Leopold was surprised to see her at the council building. She was expected across the river working in the apothecary at this hour.

"Good morning, Katherine." Leo smiled. "I'm doing well. Are we expecting you to join us in trainings today?"

"I was accompanying Adina," Katherine smiled. "I enjoy the time I get to spend with her."

"Yes, yes," Adina said. She began to organize Leopold's pile of supplies. "I enjoy our talks, too, mother, but I have a lot to do today. So we'll talk later tonight." Leopold returned Katherine's smile before she left.

"Is everything all right?" Leopold asked Adina.

Adina nodded. "Of course. Mother had a bee in her bonnet this morning is all."

Leopold didn't pry.

As their recruits arrived Adina began explaining their lesson. "Today we will be testing your skills in the woods," Adina told them. "We'll use this as a benchmark for your skills groups over the next couple of months. I intend to have you all competent scouts before the first snow."

The recruits all donned their packs and supplies and trekked south out of the old town toward the forest. The day before Adina had set specific trails for the recruits to follow, and even Leopold didn't know where they would lead. He wasn't worried, he'd always been confident in the woods beyond his house.

During the exercise recruits were sent in different directions. Adina tested Leopold as well, sending him on his own to hunt their target. She wouldn't say what it was, but Leopold was the first to arrive at the small clearing where Adina's younger sister Leah was waiting with a midday meal for them all.

Later that evening, after Adina had delivered her closing lecture to the recruits at the council building, Leopold found himself pondering the same conundrum from before. "Do you wish there was more?" he asked Adina.

"More what?" she asked.

"I feel as though I'm lacking something, like my life has stalled."

Adina was quiet for a moment as they passed through the council building. "I do wish the council would give me a quest."

"Yes, exactly. A quest!"

She walked over to a large rock under a tree to watch some horses in the field. She patted a spot beside herself for Leopold to sit. "Something to get me away from here, something to prove myself."

"You prove yourself every day," Leopold chastised. "You do so much for the people of Domum."

"We've never even seen a real battle." Her rebuttal sounded annoyed. "Why do you ask this?"

Leopold shrugged and kicked the dirt. "I have been feeling out of place."

"Well, until the council decides to give us our quest, we must both be content with our lives as they are."

I have no other choice, Leopold thought. *It's not like I could just take a trip. There's no where I want to go, nothing I want to see. I'm trapped here.*

They watched a group of young children run across the bridge. They stopped and began dancing around a small enchanted fire, laughing as purple flames sparked and flashed. Adina cupped her hands and blew into them, opening them and releasing breath toward the flame. It changed into a little orange dancing man, joining in on the rhythm of the children. They screamed with delight and swiveled to find the source. "Adina!" they shouted and ran over, the forgotten dancing man vanishing with a wave at their backs. "Do some magic for us!" they begged.

She laughed. "Isn't that what I've just done for you, children?"

"More!" they cried. She laughed again and flicked her wrist, sending orange butterflies into the air. The children laughed and jumped after them, reaching their arms as if to catch the escaping insects. Leopold laughed and watched in similar amazement.

"I will never get tired of watching magic," he said.

Adina chuckled as the last of the children chased after the fire bugs she sent into the dying sunlight. "Nor will they, I fear."

Though Leopold did not possess any magic himself, he was always impressed by those who did. His own sister, Emaline, was also proficient in the gift of creation, though none were as powerful as Adina. No one had managed to find an answer as to why Domum was touched with so much power by the gods. There was also no rhyme or reason as to why some possessed so much of the gift and others none at all. The most Leopold had ever managed once was to light a candle, but the effort had put him in bed for days. He did not understand magic, nor ever had any hope to, but he was grateful others did. Like Stace, who had saved his neighbor's cow the day before.

They finished their walk to Adina's house, and Leopold was invited to stay for dinner with her family before heading home in the dark. He heard the ruckus of men leaving the tavern across the river as he walked. It sounded as though there had been good news shared there.

Why do I feel this discontentment? Why can I not enjoy this life like everyone else? The thought of a quest sent shivers of excitement down his spine. He stared across the river to the tavern and yearned for more.

CHAPTER SIX

L EOPOLD SPENT THE NEXT several weeks attempting to bury his wanderlust. He threw himself into his work and focused all his energy on serving the people of Domum in any way he could. The harvest festival days away, and preparations were fast approaching. Leopold was beginning to feel the excitement build within him.

He watched as the council instructed the youth how to decorate for the occasion. Emaline was placed in charge of the cooking, and she was to form a team of her own to help. She was rather pleased to be handpicked by the council and took it upon her shoulders to make all of the food as perfect as possible. Aldus was placed in charge of creating a schedule that allowed for all of the border patrolmen to enjoy the festivities while still maintaining the proper protection the village warranted. Jasper was offered a promotion. It was a time of high emotion in Anora's home.

"Can you not see I am working here?" Emaline screamed. "Get out of my way!"

"Do not raise your voice like that in my home!" Anora chided.

"I'm looking for something to drink," Aldus said. Emaline threw a cup of water in Aldus's face. Aldus blinked and wiped water from his eyes.

"*Emaline.*" Anora grabbed her daughter's wrist and forced it down onto the table. "That is enough. We are all stressed, but this behavior is not acceptable. I expect more of you than these childish antics."

The fire died in Emaline's eyes as she realized her mistake. "I'm sorry, Mother," she said. She hugged Aldus. "Forgive me, Brother."

"It's all right." Aldus shook the water from his hair onto her. "I understand. Now, may I have something to drink?"

Leopold soon followed his brothers to bed after Emaline broke into tears after she'd added the wrong amount of an ingredient and thus had to use magic to repair the damage. He was beginning to feel an ache in his head from the shrieking.

The day of the festival arrived soon after the water incident, in which time Emaline had stopped speaking to her family and seemed half deranged when approached. Leopold watched as the people came together, smiling and excited for what the new year would bring. He watched little children chase each other, and then chased dogs away from the food table. Leopold watched Adina as she mingled with the people. He laughed when she produced sparkling delights and the people applauded. A young girl attempted to imitate Adina. She produced a single blue butterfly, and Adina noticed as it fluttered past her face. She turned, beaming, and sat on the floor to match the child's gaze and whispered instructions to the girl. The girl steadied herself with a hand on Adina's shoulder as her face paled with the effort. After a few moments, with a bubble of excitement from the girl, Adina's new friend had produced an assortment of butterflies. The adults around them cheered with pride.

Leopold sensed a person standing beside him. He glanced around and saw a young boy—a council messenger, from the tunic he wore—several steps away. He was watching Adina. His eyes flicked to Leopold and then he hurried the rest of the way to Leopold's side. "The council wishes to speak with you," he said. "Immediately. You and Adina." And then he hurried back to the council.

Leopold caught Adina's eye and nodded toward the road. She stood, congratulating the young girl with a hug before making her way to Leopold. She took her time, greeting those she passed with warm smiles. When she reached Leopold, he set off southward down the road, Adina at his side. "What is it, Leo?" she asked.

"I'm not sure. I was just told both of us are needed by the council."

"Well, that can't be good." Adina seemed concerned. "Why are they not at the festival?"

"I have no answer for that," Leopold said.

They arrived at the meeting house quickly. When they did, they found the full council sitting in the large hall. As they were greeted by the council, Leopold noticed they all wore the same grave expression. "Adina," Edith spoke first. She was the eldest of the council, proficient in creation magic, the council member Adina should have replaced. "We've grave news to share with you and hope you will receive it well."

Leopold felt Adina stiffen before she knelt before the council. "Whatever the council deems to share with me will be well received, Lady Edith."

"We have been foretold of a possible danger to Domum.," Judd continued. He was their own age and had the gift of prophecy. "We see many futures regarding this variant, and we wish to follow the most optimistic outcome."

"As we'd hope." Adina nodded. The words all felt very formal to Leopold as he knelt beside Adina. He felt uneasy by it.

Ibb, the youngest of the council at ten years of age, spoke next. She was Judd's female equivalent and could also see the future. "You must travel toward the kingdom Camelot. By the time you arrive, they will have suffered a great loss." Leopold was snared by this young girl's intense stare. "Go and represent us, Adina, and offer Domum's support. They will not take kindly to this offer. They will see Domum as weak to send a woman knight, but the gods have commanded you be the one with this task. We don't care that they won't accept you. We do not believe they would ever accept help from another kingdom at this time."

"That is none of our concern," an old man interrupted. Gavin, with the gift of tongues and language. "Because we will not be there to help the kingdom at all." His voice was harsh and his eyes sharp as steel. "We are there to relieve them of their pest and no more."

"What is this pest?" Adina asked in concern. "What must I do with it?"

The woman nearest them—Gloriana, who was a shapeshifter—spoke then. "It is foretold that a young woman with powerful magic will be unleashed upon Camelot. She will kill few, but those she kills will be of high standing. She will not know how to control her magic, so you must bring her home and convince her to learn from us. If not, we fear she will create a danger for Domum that would end our way of life—it would end our magic."

"Why would we bring this danger to Domum?" Leopold demanded. "If she has been dangerous in Camelot why would we risk bringing her here?"

The council room was quiet before Edith spoke again. "There is something else you must know."

Leopold waited for their justification.

"The woman you are seeking . . ." Edith spoke so softly Leopold could barely hear her. "This is where she belongs. Where she has *always* belonged."

Adina sounded as confused as Leopold felt. "My lady?"

Ibb spoke again with her high voice. "In our visions, we have seen a familiar face." Tears streaked down her cheeks, and her small jaw shook. "Judd saw that the woman you must bring home—she is the lost Megara."

Silence seemed to suffocate the room. *Megara.* That name hadn't been spoken in almost twenty years. Ibb's emotion felt out of place with her young age. The baby had been stolen from Domum by a man the council had trusted and had been mentoring. On the night this man had taken the child for reasons unknown to the village even now, many had died in the attempt to save her. That included Leopold's own father.

Anger and hate boiled within Leopold, so much so that he glared at the floor to avoid displaying his thoughts on his face. *Why should we bring her back? This girl who has brought so much pain to our home—why bring her back?* Especially if she was creating such devastation in Camelot. She was following in the ways of the man who took her in the first place. They deserved each other.

"How will I know where to find her?" Adina asked, always the clear head.

Leopold lifted his head when no one answered and jolted when he realized the entirety of the council was staring at him. Some of the faces were smiling, but most were glowering. Leopold felt the skin prickle at the back of his neck, and his stomach rolled. "This is why you must take Leopold," Edith explained. "You will not be the one to find her. He will be."

"And what if I refuse?" Leopold wasn't sure what gave him the courage to speak against the council. There were some hisses heard in the room. Leopold couldn't come to terms with returning such a dangerous woman to his home.

Edith smiled sadly. "If you refuse, Leopold, you will be the one to damn Domum."

CHAPTER SEVEN

T HE AIR WAS HEAVY when Leopold accepted his mistake before
he bowed his head once more. "I apologize for my words. I will
do whatever it is you ask."

After his outburst, Leopold remained kneeling with his head
bowed while Adina was given instructions and directions from the
council. Leopold could feel someone watching him but didn't dare lift
his head in defiance again. He stayed in his meek position and allowed
Adina to gather their instructions.

"Come, Leo," Adina said as she passed, placing her hand on his
shoulder. "Let us get ready to leave."

Leopold stood, and as he lifted his head, his eyes locked with Ibb's.
She looked fearful as she mouthed two words. *Please hurry.* Or that's
what Leopold thought he saw her whisper, anyway. He nodded toward her, turning to follow Adina out the door.

They walked from the building quietly, but once they were out
of range of listening ears, Adina stopped Leopold and glared at him.
"How dare you speak against the council like that? You humiliated

me. 'What if I refuse?' Who are you to have that choice? Once the council—the *seers*—state their claim, you listen."

"I am sorry," Leopold said, trying to keep his voice even. "It will not happen again. I will not embarrass you further."

Adina stared at him for a moment longer before shaking her head and walking away. "I doubt that, but come on anyway."

They parted ways at the bridge. Adina had charged Leopold with gathering provisions while she tracked down the map maker, Gaius. She left Leopold to begin her task. Leopold continued into the new village where his mother was celebrating. They needed to collect supplies and say their goodbyes. He suspected Anora would be able to organize some food for them.

Leopold took his mother's hand as he passed through the festival. She faced him with a smile that faded away as she gathered her skirts and followed him.

"What's wrong, Leo?" she asked once they were out of the crowd.

"Adina and I have received a task from the council," he said loud enough for her to hear as they walked. "We must leave Domum for a time."

"When will you return?" she asked.

"I am not certain."

Anora pulled him to a stop, and stared in his face. "But you promise you *will* return?" she whispered. Leopold stepped forward and kissed his mother on her forehead.

"I promise, Mother. If only for you, I will come home."

"What will you be needing?" Anora asked him, continuing into their house.

"I'm not sure. Some food and supplies."

"Will you be walking or will you take a horse?"

"I . . . don't know that either."

"Do you know what you will be doing, at least?" Anora asked, exasperated.

"Yes," he said. He decided at that moment not to tell her the nature of the quest. The thought of calling it a quest made him pause. Excitement began to sink in, but he tried to focus on the conversation. He didn't wish any pain upon his mother and worried telling her his task would do just that. "But I can't tell you." He swallowed down his smile.

Anora didn't say anything more. She bustled around their home gathering various foods. "If you can't tell me how long you'll be gone, I can't accurately pack for you. Be aware of what you have in your packs. And stay safe.,"

"I will." Leopold placed the sack on the table and retreated to his attic room to gather clothing for the trip. He had some various supplies in his possession which he added to his pack such as his father's hunting knife and the leather flask Aldus had given him years ago.

Before leaving the attic Leopold decided to go through his brothers' trunks as well to see if they had left anything useful. He found some fishing line and rope in Jasper's and a tinder kit in Aldus'. Just before leaving the room he recalled the old satchel he and his brothers once used to save the meager money they had earned. The three of them once hoped to open a shop in town where Aldus would serve as the blacksmith, Jasper a carpenter, and Leopold an armorer.

Now, the money would be used to buy more rations on their journey if necessary.

A quest, he thought. *I'm actually going on a quest. I'll be leaving the village. I'll be going on an adventure.*

I'm leaving.

The excitement he felt was unmatched.

Once he at last left his home, he found Adina walking down the road between their houses. She was heading toward the home of a man who lent his horses. Leopold breathed a sigh of relief at the prospect of riding. "Come on," she said. "There's no time to lose."

Adina knocked on the man's door, and he opened it rather quickly. Leopold was surprised, wondering why he wasn't at the festival. The man was as surprised to see them. "Can I help you?"

"The council has given us a task away from Domum," Adina explained. "I wondered if you might spare a few horses for us."

The man gazed between Adina and Leopold. "How many riders?"

"Two to leave, and three to return."

"I know you have skill, Adina, but what about him?" He jerked his chin toward Leopold. Leopold felt his pride bristle.

"We train together," Adina assured him. "We have the same skill."

The man nodded and stepped out of his house, closing the door behind him. "Come along, then."

Leopold had indeed trained with Adina, but she spent more time with horses than he did. In truth, he wasn't sure how Adina was able to put so much extra effort into their training beyond what he had done, but he did trust her knowledge and experience.

During their short stroll to the horse field Leopold observed the supplies Adina had brought with her. She also carried a knapsack across her back and another one presumably full of supplies. He hoped

Gaius had been able to give her a decent itinerary for their journey, or a map if he actually had one for their path.

When they reached the field, several horses seemed to recognize their master and came trotted over. The man accompanying them placed leads on three of the beasts, handing each the lead to one horse. He led the way to the barn with the third horse, and they gathered tack.

Adina and Leopold climbed on their horses. The man handed Adina the lead to the third, and she attached it to her saddle. When he was assured they did in fact know how to handle the horses, the man nodded at them and waved, heading to the festival across the river.

The sun was already beginning to set when the two of them—and three horses—crossed the river. They passed down several side streets to avoid the crowds of the party, agreeing to leave the village and head to the farthest watchtower before resting for the night and getting an early start in the morning. They passed out of the village without any incident and rode to the final tower. Adina rode right up to the front porch of the house beside the tower and dismounted, calling for the lead patrolman as she tied both horses to the hitch.

Leopold saw his brother Aldus open the door. "Adina! What in the world brings you here? Has something happened at the festival?" Leopold followed Adina's actions and tied his horse beside hers before joining her at the door.

"No, Sir Aldus. Everything is fine in Domum," she assured him with a smile. "We are needing a place to stay for the night. I must inform you that we will be away for at least a week. And if all goes well, we will be returning with an extra companion."

Aldus looked toward Leopold, then to Adina. "Is everything all right?" he asked again.

"The council has assigned us a brief journey," Adina assured him. "All is well."

Aldus opened the door wider and invited them in. As they entered, Jasper walked around the corner and froze at the sight of Adina and his brother in the entry.

"What are you doing here?" Jasper asked.

"The council has given us a quest," Adina said in a modest tone, but her expression did nothing to convince Jasper of any indifference.

"Well, aren't you excited for that!" He laughed. "That's all you've wanted in your life. I'm sure you're quite pleased with yourself."

Leopold worried that Jasper's forwardness would annoy Adina, but he saw that she fought a smile. "I might be," she said. Then her face returned to its typical confidence. "But that has nothing to do with it. We are to perform the task the council has requested of us and return home."

"And when will that be?" Jasper asked, his nonchalance not fooling anyone.

"About a week," Adina said in a coy manner. "We will be returning with a woman from another kingdom."

"And who might this mysterious woman be? Will she be good-looking?" Jasper smirked.

"We do not know what she looks like." Adina's tone became frosty, surprising Leopold. When he regarded her he noticed the few signs of playfulness she was previously displaying were gone. Her jaw was set.

"Then how will you know who she is?" Jasper asked, his smile fading like he had noticed, too.

"The council says Leo will know who she is," Adina explained.

Jasper grinned at Leopold. "Make her a pretty one, won't you, Brother?"

"Leopold will know when he sees her and not a moment before," Adina snapped. Jasper appeared cowed. Leopold chuckled. He could step in at any time but was enjoying their banter. His brother could use some humility now and then.

"I did not mean to offend you, Adina. I will get you some dinner and then you may take your leave for the night. There is a room at the end of the hall for your use before you spend days on your own in the forests."

Adina nodded and took her bag down the hall to the room he indicated. Leopold helped his brother with the food preparations, giving Adina the space she wanted. "I thought you were off patrol tonight, Jasper," Leopold said.

"I'm here for a few hours while the other men enjoy the first night of the festival."

"Did you draw the short straw?" Leopold teased.

"No," Jasper said. "I chose this task. I had been intending to avoid Adina. The first night is the night she tends to show off the most, no?"

Leopold chuckled. "You have never complained about that before."

"I'm not complaining," Jasper corrected. Then, after a breath, he added, "It's becoming more and more difficult . . . to deny my feelings for her, and I know she will never return them. And it is very unlikely our names will be chosen by the council as a match after all this time. I didn't want to deal with that this evening."

In Domum, most couples fell in love and chose to get married through their own agency. However, the council did choose one couple a year to be married with their blessing. Occasionally those couples were not previously courting. Those with the gift of prophecy would choose the couple to bless based on their future. The young women of the village had many superstitions and often attempted to convince the seers to pair them with the men they fancied.

"And here we are, intruding on your escape."

"Yes," Jasper mused. "Intruding."

After dinner, when Adina excused herself for the night, Leopold sat with his brothers by the fireplace. Aldus looked concerned. "You know about the likelihood of bandits, right?"

"Of course," he fought the urge to roll his eyes.

"Usually people like to travel in bigger groups," Aldus cautioned. "It's a deterrent to do so. The bandits are less likely to attack you if there is a big company passing through."

"We can handle ourselves," Leopold reminded him. "It's not like we haven't been training for fourteen years."

"There's a difference between practice and the real thing," Jasper said. "You've never been beyond the borders. You haven't ever seen a real fight."

"I don't anticipate needing to fight," Leopold sighed.

"You never anticipate such a thing," Aldus argued. "You can't it's a completely different experience to fight for your life."

"You two haven't been in such a fight either," Leopold said defensively.

"For being a part of the knights in training," Jasper shook his head. "You've been awfully sheltered. The border sees a lot more action than you realize."

Leopold blinked. "You've been in danger out here? And the council never said anything to us?"

"Of course not," Jasper seemed offended. "The border patrol could handle it ourselves."

"When we warn you about bandits, we're not discussing an unknown threat, Leo. We have actual evidence of danger in these woods."

Leopold considered their words. He'd had no idea his brothers had seen any conflict out in the woods. He wasn't sure why the council had never told the villagers, let alone the knights.

"We'll be prepared," Leopold promised them. "Thank you for the warning."

The next morning Adina woke Leopold where he was sleeping with his brothers in the main room of the home. They left without waking the others, eager to get their journey started.

As they rode Leopold mused. *I am on a quest,* he thought. His heart beat with excitement and his palms were sweaty with uncertainty. Though Leopold was glad of the interruption in his routine, he could not get past what the council had told him. "Why must I be the one to identify her?" he demanded of the trees as they rode past. "I don't even know what she looks like. I was seven when she was taken. I never even looked twice at her. How will I be able to identify her? And how am I supposed to find her at all?"

Adina was quiet for a moment. "Why does this bother you? You were quite rude to the council when they suggested it."

"Adina, my father died the night Megara was taken."

"Many people died," she countered. "We will be returning Megara to her own broken family. All she has left is her mother. Her father and her brothers all died too. So many people lost loved ones when Merlin took the youngling."

"Merlin?" Leopold was so surprised, he pulled his horse to a stop. Adina rode for several more paces before she realized she'd left him behind. Leopold didn't recall ever being told the kidnapper's name before. "The warlock Merlin?"

Adina scoffed. "Some warlock! My father tells me Merlin spoke highly of himself, but kept himself so drunk, his magic did not work. That, or he really did not possess the magic he claimed." She seemed dubious.

Leopold kicked his horse into movement and caught up to her. "Do you remember Merlin?" he asked. "You would have been in closer contact with him, with your father on the council."

Adina was quiet for a few moments. "I do remember him."

"What was he like?" Leopold prodded when it seemed she wouldn't continue.

"He was charming," she said with a shrug. "I was eight. I remember he made me laugh and smile more than I ever had before. My mother thought he was sometimes crass, but she accepted my father's wishes to have him in our home."

"Do you know what happened?" Leopold asked. "That night?"

"I don't wish to talk about it," Adina snapped. Then, with an apologetic smile, "At least, not at this time."

They rode most of that day in silence, commenting on past lessons or consulting on meals when the awkwardness grew too long. Leopold felt like his head was full of cotton. He couldn't wrap his mind around Merlin being the one who had done so many terrible things. From what he remembered the man had been invited into every home. And then one day he'd disappeared. He had asked once why Merlin was gone and he remembered his mother changing the subject. He never got an answer.

Adina and Leopold tried to avoid any traffic. They weren't afraid of any harm to themselves from other kingdoms—they were marked as Domum citizens with the blankets on the horses—but they were wary of wasting time with unnecessary interactions. Jasper had mentioned the threat of bandits and other lawless outcasts while they'd had dinner. They intended to move quickly.

"Are you at all nervous about us finding Megara?" Leopold asked. "I mean, just the two of us?"

"Do you believe the council should have sent a whole army to take a single woman away?" Adina joked as they reached the outskirts of the Camelot lands. "I do feel, had they seen the need, the council would have sent a guard or two with us. I have faith that they thought this through before sending us on this journey."

"They may have seen the future, but this woman we are collecting has *killed* people, Adina."

"Not directly—that was Merlin's doing. The council—"

"The council is not here," Leopold interrupted. "What if they were wrong?"

"Have faith, Leo," Adina said. "I believe we will be fine. We're on a quest from the gods."

Adina gestured toward a clearing just seen through the trees. They led the horses in and sat down, resting for a time as they decided what they were to do from there. "What else did the council tell you?" Leopold asked. "I admit I stopped listening after my chastisement."

"I will enter the kingdom and seek a meeting with the king. While I am there, inevitably being told no and to leave the kingdom, you will be searching the outer forest for the girl."

"Easier said than done. This forest is massive. Where do I even begin?"

Adina smiled and stretched. "Well, the council believes you will succeed. They believe you to be the only one *to* succeed. You were the first to find Leah in our training exercise in our woods."

"Our woods are familiar. I know what seems out of place there. I don't know anything about this forest."

"The skills are the same," Adina insisted. "You know how to search."

I don't believe the council really knows what they're asking of us, Leopold thought. "Well, what will you be doing in the land of Camelot to convince them of our willingness to aid them? Did the council even tell you what aid they need?"

"I'm . . . not sure yet. And no, they didn't say," Adina admitted.

"You mean the council didn't tell you everything?" Leopold asked while making a face.

Adina rolled her eyes. "The council leaves the fine details of our lives to ourselves," she reminded him.

"Well, good luck, then," Leopold said.

"And you, Leo," she said. "Good luck to you."

Leopold climbed onto his horse. "So, when are we going to enter Camelot?"

"We?" Adina laughed. "What are you talking about?"

Leopold shot her an expression full of shock. "You don't intend me to allow you to enter a foreign kingdom without any support."

"That is exactly what I expect of you," she said.

"Adina, I can't. Not with any good conscience."

"They will have a hard enough time taking a woman knight seriously, let alone if she were accompanied by a man."

"You cannot be serious. As you said, Adina, you are a *woman*. Only the gods know what Camelot will do to you."

"Precisely—the gods know. Don't worry. I'll be fine."

She placed her helm on her head, untied the spare horse, and handed the lead to Leopold.

"Adina, wait!"

She ignored him, and before he could say anything more, she mounted her horse and left. Leopold groaned in frustration and dismounted once more, tying the horses to a nearby tree and kicking at a loose stone. He watched her enter the distant gates of Camelot.

Why did the council send us on this stupid, pointless mission? He was angry that Adina had not allowed him to accompany her. *We could work so much better if we were together, and if we relied on each other. How am I supposed to find this lost girl?* Leopold very much disliked this part of the plan. *Even if I do find her, Adina at least has magic! I don't. There is no way I can control Megara if she has magic.* He never imagined this would be the use of his training.

Leopold wandered the woods a little at a time, moving the horses to each new section he searched so they were never too far away.. He stopped when he heard the twig snap. His hand landed on the hilt of his sword. "Who's there?" he called with as much force as he could muster, drawing his sword. His breath felt stuck in his chest. He didn't expect a response, but he was unnerved by the stillness.

Taking a few steps forward he looked for something out of the ordinary. Anything. He froze when he spotted a glint of light shining through the trees. The light blinked. *I don't know these woods. What could be waiting?*

A deer moved out of the trees and Leopold relaxed. He felt embarrassed. *Of course there are wild animals here. I should have expected that.* He hadn't noticed movement before but had seen the evidence of animals all around him.

"You let down your guard too soon, sir."

Leopold spun around, lifting his sword, the tip of which stopped mere centimeters from the young woman's heart. When he took in the blond hair, blue eyes, and angular face he almost lowered his weapon to give the woman a stern lecture and ask why had she followed them from Domum. A heartbeat later, he realized the woman wasn't Margaret, the council seamstress. This woman in front of Leopold was much younger, her cheeks much more hollow. And there was a scar on her cheek that Margaret did not have, but the resemblance was strong.

"Who are you?" Leopold demanded of her, though he already suspected the answer.

She studied him with an intensity he had never encountered before. It made his skin crawl, as if Leopold was the threatening stranger, not her. "You don't know me?"

"Of course not. Who are you?" he repeated.

"Hmm . . ." She walked around and appraised him.. Leopold kept his sword level with her chest. "You're not from here." She said this as if it was of great interest to her, but that it was obvious that she was right. He didn't have Domum's emblem on his clothing, and the horses that did have it were faced away from them. How did she know he wasn't from Camelot?

"What is your name?" he demanded.

"I am Meggy," she said. "Though . . . the people of Camelot are calling me the Dragon Woman." Her clear laugh rang through the trees. Leopold heard birds cry as they flew away, and chills went down his back. This was her, then, without a doubt.

How can she look so much like Margaret? He'd been picturing a much more intimidating creature, a killer in human skin, not this normal, though hungry, looking young woman in front of him.

"Why do they call you that?" he asked, turning to keep her in front of him.

She stopped walking and stared at him again, her head cocked to the side like a curious dog. Leopold felt a bead of sweat fall down his spine. *Those eyes look as though they could end me on the spot.*

"I kill people," she said. "With fire and magic. I've killed many people." Leopold continued to stare at her. He wasn't going to let her see his hesitation. "Does that frighten you?"

"No," he lied. "You can't hurt me." *I knew it, I knew it, I knew it. Where is Adina? I won't be able to stop her if she uses magic!*

She laughed, throwing her head back. The laugh was too smooth, too much like a child's. "I can't hurt you?" she asked. "And why is that?" She was grinning, enjoying this much more than Leopold was.

"Because if you do, you'll never leave this place." He was fumbling for words, trying to stall for time. "I've been sent to take you away from here."

She tossed her head, her blond hair falling in waves. "How is that? You didn't know who I was until moments ago."

"I was sent here by my people to take the Dragon Woman away from Camelot," he told her, relaxing his stance but not lowering his sword. "Your mother is asking for you." This was a lie. As far as he knew no one had told her their quest before they left, but he was fumbling for anything he could to keep her from using magic.

Her eyes became stony. "I don't have a mother." As angry as her expression was, her voice was uncertain.

"Your name is Megara. You've been living with a man named Merlin all your life."

"My name is Meggy." She glared at him, but hesitated. "How do you know about Merlin?"

"You killed him, didn't you?" he asked, realization filling him. She continued to stare.

"Who are you?" she asked him without denying it. "Why are you here?"

"I told you. I am here to take you from this place."

"What is your name? Where do you want to take me?"

"Leo! Leo, where are you?"

They both glanced behind Leopold at the sound of Adina's voice. When he glanced back again, Megara was gone. "I'm here," he called to Adina as he spun around. *But she's gone.* With her absence, Leopold felt something stir within him that he couldn't name. Even though Leopold knew she was dangerous, and an hour before he'd been praying they wouldn't find her and they could return home empty-handed, something deep within him saw this young girl differently. It was probably how everyone else remembered her, but it was connecting for him. She was a kidnapped child left alone in a world that did not want her. He wasn't sure what had changed within him, but it felt as though a blinder had been removed from his eyes and he saw the bigger picture. This young woman was of Domum. She deserved to come home.

Leopold surprised himself with the deepest desire to protect her. *I've been bewitched,* he tried to tell himself, though he knew this was not possible. That kind of magic wasn't possible, even in Domum. *Or is it?* He'd made it a point not to involve himself in things that didn't concern him, and as he wasn't gifted he'd always put the supernatural in that category. Maybe it *was* possible to influence someone else.

"Leo, are you all right?" Adina approached, pulling her helm from her head. "You look a little pale. I wasn't gone long enough to warrant such concern, though I'm glad you are so worried for my health," she teased. The smile faded from her face when he didn't respond. "Leo, what is it?"

"I saw her." Leopold's sword tip fell to the dirt beside him.

"Who?" Adina drew her sword and spun around.

"Megara," Leopold said, his throat dry. "I saw Megara."

"Where?" Adina pivoted to him.

"She was just here. She's gone now."

"What does she look like?" Adina asked, sheathing her sword.

"Like a younger version of Margaret."

"Margaret? The seamstress?"

Leopold nodded. "She is Megara's mother, isn't she?"

"Yes. I. . . I thought . . ." She seemed embarrassed.

"That she would look evil? Yeah," Leopold nodded. "Me too."

They stared at each other for a moment before they moved as one toward their horses. "How did the audience with the king go?" Leopold asked.

"As well as to be expected. King Arthur has been king since the days following Merlin's death three months ago. It appears Merlin was a dear friend of the king's He acted so arrogant, but his manners were horrid. It's as if he had never set foot in a throne room before he was appointed."

"How is that possible?" Leopold asked.

"Rumor has it, after the deaths in Camelot, the people rebelled against the king, who hadn't even known Megara existed. There was some sort of competition to prove who was the rightful king. And this man, Arthur, won."

Leopold exhaled. "Well then," he said. "So, he refused our offer?"

"As the council said he would. I asked for permission to observe on our way out of the kingdom, and if we spotted the woman, we would take her with us."

"Did he agree?"

"He said we have three days to leave Camelot. If we find her, we're welcome to her. If his people find her first . . . they have orders to kill on sight. 'We must rid the world of the magic she possesses,' he said." Adina scowled at that.

Leopold's heart twisted for Adina. The magic Megara possessed was Domum magic. *She said she killed by fire; she possesses the magic of creation. That's the same magic Adina possesses. Had Arthur known this, would he have killed her on sight too?* Leopold felt certain he would have.

"I guess that means we have three days to find her again, Let's make a plan."

"Are you humoring me? Do you believe we will fail?"

"No, of course not. This girl—she told me she killed with fire, Adina. We have to decide how to convince her to come home, and we have to decide how to do that safely."

"So, she does have magic," Adina mused. She sat on a small boulder and bit into an apple she'd pulled from her saddle bag.

"I'm not sure how we can convince her to come with us," He admitted.

"Now we're convincing and not forcing? What happened to the army you wanted to drag her away?"

Adina was teasing, but Leopold was bitter about her truths. "You didn't see her, Adina. She's not a horrible monster. She belongs in Domum."

"While I do not disagree, Leo," Adina began as she chewed, "what has changed in you? I do believe we should proceed with caution. She has magic, and she has killed people with her magic. What's to stop her from killing again? Do we want to take that threat home?"

"Do we know why she killed?" Leopold asked instead.

Adina shook her head and bit her apple again. After she swallowed, she said, "All the people seemed to know was that Merlin entered the street on fire, and while she was running away from the scene, Megara killed three more men. The fires spread and lit houses, and a family was trapped inside one of them."

An animal squeaked in a nearby bush, causing Leopold's jaw to snap shut in alarm. "But we don't know what her reasons were."

"Would there be a good reason to kill seven people?" Adina asked. "Think of your people, Leopold. If this woman is a danger to Domum, would you want to take her back?"

Leopold shook his head. "Of course not. But . . . you didn't see her, Adina. She isn't a danger. She's afraid." As Leopold voiced these thoughts, he felt his heart settle. He knew his words were true. He didn't understand, but he knew he wanted to. This strange assuredness was foreign to him. He had never once felt this quiet whisper within him, guiding him.

"How can we prove to the people of Domum that she isn't?"

"We need to convince her. If she wants to learn how to control her magic, she'll come with us."

Adina looked at the rustling in the bushes while she thought. "I suppose you're right. But they are still bound to question her."

I don't much care what the people of Domum believe. "She'll do well," Leopold said. "You'll see." *She has to. She belongs with us.*

They spent hours searching for signs of her. However, other than her path encircling Leopold they weren't able to find any other human footprints. It should have been easy—while tracking the prints she had left, they knew she was barefooted, and the soil was moist. But they couldn't find any other human tracks other than their own boot prints anywhere. They continued to search until they didn't have any sunlight left, then returned to their horses and started a fire.

His mind was stuck on her face and the feeling he had when he saw her. He'd never felt that kind of connection before, to anyone. Philipa had been only one of the women he had tried to court in his life, but he'd never felt a draw like this to them. They barely spoke and by all accounts this woman was dangerous. What was making him so confident she wasn't a threat?

The animal life was active in the forest surrounding Camelot, now that the sun had set. It put Leopold on edge, living in such a strange place with so much unknown, plus a dangerous woman they could find no trace of. He did not like it. *But I won't leave without her.* He couldn't, not now that he had met her. *There's something about her I wasn't expecting.* He wanted the chance to explore that feeling.

Leopold did not sleep that night. He thought he heard whispering a few times, but when he rolled over, he was met with only bushes and darkness. He stared at the trees above him for hours. He thought about what this woman would mean to Domum. He was certain she hadn't always been like this. The way she had examined him while they spoke reminded him of Adina. For the first time, he knew he would be the one to return Megara to Domum and return her innocence to her. He would do it, no matter the cost.

Chapter Eight

T HEY SPENT THE NEXT day calling for Megara and searching the woods. Other than a small stoat spooking the horses, they'd seen no other evidence of life.

When the sun dawned on the third morning, Leopold became desperate. He'd driven himself half mad the day before thinking of his desire to return Megara to Domum. He expressed his concern to Adina of an enchantment Megara could have placed over him. "Is it possible for anyone to manipulate another person's emotions?"

Adina stopped. "What are you talking about?"

"I know Domum possesses the powers of creation, healing, prophecy, language, shapeshifting, and willpower, but do any of those allow a person to have control over another?"

Adina was quiet for a moment, pondering. "The category you called willpower is actually psychokinesis. Children call it 'willpower' because they can't say the proper word. I suppose with creation or willpower, manipulation might be possible, but that would be an very draining strain of magic. I can't imagine anyone who would be strong enough to do it for any period of time to make it worth it."

Leopold nodded and continued prepping the fire.

The next morning as Leopold thought on that conversation, he could not deny he was relieved he was not under anyone's control, but he was disconcerted with the speed at which his intentions had changed. He had argued against the council, after all! He had not wanted to bring her home. But here he was, begging this woman to reveal herself and come with him.

Leopold stepped through a tree line then stepped back, waving to get Adina's attention. He held his finger to his lips then pointed toward the stream. He'd glimpsed Megara kneeling beside the water. Adina nodded her understanding then creeped in a different direction. Leopold was concerned that she intended to frighten Megara but had no way to convey any plans to her. *We should have decided what to do when we found her.*

Leopold watched as the young woman lowered her hands into the water and seemed to watch it for a moment before she lifted her cupped hands to her mouth.

"You know, there are easier ways to get a drink," he found himself saying. He'd stepped through the trees again. Now he tried to play off his courage by unsheathing his sword and tossing the hilt in his palm a couple times. Megara jumped to her feet and spun around. She glared at him, holding her hands up with her palms facing him. "I have more experience with magic users than you seem to think. I know how to fight them. Stand down."

"Are you following me now?" she demanded, her eyes flashing. Leopold noticed a small stoat run to her from the trees, slipping beneath her skirt. Megara didn't react.

"I told you the other day—I was sent to collect you. I can't leave without you."

"What if I don't want to leave?" Her eyes narrowed. "You should be afraid of me."

He shrugged. "Maybe, but the thing is . . . I'm not." And he wasn't. He still couldn't find any part of him that was frightened of this woman.

Leopold watched as an orange light shot at Megara from across the small stream and wrapped around Megara, slamming her arms to her sides. As the light dimmed, Leo could see ropes securing themselves around her. Megara struggled, and Leopold nodded at Adina as she crossed the stream and stood next to him. Her sword was also drawn.

"Stupid mortal!" Megara screamed at them.

Adina snorted. "You're just as mortal as the rest of us."

Megara growled. "How did you do this? I'm the most powerful—"

"You're not that, either," Adina interrupted with exasperation. "Can we agree you will stop talking until you understand the whole story?"

"I know the whole story," Megara hissed. "The last person who 'told the whole story' died! And I laughed!"

"You didn't laugh," Leopold said. Both women looked at him. Adina seemed amused, and Megara sneered at him.

"How do you know?" she demanded, her chin held high. He didn't know, but it felt right.

"Even if you were as evil as you're acting, you wouldn't have laughed ." Leopold watched her for a moment. "It was Merlin. As terrible of a man as I'm sure he was, you stayed with him all this time."

Megara didn't show any reaction other than whispering words Leopold didn't understand. Adina raised her hand, and a gag appeared over Megara's mouth.

"She uses spells," Adina explained to Leopold with surprise. "That's at least one advantage we have." She addressed Megara. "Are you willing to come with us peacefully? Or will we have to force you? Either way, you are coming with us."

All three stood in silence before Megara walked forward, her head held high with as much dignity as she could manage. Adina led her to the horses. Once to them, Leopold held Megara's shoulders and stared in her face. "If we untie you, would you ride beside me without fighting? Without any attempt to hurt us?"

"Why should she ride next to you?" Adina demanded.

"If she misbehaves near me, you would have a chance to tie her up again. If she misbehaves beside you, it would be to incapacitate you in some way," Leopold said without looking at Adina, knowing he was making up an excuse to be near Megara.

Adina couldn't deny the logic, however. "All right. If she'll agree."

They waited for a moment, watching Megara. She stared back at Leopold, her eyes puzzled before she nodded. He undid her gag and the bands around her torso. She rubbed her arms before speaking. "Thank you," she whispered. All the malice was gone from her voice. She walked toward the horses, reaching forward and stroking Adina's mount down the center of its face. Adina had drawn her sword again, but now she and Leopold looked at each other. Adina sheathed it before walking to the horses herself.

"Are we ready to go, then?" Megara asked.

Leopold watched her eyes a moment, nervous about their ride home, before helping her mount her horse and then climbing on his own. They had given her the more docile beast and he was grateful for it—she appeared out of place upon its saddle. Leopold tied a lead rope between her horse and his so it would follow him.

They didn't dare ride too quickly due to Megara's inexperience, but they were anxious to leave Camelot's lands before any guard could find them. They were certain to be found by men who knew the land better than them. They did not stop until after the sun had set, when they were sure they were out of Camelot. Adina dismounted first and set to starting a small fire while Leopold helped Megara off her horse. Her eyes were locked on Adina, and Leopold thought he could see fear hidden there when she watched Adina create a fire with nothing more than her hands. When he blinked, the expression was gone, and her chin was raised in defiance.

She walked over to the fire and sat next to it. Adina hesitated then moved away to sit on the opposite log. Megara turned to Leopold. "Are *you* frightened of sitting beside me?" she asked with an accusing lilt to her voice. "You just spent hours beside me on a horse, but sitting next to me beside a fire frightens you?"

Leopold gripped the hilt of his sword and walked to her, sitting closer to her than the situation warranted. "I told you before, Megara. I am not afraid of you."

"My name is Meggy," she snapped. They all listened to the fire crackle and hiss. "Are we going to have any dinner?" she asked. Before they could say anything, Megara added, "I can get us meat, if you trust me to go for a time. I'll be back. If you'll . . . trust me."

"And if we don't?" Adina asked.

"Then we don't get fresh meat. And I'll understand."

Adina turned to Leopold for support. He sighed. "If you say you can get meat, I'll come with you."

"I have to do it alone," Megara said, her voice sharp. "Please. It—it's the only way I can do it. Please."

Megara looked between Adina and Leopold. He was struck again by how young she appeared. He knew she was twenty, but her mannerisms and physicality made her seem younger. "All right," Adina said, surprising everyone. "You have nowhere to go. We'll find you again if you leave."

"That's not likely." Megara smiled as she stood. "But I will be back."

Leopold stared at Adina after Megara had left the circle of light. "Why did you let her go?"

Adina poked at her fire with a stick and shrugged. "Like I said, where's she going to go?"

"I didn't expect you to believe her."

Adina hesitated. "I remember her birth, Leo," she whispered. The trees seemed to still around them as if they were listening.

"What do you mean?"

"My mother was asked to attend her birth. I begged to come along, but she said no. I followed her though, sneaking so she wouldn't see. It was after mother was removed as one of the council healers. And there was a complication. Margaret almost died. I was outside with Megara's brothers the whole time. The screaming was terrible. I was so scared. But my mother saved Margaret."

"Forgive me," Leopold said. "How does this relate to allowing Megara to hunt for us?"

Adina spoke in an uncertain tone. "She looks like Margaret. And . . . when she was asking permission, I saw Margaret when she begged my father to send search parties for Megara and Merlin. It was pitiful, but you couldn't help but feel sorry for her."

Leopold didn't mention that he'd compared her to Margaret, too. *Is that why it's so easy for me to trust her? Because she reminds me of Margaret?*

Within minutes, Megara stumbled through the underbrush, carrying two rabbits by the feet. Her hair was more chaotic, but there wasn't anything else different about her. Adina stood and took the rabbits, shock plain on her face. Megara sat down a few feet from Leopold.

Leopold sat next to Megara again. "How did you do that with no weapon?"

She kept her gaze on the glowing embers. Her voice wasn't much louder than the popping of the wood. "I see how you both look at me. I'm a monster. I know this, you know this—yet you're taking me to your home."

"Your home too," Leopold corrected. "We're taking you *home*."

She was quiet for a moment before she continued. "I'm dangerous, yet you see no problem with taking me to where your mother lives."

The council sent us to collect her. The seers had seen me specifically be the one to bring her home. After so many years, why now? And she's almost at Adina's magic. Does that mean once Megara learns how to use her powers, she'll be more advanced than Adina? Would that earn her a spot on the council? After they helped train her in magic, would she attack those who had saved her?

Leopold watched Megara's face. He did not have the power of prophecy. He did not have any abilities at all, despite all of that he knew Megara was not evil. She did not want to hurt anyone. "Meggy," he whispered. She tore her eyes from the fire. "Meggy, I trust you to do what's right. Once we take you home and you see what you've been missing, you'll find your place, and you'll be okay. You're one of us."

"Dinner's ready," Adina interrupted and stood with the rabbit on the spit. She took the first bite before passing it to Megara.

After they'd eaten, Leopold watched Megara as she lay on her back in the grass. He saw a noticeable difference in the way she behaved. Her shoulders were relaxed, her eyes brighter. It was like the night brought out a different person. Adina sat farther away, next to the horses, her hand resting on her sword, appearing poised and ready for action. But she didn't seem to feel threatened, just prepared.

Leopold walked over to where Megara was laying and sat a short distance away. "What do you think about us taking you home? Are you excited? Nervous?"

Megara shrugged. "I can't go back to Camelot. This is the next step, I guess." She continued staring at the stars. "Are we traveling far enough that the stars will be different?" she asked. "Where's Domum?"

He almost chuckled at the way she sounded out their village's name. "Tomorrow we will reach the first lookout points."

"The first?" she asked. Leopold nodded.

"The council is very protective of Domum. We have lookouts a day's ride from the village, then one closer to the border as we get nearer." Leo wasn't sure if he should be divulging all of the village's secrets to this stranger, but it was going to be her home too, wasn't it?

. "Do you really know my mother?" Megara breathed the question and Leopold had to strain to hear her.

"Yes," Leopold matched her volume. "You look so much like her."

"What's she like?" Megara rolled over and propped her head up with her hand. "Is she kind?"

"Probably one of the kindest, but all of Domum is polite."

"I don't care about the rest of them. I just want to know about her." Megara's eyes were hard while she said this, but then her eyes softened. "What else?"

"She's a seamstress," Leopold said. "She works for the council. She is like a second mother to everyone. They all go to her for so many things. I've done so myself at times. I love my own mother, but Margaret has something special about her."

"That's her name? Margaret?"

Leopold nodded.

Megara lay down and gazed at the stars once more. "I hope I don't disappoint her. I've already lost one parent. I don't want to lose another one before I even know her, before she knows me."

Leopold was quiet for a moment. "Is that how you saw Merlin?" he asked. "As a father?"

Megara nodded. "I stayed in his cellar. He was the only person I knew."

"In the cellar? Your whole life?" Leopold felt disgusted. How dare someone trap another human like that? Domum had jails but they were never used to keep anyone incarcerated.

"Well, I mean I enjoyed dinners with him after sundown, when there was less chance of people hearing me. My father—I mean Merlin—was a good man."

"No," Leopold said. "He was not. He stole you, Megara."

"I know that now. And my name is Meggy," she reminded him.

"You don't know what he did," Leopold snapped. "Your father and brothers, my father—they all died protecting you!"

Megara sat up, staring at him. "*Your* father?" she asked. "Is *that* why you came? You wanted to see the woman who killed your father?"

"You didn't kill him," Leopold growled. "The bastard Merlin did." He had heard the story so many times in his life.

Megara glared at the sky. "And my brothers and my father."

"He didn't poison them," Leopold said. Megara closed her eyes.

"Then how did they die?"

Leopold watched how the firelight played on her skin before responding. "Merlin was gifted with the sword. Your father tried to rescue you, and your older brothers got in the way. I would have done the same for my sister."

"You have a sister?" Megara asked as if desperate for a change of subject.

Leopold nodded, looking toward the southwest, toward Domum. "And two older brothers."

"Do you think Domum will accept me?" Megara was calmer and laid down.

Leopold considered. "I think they will be nervous at first. They won't know what to expect. After all, we didn't know you were alive all this time. Then we discover you've lived with the murderer Merlin your whole life . . . you'll have to show them you mean them no harm."

Megara glanced toward Adina. "She has magic. She started the fire... controlled it. I wasn't able to do that. The night Merlin died. The night I murdered my father, I hadn't meant to kill him. Only hurt him so he wouldn't hurt Superus."

"Superus? I thought you didn't know anyone."

There was a loud squeak and hiss behind him. Leopold leaped to his feet and drew his sword, turning around for the source of the sound. His sudden movement alarmed Adina and the horses. "What is it?" she called, also standing and unsheathing her sword.

Megara laughed. "It's fine! It's fine." She reached down beside her and lifted a wriggling and spitting stoat. "This is Superus." Leopold stared before he sheathed his sword and waved Adina off. It was after he sat down that Adina followed suit.

"You burned Merlin... because he threatened a stoat?" Leopold's heart thudded in his chest in fear. Was that all it took to offend her? Insulting an animal?

"No," Megara said, stroking the stoat as it curled up in her lap. "That's not it." Leopold waited for her to continue, and she sighed.

"That night, Merlin had come home drunk. It wasn't unusual—he often did that. But he was angry with me for some reason. And . . . he said so many things . . . and then he started beating me. He pushed me down and was kicking me. Superus tried to help me. He was biting and scratching Merlin. I was afraid of Merlin hurting him too, so I set his cloak on fire. Then when he took it off and started stomping it to put the fire out, it spread over him. It kept getting worse. I had no control over it. But Adina can control fire. Did she learn how to do that? Or is she just that good?"

Leopold hesitated. "In Domum, many people have magic. If it's strong enough, they begin lessons when they're young, and they're taught by the council."

"What is this council?" she asked. "Do you not have a king to rule, so this council rules you?"

"The council governs our people. They are the most powerful magic users in the village. Adina's father is on the council—he is a healer. So is her mother, but she was replaced on the council when someone else was better than her."

Megara sat straight up, open-mouthed and staring at Adina. "She's a princess?" Her voice was an octave higher than usual.

Leopold huffed out a breath. "Not really. She should technically be on the council, but with her father there, she can't be."

"What a world this is," Megara mused.

"Yes," Leopold murmured, watching Megara as she rolled back to the stars. "The council is in place as guides. They take apprentices for each of their kinds of magic."

"There's different kinds?" Megara asked, though her voice was flat.

"Yes, there are six kinds. Willpower, or psychokinesis, is the control of inanimate objects, though I'm told this is the most draining kind of magic. Language, where one can speak every tongue, including that of creatures like your stoat or the horses. Shapeshifting, changing one's appearance. Prophecy, viewing the future, though this magic is the most emotionally draining. Healing, which explains itself. This is the magic Katherine and Uther—Adina's parents—possess. And creation, which is what Adina has, and what you seem to have. The ability to create something that didn't exist before."

Megara absorbed the information. "So . . . how does one end up on this council? Do they get elected? Stay until they die?"

Leopold shook his head and picked at the grass. "No, not necessarily—sometimes. The council members are usually challenged. Anyone can appear on the council as long as they were born in Domum and have proven they are more proficient than the current member on the council."

"And how do they do that?" Megara asked.

Leopold shrugged. "Honestly, I'm not sure. I don't have any magic myself so I never asked, and they never told me. As long as we have honest people on the council, it doesn't affect my life too much." *Until they tell me I'm needed for a quest.*

Megara rolled away from Leopold. "I'm going to sleep now, if that's okay," she muttered.

"Of course," he said as he stood and walked toward the horses. "Adina," he said, "I think it would be more appropriate for you to guard her at night. I don't feel comfortable watching her sleep."

Adina smiled and stood, pulling a blanket from her horse. "I understand," she said. "I don't mind. I admire your determination to keep her virtue intact." She winked and walked to Megara. Leopold rolled his eyes and walked between the horses and made a bed there, annoyed about the teasing.

He awoke to darkness. It took him several heartbeats to realize what had awoken him. The women were conversing nearby. He held his breath and didn't dare move.

"I don't know what to expect," Megara was saying.

"From the brief glimpse I had of Camelot, Domum is leagues above them."

"I didn't know Camelot," Megara admitted. "I can't speak to what that would have been like."

"You never interacted with any of them?"

"Once," she sighed. "One time I left the house when Merlin was gone. He appeared when I was on the porch though. I said maybe two words to a couple of soldiers past the garden."

"So, Merlin was the only person you've ever spoken to?" Adina asked. Leopold imagined Megara nodding. "You are very intelligible for such a life."

"Is that meant as a compliment?" Megara's voice was icy.

"I mean it in the best way," Adina confirmed. "I truly had no indication that you had been so isolated."

Megara didn't respond at first, but when she did her voice was calmer again. "Are there many people in Domum?"

"Not nearly as many as Camelot, but you can't really use that as a comparison, can you?" Adina deliberated. "I don't know how to properly depict the number for you. But, yes, from what little you know, Domum will likely be very overwhelming."

"Do you have any advice for me?" Megara asked in a small voice.

"Be very transparent. The council must know everything you can tell them."

"What does everyone know about me?"

Adina tittered. "Your story isn't taught broadly by any means. However, Merlin was involved in the lives of many of the villagers. Everyone knows his name. And if everyone knows Merlin's name, they know the name Megara along with it as the child he stole from us."

"Do they know what I did to him?" The words were almost too quiet for Leopold to catch.

Adina lowered her voice as well. "The prophets and council are aware something happened, but not all of the details."

"How does that work? The prophets?"

"I don't really understand that magic, myself, but from what my mother has told me they speak directly to the gods, if not having revelation given by them to their minds."

"The gods?"

Adina hummed. "This is a lot of information for you and it is very late. Please try to get some sleep, Meggy."

Leopold stayed awake for a long time after their conversation ended, trying to decipher what his feelings were telling him. The woman had clearly been mistreated by Merlin in drastic ways they could never understand, because Megara herself was unaware of the abuse.

I hope the monster suffers in the abyss for the rest of time.

They returned to the road as the sun was rising. Adina had designed and made a sort of warning system for if Megara had tried to leave, that way she could get some sleep as well. Leopold yawned on his horse, himself having had too much in his head to sleep.

Around midday, before they reached the first watchtower, Adina declared she wanted to wash before they reached the village. When they reached the lake, Megara and Leopold stayed near the horses while Adina went to wash. Megara had been quiet for the last several hours of their ride. She spoke when Adina stepped away.

"Does Adina trust me?" she asked.

Leopold looked at her as he sat on a boulder. "Why do you ask?"

"I'm worried she will tell the council I'm dangerous and harm my chances of fitting in," she said. "I want to be welcome."

"Adina will be honest when we see the council," he said with a smile. "Meggy, we've been with you since we found you. Adina is very honest. We know you need to learn how to use your magic. You could've killed either of us on this trip. Unless you're biding your time until you really can kill us and everyone in Domum, which I doubt, I'm willing to vouch for you myself."

Megara smiled. "Thank you, Leopold."

"Haven't you heard?" He smiled as he pulled his boots off. He heard Adina returning and he decided he would do the same as her and clean the grime off before seeing the council. "Everyone calls me Leo."

Meggy grinned at him.

Adina returned, plaiting her hair, and Leopold walked to the lake. He listened to Megara laugh at something Adina had said, though he couldn't hear what it was.

Leopold was almost finished washing in the frigid water when he heard someone approach.

"Leo," Megara called. "What about sweets? Are there sweets in Domum?"

Leopold jumped and spun, instinctively lowering his hands to cover himself. "Megara, not now." She was standing at the lake's edge.

"My name is Meggy," she reminded him, as if it were second nature now. "And why not now? What's wrong with now?"

"Meggy." Leopold laughed in the awkwardness. "I'm washing."

"I see that."

He wished he had anything else to cover himself. Something bigger than his hands. "It is improper for an unmarried woman, like yourself, to see me while I wash. Any woman, at that, as I do not have a wife."

"I'm confused."

"About what?" Leopold demanded in exasperation. *Maybe I can catch a fish or something to cover up.*

"If I were married, or you were married, would I be able to ask about sweets?"

Leopold heard Adina's laugh behind the trees. She had attempted to stop Megara, it seemed, but had stopped short of the view herself. "Megara," she called. "Let's allow Leo to finish washing, shall we?"

"I just want to know if there are sweets in Domum!" she complained, heading to Adina.

Leopold hurried and redressed and returned to the women. "Are we ready to go?" he asked, Adina snickering at him.

"You never answered my question," Megara said, upset. "Are there sweets in Domum?"

"Yes." He sighed. "There, indeed, are sweets in Domum." Adina guffawed.

CHAPTER NINE

L EOPOLD WATCHED MEGARA CHEW on her lip when they saw the cabin. She appeared so anxious, Leopold's heart ached for her. What was it like, returning to a home you'd never known to live with a mother you couldn't remember? They passed by the first watchtower with no trouble. A shapeshifting patrolman was sent ahead of them as a wolf to alert the next tower of their arrival. Megara had stared open-mouthed as the man shifted and ran away.

"Remember," Adina said as the last tower came into view, "the council wants to speak with you first. Don't speak to anyone else, and don't run off."

Megara nodded. "I'm not running, Adina. I want to do this right."

Adina glanced at Leopold, and he could see the trepidation in her eyes as well. They had accomplished their task of bringing Megara home, and they knew the council intended to teach her, but what would happen when they discovered what she had done? Leopold hoped they would see she hadn't meant to hurt anyone.

Leopold straightened when he saw the riders coming to meet them. "Leo!" One of them waved. It was Jasper. Leopold returned the wave and urged his horse a little faster, passing up the women. They met halfway and clasped hands. "It's good to see you, little brother."

"Why weren't you at the first tower?" Leopold asked.

"That is a discussion for dinner with the family." Jasper grinned. "Let me meet the woman!"

"Adina doesn't want anyone to speak to her yet," Leopold said. Jasper caught his tone and became serious, a rare occurrence for him, as he retied the knot in his dark hair

"Is everything okay?" Jasper asked.

"At the moment, yes." Leopold lowered his voice as the women got closer. "Another discussion for dinner."

Adina passed and she nodded, not sparing a glance for Jasper. Her disregard made his face fall, but he didn't make a scene. Leopold felt for his brother. He knew Jasper had been pining after Adina for years with no reciprocation. Jasper turned his mount and kept his horse equal with Leopold's. The other patrol riders followed on their horses and took up the front of the procession as they walked into the village. The wolf from earlier ran toward the first watchtower. Leopold stayed beside Jasper as they walked past the village border.

The people on the roads stepped to the sides and stared at the procession. Women gathered their children and stopped their chores. Men halted their work to watch the horses ride by. The patrolmen escorted Adina, Megara, and Leopold across the river and to the doorway of the council house. Adina dismounted and helped Megara down as Leopold dismounted and followed them into the building. The patrolmen promised to return their horses.

Leopold watched Megara as they walked into the council's presence. Her arms were wrapped around her chest and she was watching all the men and women with nervous eyes. He stood next to Adina near the edge of the room. Their jobs were done—Adina had brought the Dragon Woman home, and Leopold had found her. They were still in the room because they had yet to be dismissed by the council. Leopold hoped they would be allowed to stay. He didn't want Megara to feel alone. They may have started this journey as Megara being Leopold's reluctant errand, but this young woman belonged in the village. Leopold found himself grateful to have been the one to go find her.

"Recite your name," Adina's father Uther—the male healer—requested, not unkindly.

"Meggy." She spoke with her chin held high. Leopold wasn't sure if her mock confidence would damage their view of her or not, and he wasn't sure if they could see how frightened she was.

"Is this what you call yourself," Edith asked, "or what you've been called?"

"Megara," she corrected herself. "My full name is Megara. Merlin . . . he . . . I go by Meggy."

"Tell us about your life, Meggy." The youngest girl of the council, Ibb, smiled at Megara in encouragement. "How have you lived?"

Leopold heard the ice in Megara's tone as it changed but wasn't sure anyone else could. "I was raised in a cellar by a man named Merlin. When I was young, I was allowed out at night to play with the mice beside the fire and eat dinner with him. He would read me stories. Once I learned to read, I was no longer allowed out to play. He continued to allow me out of my cellar for dinner, where we would discuss the magic I would read about during the day."

"You learned magic from books?" Judd demanded. His face was stony.

"Y-yes." Meggy seemed surprised by his harsh tone. She took a deep breath. "Merlin taught me some very basic things when I was a child, but the rest I learned from his books."

"What kind of things did you learn?" asked Gavin, a man old enough to be Leo's father.

. "I learned how to turn things into something else, how to create things, how to curse things." Her voice sounded flat.

Leopold held very still. He had not known she had so much knowledge of magic. She'd never let on. A murmur went through the hall with the word "curse." "What kind of curses?" Ibb asked.

Megara seemed uncomfortable as she shifted. She looked at Leopold and Adina continuing in a smaller voice. "Merlin asked me to charm a sword and a stone once. Another time, he asked me to charm a goblet so any man who drank from it would be poisoned, but the women and children would remain safe."

The murmur resumed. nodded his head in support when she turned to him, trying not to show his disgust. The old man had used Megara, corrupted her magic. He'd corrupted her soul. And she knew no difference.

"How did these ventures affect you?" Edith asked Megara.

She focused on Edith again. "The sword was decently difficult. I had to rest for several hours afterward."

"And the poison?" Judd asked.

Megara hesitated again. "I was younger. That was one of the first experiments he had me do. I slept for several days, but he also kept dinner from me during that time, so I'm not sure for which reason I slept."

Another murmur swept through the council. They had a mixture of expressions from pity to anger on their faces.

"What else have you learned, Meggy?" Ibb asked.

"I'm not sure," she admitted. "I learned the theory for many things, but I did not have need to practice most of it. I do know how to change my form into that of animals." She took a deep breath. "I hid from Leopold and Princess Adina as a stoat. They did not know."

The incorrect title went right by Leopold, who was both impressed and shocked; he felt as though he'd been lied to. He couldn't help it. *She was there. The whole time. Why was she hiding?*

"She needs to use words." Adina surprised them all—including Leopold, who jumped—by stepping forward. She smirked at him before turning to the council with her usual stoic expression. "I've watched her these several days. She accesses her magic by speaking. She was not trained in silence. It would be hard for her to tell you all the things she can do if she doesn't even know what she cannot do."

It was as though the council had forgotten they were there, several seemed to feel the pair of them were intruding. "Adina." Her father nodded. "You were not intended to participate in this meeting."

"If that were true we'd have been dismissed when we arrived. This meeting was convened in order to judge whether Megara was a danger to the village, arranged to decide Megara's fate. Council, I tell you, Leo and I have been the only ones to spend these many days with her. Of all who should know the danger Megara could inflict, it would be us."

There was more quiet. Leopold could feel Megara staring at him. He watched Adina's father and Edith without breathing, wondering if they'd send Adina and himself from the council room or if they would be allowed to stay.

"She is right," Edith said. "Leopold and Adina were sent to retrieve Megara; they do have a right to be involved in this decision. They risked their lives—"

"They obviously arrived safely," Judd said.

"All the more reason they should be allowed to share their experiences." Edith seemed the most patient woman in the world when it came to Judd.

Uther waved Adina and Leopold forward. "Come, give us your report."

CHAPTER TEN

L EOPOLD AND ADINA SAT outside the council house an hour later. They had been dismissed by the council after they had delivered their statements each in turn. Now they were waiting to hear the verdict. "What do you think will happen?" Leopold asked Adina.

"I don't know." She sighed, leaning against the wall and picking weeds from the grass. "I'm hoping they'll believe us."

"If they decide she is a danger after all, what would they do?"

"I don't know that either. There is no precedence here. I hope they would seclude her until they could teach her." This made Leopold frown at the sky. "But I have no idea what they could do. They sent us on a long, pointless journey if they decide to kill her."

"Kill her?" Leopold felt his heart race as his gaze snapped to Adina. *They couldn't do that, could they? Something like that would have to be brought to the village, wouldn't it?*

They waited where they were until the sun was setting, then heard the door open. They both stood and faced it as each of the members of the council left the house one at a time. Most of them smiled as they passed. A few of them glared. Once Leopold counted twelve people, he held his breath. Would Megara follow?

He saw her walk out, her blond head bowed. Leopold's heart pounded as he waited. "Meggy?" he asked. Thoughts about public executions raced through his mind. She raised her head, her face split in a broad grin.

"They've decreed that I'm not an imminent danger to Domum!" she exclaimed. Leopold fought his impulse to hug her and grinned back. The relief made him weak.

"That's wonderful news, Megara." Adina smiled, also appearing relieved. "What else have they said?"

"They're going to take turns training me, since it seems I have some of each of their magic. They want to see my proficiency in each skill. I start tomorrow."

Leopold thought about the few who left the meeting with negative reactions. He doubted they would enjoy teaching her. "Where are you to sleep before then?" Adina asked, heading toward the horses they had yet to return.

Megara bit her lip. "They . . . they didn't mention anything in specific . . . but one of them did ask if I was going to need a guide to my mother . . ." She looked at Leopold. "I told them you could help me, if that's okay."

"Of course." Leopold smiled.

"He will also escort you to and from your lessons," Adina said with a simple smile.

"I'm supposed to be with you every morning, Adina, unless—"

"Unless I give you another task." Adina smiled. "And I'm giving you another task. You're to spend your days with Megara until she's accustomed to Domum."

Leopold nodded, and she returned the gesture. She then mounted her horse and took the reins for the others. Leopold lifted his bag onto his shoulder and waved Megara forward. "All right, let's go find Margaret, shall we?"

They walked across the bridge into the newer parts of Domum. Leopold did his best to point out important landmarks to her, attempting to distract her from the stares of the people around them. He pondered how recently he'd been bored with his life in Domum. Now he was viewing the village with a fresh perspective as he imagined Megara was viewing it.

As they walked past the town center, Megara had eyes for everything. It was as if she'd never seen one before. *She spent her life in a cellar,* Leopold reminded himself. *The only city she's seen was Camelot the night it burned.* He grinned at her then took her hand, surprising them both and making her look frightened for a moment before something in Leopold's face made her relax. "Follow me," he said, leading her toward a stand at the edge of the center that was closing for the night. "You'll like this."

Leopold dropped Megara's hand and rushed forward to touch the saleswoman's shoulder. She smiled at him. "Leo!" She laughed. "What can I do for you?"

"Forgive me, Rohese. I know you are closing up. I was hoping to purchase from you before you do."

Her eyes flicked to Megara before she smiled in a wince at Leopold. "O-of course. Anything for you, Leo." She pivoted to her stand then back to him, holding out a bag with candied strawberries. Leopold exchanged some coins for the candies and Rohese hurried to clean up and move along.

Leopold smiled at Megara and offered the sweets. "Are you sure?" she asked, her eyes pivoted to the candies. "You paid for them. I don't want to take food from you."

Leopold shook his head. "It's fine, really. Please take one."

Megara took the smallest berry and placed it on her tongue. She closed her eyes and smiled. After she'd finished, taking longer than Leopold thought possible, she opened her eyes and grinned. "That was wonderful!"

"Take another one." He laughed and led her down the road, still offering the candy to her. She took another one, this time taking the largest after using her eyes to ask permission. Leopold smiled and watched her place it in her mouth delicately before he tossed one in his own mouth.

They finished the berries as they came upon Margaret's house. Leopold stopped their progress in the path and left them staring at it. "This is it," he said. "This is Margaret's house. She moved into a smaller one after . . . well, when she was alone." The home was modest. He knew from the shape of the exterior that it had one bedroom and one main room. There was a small garden off to the side with a few chickens within its gate. Smoke rose from the chimney, indicating Margaret was cooking.

Leopold saw the curtains move beside the door. Megara hesitated before taking a single step forward.

The door swung open then, and Megara jumped behind Leopold's back. Margaret stood in the doorway of the house. Her mouth was parted, her chest heaving. Suddenly Margaret appeared her age, the wrinkles around her eyes in sharp contrast. Her frame also seemed twice Megara's, forcing Leopold to acknowledge how unhealthy Megara looked. Her hair wasn't as shiny as Margaret's and instead was matted and dull by comparison. Her bones pointy at every bend. Leopold's heart ached with sympathy. *I should have made her eat more on the journey.*

A tear slipped down Margaret's cheek. "Meggy?" She spoke it aloud but not to be overheard by passersby.

Megara's hands gripped the fabric on his back. "She knows my name," she breathed.

"Of course." Leopold turned to her, breaking their connection and taking her hands in his. "She's your mother."

"But . . . she knows *my* name."

"Come," he said. "Meet her."

Leopold walked backward, leading her one step at a time. He took her as far as she braved until they reached the house. Margaret held out a shaky hand and bit her lip, as Megara did when she was nervous. Leopold saw Margaret's other hand rotating a smooth rock over and over. After a moment, Megara reached a hand toward her mother. Margaret clasped her fingers around her daughter's and closed her eyes, breathing out a small sob.

Megara stepped forward the last step away from Leopold and wrapped her arms around her mother. They were the same height, Megara a hint taller. They entered the house and closed the door without further acknowledgement of Leopold. He walked away, tossing the rest of the berries into his.

He arrived home and his mother and sister ran out to meet him, hugging him. He laughed and held them both in turn. "Hello," he said, grinning.

"That was a quick trip," Anora said. "Did you run into any trouble?"

"What is Megara like?" Emaline asked.

"Let's eat dinner and I'll tell you all about it. One week was too long without your cooking."

He led them inside, noting as he went the size difference of his home and Margaret's. His home was two stories tall. He and his brothers slept upstairs amid old trunks and family keepsakes. Downstairs were large storage areas for food, a decent kitchen and dining area, a room for them to accept guests and sit around the fire, and Anora and Emaline's bedroom. Leopold sat down at the dining table, and Anora placed the remains of their dinner in front of him. He dug in and told them the story of his travels from the moment he'd left the harvest festival.

"That's all very well and good," Emaline said. "But I want to know about *her*."

"Emaline, I'm sure he's tired enough for the day," Anora chided.

"No, it's all right," Leopold said before taking another bite and speaking through the food. "What do you want to know?"

"Is she beautiful?" Emaline asked. Anora hummed disapprovingly, but Leopold swallowed and answered her question.

"She looks like a younger version of Margaret. The first time I saw her, I thought she *was* Margaret, following us. But she's very undernourished. Merlin kept her in a cellar her whole life. She didn't eat much. It sounds like she was lucky to have a decent meal a day."

Anora gasped. "That's terrible!"

"Yes," Leopold murmured, staring at the table of food and marveling that he'd never known a hungry day—not the sort she would have experienced, anyway. "It must have been."

"I heard she killed him," Emaline said with an almost reverent voice. Leopold heard Anora catch her breath.

Leopold chewed another bite and took a sip of his watered wine before speaking. "She did," he said, choosing his words carefully. "It was to protect her friend, " he said, realizing he hadn't seen the stoat since the day Megara had introduced them. "She didn't care about herself, even though he was beating her to death. She tried to distract Merlin by burning his cloak, but the fire she conjured wasn't easy for her to control, though she seems to be very powerful. The fire spread to the rest of his body. When she was running away, she ended up killing three more men in the same manner. After that, the fire spread to a home and killed a family. I'm not sure if she knows that bit or not, though. She's been hiding in the forest from that night on."

"So, she does have magic," Anora said. "A true woman of Domum."

"Yes." Leopold swallowed. "Though . . . I learned today she has more than creation magic."

"What do you mean?" Emaline demanded.

"She also knows shapeshifting, and the power of language, too. I'm not sure what else, but the council is going to take tutoring her."

"There's never been anyone to use all kinds of magic," Emaline snapped.

"I know, but she can." Leopold stood. "I should go to bed," he said. "Adina has assigned me to escort Megara around Domum for her lessons. I'm not sure how early she wants to begin."

Anora nodded and smiled at him. "Of course. You've had a long journey. I hope you sleep well."

Leopold took his dishes to the sink before walking up the stairs to the attic and lying across his bed. He fell asleep soon after, still dressed, his mind exhausted.

Chapter Eleven

T HE NEXT MORNING, LEOPOLD woke before the others. He took a loaf of bread off the counter and a strip of jerky from one of the jars and left before the sun rose. He enjoyed listening to the birdsong as he walked, and the various animals throughout the village began to wake as well. The morning smelled fresh. He walked across the bridge and came to Margaret's house as the door was opening and she was making her way out. Her face was serene. Her eyes crinkled when she saw him.

Margaret hurried to Leopold with a grin and hugged him close. "Thank you," she whispered in his ear. "Thank you for bringing my baby home. I never thought this day would come."

"I'm happy to be able to help."

"Seeing as how Meggy will be with the council, I am heading to the shop. No use waiting around when there's work to be done. Meggy will be out soon." She smiled once more before making her way to work.

Leopold stood at the base of the path and waited for Megara to make her appearance.

When she opened the door, Leopold couldn't help but stare. She had cleaned up and looked like a new person. Her hair had been cleaned and was braided, no doubt the work of her mother. She wore a new dress, one of fine material only the council's seamstress could afford. It was loose on her, likely one of Margaret's they'd attempted to adjust, but it was clean and neat.

"Are we ready?" She giggled in excitement and pulled on his arm. Leopold couldn't help but laugh at the difference from the girl he had left in this spot the night before. "Come on! Where to first?"

He laughed. "All right, slow down, slow down. I'm sure they'll want us to meet at the council room this morning."

"Then what are we waiting for?" she asked. "Let's go!"

They walked down the road at a brisk pace. Megara would move a few steps ahead and then turn and walk with Leopold a few more steps before moving ahead again. Occasionally she would jump and spin, her face tilted to the sun. This attitude was one Leopold had not seen from her yet. He couldn't help joining in on her pleasant mood and laughed along with her.

When they came near the council house, they found Edith waiting outside the door. She smiled when she saw them crossing the bridge, but Megara slowed her walk and bit her lip. Leopold bumped her shoulder to get her to look at him and then smiled at her. She smiled back, still biting her lip, then straightened her shoulders and lengthened her pace to reach Edith before Leopold.

"Good morning, my lady." Megara curtsied.

Edith chuckled. "Oh, child, we don't curtsy here. Especially not to me."

"How do the people of Domum show their respect?" Megara asked, her eyebrows crunched in confusion.

"Some bow to the lead healer, but to the rest of the council, just bow your head. There's no reason for anything more toward us."

Megara hummed before changing the subject. "What am I doing today?"

"Today you and I will be evaluating your skills in creation." She faced Leopold. "I hear Adina has requested that you stay with Megara throughout these lessons?"

"Yes, my lady."

"A wise decision," Edith said. "I trust every member of the council, but I do not believe all will treat Megara fairly. A few did not believe we should allow this training. I'm grateful for your added eyes, Leopold."

"It is my pleasure," Leopold said. "I am grateful for the opportunity to spend this time with Megara now that we're home." He froze, hearing how those words sounded and hoping no one read too far into them.

Edith nodded with an amused glint in her eye. "I see. Well, we should get started for the day." She turned to Megara, reaching out her hand. "Come along. We have much to do." She led them to her home a short distance away. They remained outside near the river.

Leopold didn't understand much of what transpired during the lesson. He was amazed by what Megara could do when she spoke her Latin words. She could do anything Edith asked. However, he was surprised by how much it drained the strength from her. Her magic in the woods had been much easier for her. Now she had to rest and was moved to tears on several occasions. Edith would reassure her and allowed her the moments needed to regain her composure before they started again.

Leopold was in awe watching the women work. He had a hard time pulling his eyes from Megara, but whenever she glanced at him he couldn't meet her eyes and would glance away. He found pleasure in the secret glances.

At lunch, Edith sent Leopold away to fetch them food. She handed him coins from her own purse and told him where to go. He tried to hurry, but he had the feeling he should allow them time alone. Not only could it allow different results, but maybe it would show Edith that he wasn't obsessed with the intriguing new woman. He hoped at the very least it allowed Megara to feel confidence in her ability to converse with the woman.

When he returned, he found Megara sipping water from a glass with twitching hands Ibb was offering her. Edith stood to the side, watching the interaction. Leopold was concerned. She was pale and shaky. He hurried to her side and was intercepted by Edith who subtly shook her head and took the meal from his hands.

"My name is Ibb," she told Megara, her voice still high and childish, her eyes showing an unnerving maturity. "I wanted to see how you were doing today."

"Thank you for the water, Ibb," Megara breathed. "I think I'm doing okay." She looked to Edith for confirmation.

"You are doing very well, Megara." Edith smiled. "This gives us a very clear line on where you are with your skills, and intriguing insight into our magic. I'm curious to see what my findings can do for the other people of the council."

Ibb took the empty glass from Megara. "I should be returning. Enjoy the rest of your day, Megara!" She ran away, her thin braids flying in the wind.

Leopold returned the leftover coin to Edith and took a seat on the ground. Edith had set a small tea table for herself and Megara. They sat in the shade of a tree behind Edith's house where they had a view of the river. "Tell me what you think of Domum, Megara," Edith requested.

"I haven't seen much," she said. "But what I have seen is wonderful. It's so big and busy and fun. I am . . . afraid the people won't like me."

Edith nodded while she bit into her bread. "Well, you are known around here," she said. "Just not in the way most people would like to be. It will take some time for them to *know* you, but they'll come around."

"And how do you see me?" Megara asked, her voice guarded.

Edith turned to Leopold with a smile, that amused glint in her eyes once more. "What do you think, Leopold? What do you think of our Megara?"

Leopold thought about his earlier mess of words and knew he must speak with caution. "I think Meggy is very perceptive," he said. "I think you have so much power, but you are more than your magic. And once you see that, you'll be unstoppable."

"Quite insightful, Leopold," Edith said, her eyebrows lifting. She faced Megara and took her hand. "And I agree with every word."

After they finished with their meal, Edith began their training again. Leopold watched, trying to understand the things he was seeing. Had he tried any of this, and he felt he *could* with the instructions for non-verbal control Edith was giving, he knew he'd be on his deathbed for a week until his strength returned. He compared his views of Megara, struggling red-faced and sweaty, with the memory of all of the times he had seen Adina create things. *She just breathes those butterflies to life. I've never seen her struggle like this.* It wasn't that he thought Megara was inept—she wasn't. It was interesting to see the differences.

Edith decided to end their lessons as the sun was beginning to get low in the sky. There were still a couple of hours until sunset. Edith walked away, promising another day of assessment in the morning—though with a different member of the council.

Megara seemed exhausted. Leopold was worried she might fall over. "Are you ready to go home?" he asked her. "You seem like you need to head to bed."

She yawned. "Let's wander. I want to see where I was born."

Leopold led her toward the shops surrounding the town center. She wandered from cart to cart, observing all the food and items for sale. The carts had amazed him when he was a child. It was a reminder of their beauty to see Megara admiring them for the first time. The healers had their own shops, and so did the prophesiers. Margaret's mother worked in a dressmaker's shop even though she did not possess magic herself. Some people preferred buying from those without magic.

One man saw Megara's gaze captured by a glistening blue figurine. He made some flourishing movements and offered it to her. Leopold tried to get a better look and almost scoffed out loud. It was a very poor rendition of Adina's mother, Katherine. *I'd be offended if that was my lookalike*, he thought with bitterness. He studied the artist's other merchandise, and it all seemed subpar, like Katherine's statue. Leopold didn't like the greedy expression on the artist's face when he made Megara laugh. Leopold felt it twist his gut in two. On the one hand, he loved to hear Megara laugh. On the other hand, he wanted to get away from the shopkeeper.

"I do not believe I have seen ye here before, m'lady," the merchant drawled with an exaggerated accent. "What be thy name?"

Leopold rolled his eyes at the act. Megara giggled.

"Meggy," she said. "My name is Meggy."

The man clutched at his heart. "A name worthy of a goddess," he whispered loudly. Megara giggled again. "Come, let me capture your beauty. Come, come." He pulled Megara around and sat her on a stool before waving his arms around, splashing colors into the air where they waited for further instruction and shaping. After a while, Leopold looked back at the show and saw a figure being formed with the magic. He supposed it resembled Megara. He could see how this stranger would think it was her. But he hadn't captured her smile properly. And her eyes weren't as excited. And the statue's nose was too broad.

Megara took the finished product tenderly. It had finalized in a material similar to glass or porcelain. She stared at her image. She didn't seem to be listening to the man as he continued to rain down compliments. She stood and spoke over him, her voice cold. Leopold watched her, noting the sudden change in mood and not knowing what triggered it. "I can't pay you for this. I have no money."

"Oh, no charge, m'lady, no charge at all," the man gushed. "Not for such a beautiful—"

She pushed it into his hands. "I'm sorry you spent so much time on it. It really is pretty. But I can't take it."

She hurried away, weaving through the crowd. Leopold was stunned. He looked apologetically at the shopkeeper, who seemed offended. Leopold hadn't seen her this cold since the day they'd found her in the woods. *What happened?* he wondered as he raced after her.

He caught up to her, very lost at a crossroad. "I want to go home," she said. "Now. Which way is home?" Leopold pointed, and she started stomping down the street. She kept touching her face. Her eyes were glazed over as if she wasn't walking with anyone. Leopold wasn't even sure she knew she was going, as she almost collided with trees and people a couple of times and he had to redirect her.

"Meggy, what's wrong?" he asked. "What's going on?"

"My face."

Leopold waited for more, but that was all she said. "What about it? I promise, he didn't do it justice—"

"My *face*." She spun, pressing her hands against his chest. They were wet and left marks on the fabric. His breath caught with the contact. Her cheeks were wet too. "Leo, the first time I saw my face was the day before Merlin . . . before I . . ."

Her eyes begged Leopold not to make her say it. Leopold covered her hands with his own. "Meggy, what's wrong?"

"I didn't even know what I looked like. All my life. I didn't know until *he allowed me* to know. And he only allowed me because it would accomplish his task." Leopold thought about this before pulling her in the opposite direction toward the town center, the bridge, and the old homes beyond. "Where are we going?" she asked, sliding in the dirt at the change of direction.

"Just trust me," he said, then hurried her along.

He ignored his sister in the yard as they bustled around to the rear of his mother's house. Leopold led her to where he kept a small bucket and shaving mirror. He stood her in front of the mirror and pointed into it. "This is Meggy," he said, his chest heaving. It hadn't been an exerting walk, but he'd worked himself up with the audacity Merlin had possessed to prevent this woman from seeing herself.. "This is the woman we brought back from Camelot, a beautiful, brave, and intelligent woman."

He watched her touch her hair and the neckline of her dress. She stared, her lips parted. "I . . . look different than I did with Merlin."

"Of course you do," he said. "Because he's not here. We didn't bring him with us. We brought you. And you are beautiful, strong, and safe. I watched you today. I watched how hard you were trying to do what Edith asked. You are trying to do the best you can to *be* the best you can. And it shows on the outside."

Megara's eyes filled with tears. She smiled at her reflection, then gripped his hand. "Thank you, Leo," she whispered.

He nodded, aware of how her mood had shifted once again, and they walked into Anora's dining room, Megara still holding his hand. Her grip was warm and sent goosebumps up his arm. Emaline was standing in the kitchen, a bewildered expression on her face and hands on her hips. She blocked the exit and held her hand out toward Megara. "Hello. I am Leo's sister, Emaline. I haven't met you before. You blew past me with my brother, and now you've been crying so I'm wondering what sort of abuse he put you through. Pleasure to make your acquaintance."

Leopold wanted to melt through the floor, but Megara sniffled and took Emaline's hand. She dropped Leopold's hand to do so and he found he missed it. "I'm Meggy," she said. "And Leo was helping me. He didn't hurt me."

Emaline's mouth dropped open. "You're *Megara* Meggy?" she asked.

Megara stiffened and pulled her hand back. She tried to play it off with a teasing tone. "Depends on what you've heard." Leopold heard the hesitation in her voice.

" Ibb said she went and saw you at Edith's. She says you're so powerful and wonderful! She also said you are super nice. She didn't tell me how pretty you are."

Megara blushed and glanced at Leopold. He smiled, but was embarrassed by his sister. "I should be taking Megara home," he said to interrupt whatever his sister was going to say next.

"It was good to meet you, Megara," Emaline said.

"It's Meggy," Megara said.

Emaline was surprised but nodded anyway and stepped out of the way. Leopold and Megara walked out of the house and down the path toward the main road. They continued until Megara inhaled as if to speak. Then she shook her head.

"What is it?" Leopold asked.

"Is that how they will see me forever?" she asked. "A powerful sorceress who disappeared for two decades? Will I not be anything else here?"

Leopold thought for a moment before he spoke. "Yes. They'll always know you're a powerful woman because there's no way to hide the magic you possess. And they'll know your history because, well, everyone does, but I don't think it's a bad thing."

"It's not a bad thing that I'm well-known for my ability to kill people?" Megara demanded.

"It's not that, though." Leopold stopped her and locked eyes with her. "Meggy, my sister never once mentioned Merlin. You will have a hard time finding anyone here who is angry you killed him."

"It's not just that I killed Merlin," Megara cried. "I killed seven other people. You keep forgetting! I killed those men who chased me, and then the fire—"

"I don't forget. You didn't mean to do that," Leopold countered. "You didn't even mean to kill Merlin. No one will blame you, Meggy. You weren't taught how to use your magic properly. We have children in the village who have done some pretty reprehensible things with their magic, but people get over it. It's. . . part of learning to control it."

Megara continued down the road, though slowly, and Leopold knew she didn't know where she was going. He walked beside her to Margaret's house, unsure what else to say. Her outbursts were confusing, and he didn't know how to respond to them.

After Leopold left Megara, he was looking down, not paying attention to where he was going. Hands reached out and grabbed his shoulders. "Leo!" Leopold jerked his head up, surprised. It was Jasper. "Come with me," his brother demanded. "Hurry!"

They ran across the bridge toward the council house. Jasper pushed his way through the door, dragging Leopold by his shirt. "Council, please, listen to me," he yelled, getting the voices in the room to quiet. "There is an army hiding in the woods near the farthest watchtower. Our spies say they plan to attack in two days."

PART III

PART III

Chapter Twelve

T HE FLURRY OF MOTION around him was lost to Leopold. He could think of one thing: his family. They were in danger. Never had Domum been under attack by an army in his memory, in his parents' memory. The worst had been Merlin's betrayal. Domum was so far removed, why would anyone bother? This didn't make any sense. He rushed from the room, following Jasper as he took off with instructions for the militia from the council. "Jasper!" he called. "Wait!"

Jasper turned and clutched Leopold's shoulders. "Get Mother and Emaline to safety. And you, stay alert."

He ran for his horse and galloped away to deliver the instructions he'd received. Leopold found Emaline still at home and grabbed her arm, dragging her toward the town center where their mother worked, explaining what little details he knew. They raced together through the streets, which were starting to fill with panicking members of Domum as the council's messengers spread the word. Leopold and Emaline found Anora as she was leaving work, the people around her screaming the news. Her eyes were wide with fright as she saw her youngest children running toward her. She took Emaline's hand, and they found their place in the village center to hear instructions from the council.

"My people!" Uther called for attention, his hands raised in the air. Adina and her mother were on either side of him. Leopold wasn't sure where Adina's sister was, but his mind didn't rest on the thought. "People of Domum," their leader called when the sound quieted around him. "As you've heard, our home is being approached by an army of unknown men. Please, do not be afraid. Though we may fear the worst and we don't know why they are here, take heart. We are more able to cope with this than any other kingdom. So many of our people have powerful magic and can help. Any of you who have magic within you, please meet at the council house. We have instructions for you. Those able men and young men who do not have magic, please meet at the watchtower. Women and children, Katherine will have instructions for you. There is a job for everyone! We need your courage and strength at this time. Take up arms and defend your homes!"

Leopold had no magic and knew he should be heading to the gate, but he followed Emaline as she made her way to the council house, leaving their mother in the square to listen to Katherine. Leopold pushed through the crowd, searching for the blond head he prayed would be near the council house.

He found her right at the steps, the front row. He breathed a sigh of relief. *Where else would she be?* He tried to tell himself that Megara would already be interested in protecting Domum, but he couldn't lie to himself. He knew she still felt unsure, but seeing her standing at the front reassured him.

He pushed through the crowd to reach her side. She stared at him with wide eyes. She was hyperventilating, panicking. "Leo, what do I do?" she asked. Her voice was higher than normal.

"Just listen to what they say," he told her. "You'll be okay, I'll see you after. Emaline will stay with you." Without pausing to consider, he kissed the back of her hand, glimpsing Emaline's wide-eyed gape, and ran across the bridge toward the watchtower.

He arrived at the watchtower late enough to miss the beginning of the militia commander's instructions. He couldn't train everyone as knights overnight, but he gave tips that could be helpful and advised on weapons. He recognized Leopold standing in the crowd and used him as an example, then asked Leopold to help distribute good weapons.

As the day passed, Leopold felt his mind being stretched in two directions. He loved his home and he wanted to make sure it and his family were safe. On the other hand, he was also trying not to focus on Megara's progress. He didn't know what was going on with those with magic. Was she being successful? Was she scared? Were people wary of her presence?

His attention was brought to his training when he felt a firm hit on the side of his head. He looked back, and one of the knights he knew well was frowning at him. "Get your head out of the clouds, Leo!" he said.

"Sorry," Leopold murmured and then started into the bout in front of him.

When the sun began to set, the people were released to their homes, searching for their families. There was no more time for instruction. If Jasper was right, the army would be upon them the morning after next. They would spend the entire next day setting defenses around the village and begging the gods for peaceful negotiations.

Leopold disarmed and then rushed to the council house, being one of the last to leave the tower. He found Adina speaking with Emaline and Megara. Emaline had dead eyes—she looked as tired as Megara had after her lessons. Megara's face was soaked with sweat, and her eyes were red as though she'd been crying as well. Adina's hair was falling out of its plait. All three appeared like they'd already been in battle.

Emaline hugged her brother and he wrapped his arms around her shoulders, all the while watching Megara. She cried again. "I'm sorry," Megara sobbed, her arms wrapped around herself. "I didn't mean for this to happen."

"What is she talking about?" Leopold asked Adina.

Adina sighed. "New reports have come. The army is flying Camelot's banner."

"Camelot?" Leopold asked, his heart dropping into his stomach. He thought about Camelot's threats to eradicate magic.

"They followed us here," Adina said. "We think they've been hiding in the woods, planning their attack. As soon as we told them who we were, they must have planned this. The council, Judd, believes it has to do with our magic."

Leopold gazed at Megara. *She killed with magic. They must have wanted revenge more than we'd realized.*

Leopold let go of his sister and put his hands on Megara's shoulders. "This isn't your fault," he insisted, trying to make her meet his eyes.

"They found Domum because you had to come get me. They want to kill me."

"We don't know what they want," Leopold reminded her. "They could just want to talk."

"A whole army just to talk?" Adina asked in doubt.

Leopold glared at her. He knew Domum had slim chances. He knew it was bringing Megara home that triggered this, but he didn't know why.

"What if . . .?" Megara began before hesitating.

"What if what?" Adina asked.

"What if I gave myself to them?" she asked. Her posture straightened and knocked Leopold's hands from her shoulders, her gaze hardening.

Emaline took Megara's hand. "Absolutely not. We just got you home, Meggy. You're not going back."

Leopold's mind filled with the memory of the last time Domum was faced with this level of terror. *Merlin, you bastard,* he thought. *Why couldn't you have left us in peace?* All of this began with him taking a child. And no one even knew why! What would life have been like had he left them alone? What would have happened had he ignored the baby toddling around? *Our fathers would still be alive. Megara would have had older brothers. She probably would have been on the council.*

She probably would have been on the council.

Leopold laughed humorlessly. "Megara, you are our only hope."

"What?" she scoffed.

"You're the only one who can save us. You have to use your magic. You have to teach Adina what you did in Camelot."

"No!" Megara retreated from the three of them, seeming to fold in on herself as her shoulders slumped once more. "I won't. That's

145

what got us into this mess in the first place. My magic brought them to Domum. I can't use it."

"You can't deny who you are," Emaline disagreed.

Leopold was torn. He had never known much about magic and it never bothered him, but he wasn't sure how to respond to this. Her refusal to use magic would have rolled off his shoulders before, but now he could feel frustration boiling beneath his skin. She had an ability which could be used to save everyone, and she wasn't going to even try. He knew he couldn't say any of this though, it wasn't his place.

"I can and I will." Megara glared at them all, straightening her shoulders again. "I'm not doing it. I've brought enough anguish to Domum, to my mother. I will not let you use my magic like *he* did."

Then she ran away. Leopold was afraid to follow, though he desperately wanted to. He didn't mean to use her like Merlin did. He knew they had one hope against Camelot, though. He didn't know how to convince her, or even if he should.

"I could go after her," Emaline offered without hope.

Adina shook her head. "She's made her decision. Domum will not force anyone to fight. We must continue our preparations on our own."

Leopold went home with Emaline, dragging his feet. He still didn't know if he should go after Megara. When they walked in the door, they found a table full of food, his older brothers sitting there. Aldus stood and grasped Leopold's forearm with a grim expression. "Do you think the men are ready?" he asked.

Leopold gave a small smile. "I wasn't paying much attention to the other men. The knights and the commander gave me other jobs. What are you doing here?"

Aldus sat down with a sigh. "The commander asked all the patrolmen to come in. We know of the danger—we know where they are. He wanted all the families to be reunited before the battle for a final goodbye."

"It won't be final," Anora insisted as she slammed a bowl onto the table. "And I won't have you talking like that, Aldus."

Her hair was frizzy and her eyes wild. All the men lowered their eyes in shame. "Sorry, Ma," Aldus murmured. "I didn't mean it like that."

"Yes, you did," she said. "I won't have you lying, either."

They went to bed with full stomachs, having forced themselves to eat for Anora's sake.

For as much as she wouldn't allow talks of final goodbyes, Leopold thought, *why do I feel like that was my final meal?*

Leopold and his brothers lay without speaking for several minutes after Aldus extinguished the candle. Finally, Jasper spoke. "Ma said no goodbyes," he said. "But you both need to know how much I . . . Aldus, I admire you. I admire your courage and your strength. I always wished I could be as focused as you. Leo . . ." Jasper rolled over, and despite the dark, Leopold could tell his brother was facing him. "Thank you for always being humble and for putting others first. You taught me how to slow down. So, thank you."

"Thank you for teaching me to be strong," Leopold responded, staring upward toward the ceiling. "And for always being there."

Aldus was quiet for so long, Leopold thought maybe he had fallen asleep. Then they heard his bed shift, and he came to them in the dark.

He stood between his brothers' beds and put his hand on their heads, tousling their hair. "You two are the reason I am who I am. Thank you."

Megara's face flooded Leopold's mind. He should have said more. He should have said goodbye to her. If she wasn't going to join the fight, that could have been the last time he spoke with her. The thought made his heart feel like it could sink him in the river.

The next morning, Leopold woke to the sound of silence. Not even the cattle outside the window were making noise. The entire world was still. *Do the animals know what's coming? Are they frightened? Do they fear for their loved ones? Are they angry that their home is being invaded?* He didn't know the answers, but the questions pelted his mind.

He rolled out of bed and dressed. He didn't know what to expect from this day. It would be all about preparing the village for the fight. The council could talk of negotiations all they wanted, but everyone else knew the truth. Death was coming. It was almost to the gates.

He reached the front door as the bell in the town center sounded. It was calling the people of Domum to the council. He obeyed, watching the crowd glumly for the familiar blond head he wished with all his heart would be there.

He knew she wouldn't be, and therefore was not surprised to find her missing from the crowd. He stood beside his family. His mother reached out and held his hand in a tight vise. He watched the council leader, whose face was pale and sweaty. "My people . . ." He spoke with less assurance than he had the day before. "My people, I hope, for all our sakes, that we have fortified our home well. I hope we will be able to spend the rest of this day fortifying our borders. Each member of the council and each member of my family will take separate quadrants of Domum to get ready. Allow us your strength to defend our home. We will not demand that you fight. If you feel that fleeing into the woods is best for your family—" There were lots of murmurs in the crowd at this, and the healer slumped, saddened. "You will not be pursued. No one shall spare a second glance. Do what you feel is best for your family. But leave now, as we do not have the resources to protect you, and we would wish you safety. Take this time to go as far as you can before the fight begins."

He stopped speaking and looked around. He seemed relieved at first when no family left right away, but then Leopold saw at least three families peel away from the edges of the circle. Adina's father did not hide his dismay well, but did not comment on it further. "We must brace ourselves," he said, seeming to build himself up with his final strings of courage.

With that, the crowd broke apart. Leopold watched his mother and sister follow Edith. His brothers followed the commander. Leopold's eyes fell on his lifelong friend, his partner in all adventures, and went to her. Adina appeared as though she had gotten no sleep the night before. He didn't blame her. He was surprised he'd slept at all. "What's our quadrant?" he asked when he approached her.

"We're taking the far edge beyond the harvest fields." She yawned. "We'll be preparing cells for possible prisoners."

He nodded and headed that way on his own, knowing Adina would wait for more volunteers before following. He didn't come this direction in his normal duties. No one did. The prison cells had sat empty for many years. He couldn't actually remember the last time amyone had filled one. *The people of Domum are too peaceful for their own good.* Leopold felt an immense sadness knowing it was possible that lack of aggressive drive would leave many of their people dead at the end of this.

The walk to the prisons took longer than he expected. He knew there was a path through the middle of their largest harvest field and it led to a bridge over the irrigation stream. At the other end of the bridge was the large clearing with the prison in the center of it. It was rundown. Leopold could understand why they needed to repair it.

Throughout the day, the village worked hard to stockpile supplies into the square and protect their homes. There were expressions of despair passed around when Leopold paused to observe. Tears were shed as mothers worried for their children. They took a break for a midday village meal. A few of the men decided to start sharing good memories, trying to lift up the women and children so they could get more work done. There were many chuckles, and it did put a lighter step into everyone's gait, but it wasn't enough.

By the time the assigned tasks were done, Domum's borders were unrecognizable. There were sharp trees made into spikes on three sides directed outward, intending to create a physical barrier. They wanted to direct the battle to one direction. They could fight a battle from the front, but they stood even less of a chance if they left blind spots open. Camelot had no way to attack from the river.

Leopold saw that those studying creation were creating traps and danger zones for the invaders. He knew Ibb and Judd were leading the other prophets in a meditation as they tried to find every possible outcome. There was a group of healers, and Stace, who had healed his neighbor's cow a lifetime ago, was assisting those who were struggling. A group of people were forcing boulders and other large objects across the fields. All the magic users were at different levels of skill. Some were needing to take frequent breaks so as to regain their strength, but everyone was trying to do their best for their people.

Leopold's heart warmed with pride. *I'm a man from Domum,* he found himself thinking. *I am from the village with the most care, courage, and power. We are one, and we will survive. We can survive this.*

Though he still didn't see Megara anywhere, he felt peace. The village would try their hardest, and that was the best anyone could ask for.

CHAPTER THIRTEEN

A T THE END OF the preparations, Leopold joined everyone
else in the town center. There was more crying and so
many embraces. Leopold saw Adina walking among the children,
kneeling down and giving each of them kind words in turn. They
all cried and hugged her. He wondered how she could hold so
much strength within her. He saw her approach the young creation girl from the harvest festival. She knelt and blew a single
butterfly onto her finger, then set it on the little girl's shoulder
and whispered something to her. The girl stood a little straighter
and put her fists on her hips. He saw Adina chuckle and say one
more thing before hugging the little girl and moving along in her
task. *Adina never needed a quest to prove herself. The people already
trust her with all their hearts.*

As Leopold was gazing around, he saw a flash of yellow out
of the corner of his eye. He turned his head and saw Margaret
staring toward the path that led to her home. Leopold walked to
her, clearing his throat so as not to sneak up on her.

She saw him and nodded. "Hello, Leo," she said. She sounded very tired.

"Are you all right, Margaret?"

Her eyes filled with tears. "Meggy hasn't left home all day. She's been sitting in the house since this morning. She's afraid. She blames herself."

Leopold squeezed her hand. "Are you all right with me going to speak with her?" he asked. Margaret searched his face for a moment before nodding.

"Be gentle," she pleaded. "I just got her back. I don't want her to run away and leave me."

Leopold nodded then walked toward Margaret's house. He thought about what he might say, but by the time he reached the home, he still didn't know. He knocked on the door and didn't receive an answer. "Meggy?" he called. The silence was cold and still. "Megara, open up or I'm coming in."

He was about to open the door when he heard footsteps beyond it. "Go away, Leo." Her voice was soft, broken. "I don't want to fight."

"I'm not here to make you fight," he told her. "I'm here to see you."

She opened the door and leaned against it. Her eyes were red and swollen, and she hiccupped. "I'm fine," she said.

"You can't lie to me, Meggy," he said, wiping a tear from her cheek with his thumb. He wanted more than anything to pull her into his arms and say that goodbye to her, but he didn't. He jumped when something brown and furry climbed onto her shoulder and hissed at him. He took a step away until he realized it was the stoat from Camelot. "Has he been here the whole time?" he asked. She nodded with a slight smile.

"He said he couldn't let me go alone. I'm his family. Stoats don't stay with their families, but I named him, and he liked how I took the time to. He grew attached."

She took him from her shoulder and held him in her arms, petting him. Leopold watched her face. "May I come in?" he asked. She hesitated then nodded and stepped aside.

He walked into the small home. He couldn't see anything, the house was so dark. He couldn't spot a single candle anywhere, and the fireplace was not lit. "Have you been like this all day?" he asked.

"It was warmer when the sun was up," she said.

Leopold walked to the fireplace and felt along the mantle with his hands until he was able to find supplies to start a warm fire. He sat beside the fire, and after a moment, Megara joined him on the stool next to his chair. "Meggy, I don't want to hurt you. I don't want you to think I'm demanding your help, either. But I do not believe we will be able to make it through this *without* your help."

"I will not use my power," she insisted, watching the flames lick up the wood. "I will not be the reason people die."

"And what if you *not* helping gets people killed?" Leopold insisted.

She looked away from him. "Then they are meant to die, and fate has spoken."

"You're a stubborn woman, Megara," Leopold growled and stood. "But if that's the way you see it, fine. I will be in that battle. I will defend our home while you hide here in the dark and pretend this isn't happening." He hadn't intended to argue with her, but he couldn't understand her refusal to protect her family.

Megara slammed the door behind him as he sighed on the step. *How can she even allow herself to be like this?* he thought as he stomped down the road, his hands in fists. *People could die! And she's just going to sit there and hide.*

Maybe she is a coward. She was raised by one, after all.

He felt a little guilty thinking these things, and it conflicted so much with his desire to protect her and hold her close, but he couldn't help it. He was so angry she would allow the people of Domum to fight and die while she didn't even try. He watched even the elderly of Domum teaching the children what they knew. *The last time there was this much danger was when Merlin was taking a baby. People fought as hard as they could to keep that family together. And now that victim is sitting in her house, safe at home, and allowing people to die for her all over again.* It infuriated him. He'd never met a more selfish woman.

And yet, even through his anger, he felt the immense desire to protect her. *If this army is here to kill her and she refuses to defend herself, she'll be too easy a target.* He couldn't allow that, either. As he crossed the bridge into the old town, he vowed that if he had the chance, he would do what he could to make sure she survived this. If he had to stand at her door and stop every person from entering, he'd do it until he died, even if he thought Megara was being unreasonable.

Just as he was reaching his mother's house, Leopold heard the village bell begin to trill, and a scream ripped through the night. His blood transformed to ice and his heart felt as though it had stopped. The army had arrived.

He was running before he knew what he was doing. His feet thudded across the bridge faster than he thought possible as he raced toward the scream. He slid to a stop when he reached the northernmost part of the village. Other men had come too, though they'd thought to bring their weapons. A boy, not quite a man though he wasn't a child, stood in the front of the crowd, pointing toward the looming darkness. The breath caught in Leopold's throat as he stared. Here they were. This was no "small army," as he'd been told. This was a *full* army, with twice as many men as there were people in Domum. *We're doomed*, Leopold thought even as another family took their children in their arms and ran southward. *We're all going to die.*

"Leo!"

He saw Adina rushing toward him. She threw him an orange tinted sword—one she had clearly just created. He caught it and turned to the front, sensing the sword was almost a perfect replica of his own weapon he'd left behind. More men joined behind him, those with magic moving to the front and reciting their strategies. Uther rode by on his black steed, the militia commander and three knights behind him on their own mounts. They raced to meet the figure riding out in front of Camelot's men. Leopold heard women behind him begin to whisper prayers to their gods and begging for a peaceful resolution.

The people of Domum held their breath as they watched their leader attempt to reason with the leader of the Camelot army. Leopold heard a scream of anguish and the cry for revenge before his eyes even registered what he'd seen. Then he saw Adina's father fall from his black horse, decapitated. The Domum knights retreated and galloped to their people, who were now leaderless and waiting for their doom. Leopold felt as though he'd swallowed a boulder.

"Defend Domum!" Katherine screamed from somewhere near Leopold. "Avenge Uther!"

"*For Uther!*" the people of Domum echoed as they took up arms and rushed forward.

The sounds around Leopold seemed to mute as he rushed forward with his people. Colors sharpened. His body fell into the familiar movements he'd been learning for fourteen years. It was easy for him to differentiate between his people and the army of Camelot. The men of Camelot were clothed in red and gold, wore armor, and most had the kingdom's emblem on their chests. The people of Domum were in simple clothing, and only the knights wore silver armor. Leopold himself had not been wearing any protection before the battle began. He held a simple shield which he had found discarded on the ground before joining the fight. Men fell all around him. A few were men of Camelot, yet most were farmers of Domum. Leopold did not allow himself to study the faces of his people as they fell. That would come later. For now, he needed his wits about him.

Leopold fought with vigor. His fighting style was different from Camelot's. They relied on brute strength to cut down their foes. Leopold relied on stamina and dexterity. His mind took him deep into instinct as he fought for his life and home as hard as he could. He allowed his training to command his actions.

Leopold faced one opponent who made his mind wake up. He realized the adversary was his age. He was built the same as Leopold. He was strong, but his eyes were frightened. Leopold forced himself to use that fear and pushed the young man back hard. Leopold stabbed him, and the knight dropped his shield to clutch at his sword-wielding arm. Leopold kicked the man to the ground and plunged his sword into the man's chest. The light left the man's eyes and Leopold took a shuddering breath. *I just killed a man*, he realized with a jolt.

Leopold straightened and turned to the next enemy. He noticed some of those with creation and willpower magic were climbing onto

the roofs of nearby homes. He glimpsed shapeshifters joining the fighting ranks as various predators, most as wolves and
bears. He recognized most of the magic users had never received
hand-to-hand combat training. They needed to be protected.

He was coming to this realization when he watched a group
of men break off from the battle and head toward the first house
at the edge of the forest. A young woman had climbed onto that
roof and was positioning herself to fight. Leopold shouted and
chased after them, a few Domum farmers following on his heels.
The young woman's head popped up at his shout and Leopold
realized it was Emaline, her eyes wide with panic, and blind fury
filled him. He raced forward and brought his sword in an arc
against the man closest to him in the group of soldiers before they
realized they'd been followed. The man's head left his neck with a
sickening *thwip*.

Emaline shot something red over Leopold's head, and he spun
to see anotherman from Camelot being chased by a creature of
fire. The blaze followed the knight to his platoon, and Leopold
watched it consume the entire gathering. Leopold stared at Emaline in shock. Her face was set in chilling determination as she
mouthed one word. *Meggy*.

He returned to the fight and kicked the knees of a man with
his hands around the throat of one of the healer women. Leopold
stabbed him from the side, pulling the woman from his grip.
As Leopold forced himself to watch the life leave the soldier's
body, a memory filled his mind—Adina sharing King Arthur's
abhorrence of magic. *They don't care who they kill.*

They just want to kill as many as they can.

As Leopold pushed the healer toward the village, he looked around, his chest heaving, and he realized what the army's intention was. There were more troops who were targeting the houses with magic wielders on the roofs. *They're going for the magic. They want to kill the magic.*

The whole picture filled his mind as he thought about this. *Meggy killed Merlin with magic. They'd allowed Merlin into Camelot because he benefited them and befriended them. Meggy killed him, and some of their people. They learned there was a village full of magic when we went for Meggy. Adina must have told them we know how to teach Meggy how to use her magic. The king must have decided to kill all of Domum. Rid the earth of magic.* Leopold had never imagined Arthur would go so far out of his way to achieve this.

Leopold knew there was little hope the moment these thoughts filled his mind. This was why Camelot had brought such a big army. Even with odds in their favor without the massive numbers, they were taking no chance against the magic. They didn't care how many people they lost—they had more to replace them. They were going to wipe out the village and make their magic extinct, no matter the cost. *Who is this king? What king would demand this type of disregard of his own men?*

As he continued to fight through the men in front of him through sheer instinct, his attention was grabbed by a woman screaming past him. He saw Adina locked in a fierce attack, using her magic in the form of a bright orange cannon, against a man astride a horse. Leopold recognized the markings on his tunic—this man was Camelot's king. It was made clear this was the one who had murdered Adina's father.

Leopold fought his way toward Adina, trying to help her. She was using every tactic she'd learned from the knights and all of the magic she'd learned from her mentors. But she wasn't fighting with a clear head—she was fighting for revenge.

Leopold was almost to her side when he realized another man was working his way toward her. It was Jasper, his eyes ablaze with fury. He got to Adina before Leopold could and joined her in the fight. When the king saw that a man had joined Adina, he turned his horse and retreated behind his forces. Adina and Jasper fought off the men closing in around them, their backs together. Leopold stopped trying to reach her, trusting his brother to safeguard his friend.

As the sun started to set, Leopold began to feel what felt suspiciously like hope. They couldn't keep fighting in the dark—they'd have to rest soon. Both sides would need to gather their dead, and both sides had many comrades who had fallen. Both sides would have to wrap their wounds. This would give Domum the chance to heal their forces with magic. *We might have a chance.* Leopold hadn't stopped to evaluate the damage to their numbers, but he'd seen so much magic flying around that he knew Domum was on equal grounds despite the gross number difference.

Leopold at last heard Camelot's call to retreat. The people of Domum shouted jeers as their opponents fled, though everyone knew this war was not over. As soon as the men of Camelot were gone, the people of Domum gathered their dead, and the injured were sent to be healed. Leopold evaluated his own injuries before staying to help move the dead, deciding he could stop by a healer later.

As he helped to carry the dead to the area to be laid out for final farewells, he felt sick as he saw the children who had been killed. Homes had been invaded and the children dragged into the streets.

The elderly who were too frail to fight lay broken, the expression of terror suspended in their dull eyes.

After all of the Domum dead were collected, the townspeople retreated within their borders and allowed the knights of Camelot to gather their own. The people of Domum hadn't known where to rest their dead that evening as there wasn't enough time for proper burials, so they were laid together in the village center As his neighbors returned home, Leopold headed toward his home for some rest. His eyes were caught by a woman with blond hair sitting near the bonfire, facing the flames. Leopold froze when he saw a man in glimmering armor sneak from the shadows toward her. He sprinted toward them, screaming to get the attention of anyone closer. A Domum man rushed forward and cut down the knight.

The woman turned from the fire with Leopold's shout, her hand at her throat, a small stone clutched in her fingers. Leopold realized it was Margaret, not Megara, her eyes wide with fright, her chest heaving as she watched the Domum man cut down her attacker. "Leo!" she sobbed as she rushed forward and clutched him in a hug. He patted her before continuing his journey to the healers after she thanked her real hero.

Leopold sat beside the fire later that night, taking his turn for watch.. The healers rested together in the council house, sleeping or eating to regain their strength under protective watch from the Domum militia.

There hadn't been a single wounded who hadn't been healed, even brought from the brink of death. Leopold had watched men who he'd mistaken for dead hand bowls of broth to women and children for supper. Every scratch had been healed as though it had never happened—missing limbs were reattached. Some men appeared as though they had never fought, though Leopold knew they had from the blood-soaked clothing they wore. Some wounds had been healed poorly, but they were alive. Leopold felt a renewed sense of gratitude for this magic they were fighting to protect.

Emaline sat beside Leopold and laid her head on his shoulder. Her energy was drained, and he could feel how weak she was when he took her hand. "We're going to lose, aren't we?" she whispered to him.

Some with magic who hadn't the energy to make it home had laid in the dirt or on a log or wherever they could and fell asleep. They had a few hours to regain their strength, but he knew it wouldn't return completely. The healers couldn't restore the energy to those who were fatigued from magic, especially for those who didn't have a full grasp on it. It wouldn't return at all for the remaining battle for many of them. "Go home and get some sleep," Leopold told her instead of responding to her question. "It'll be a long day tomorrow."

CHAPTER FOURTEEN

J UST BEFORE SHIFT CHANGE, Leopold felt the hairs prick on the back of his neck. He listened hard for any sound and heard a whisper of skirts against the ground nearby. He sat as still as he could, holding his breath and listening. The fire was low, enough to light the firepit. He couldn't see any movement, but he heard a whisper that sounded like a shift of leaves. Within seconds, he felt a slight pressure on his foot. He stood, unsheathing his sword as he looked down. The stoat placed a small paw on Leopold's own foot, matching his gaze. It had a white spot on its nose he hadn't noticed before. They stared at each other for a moment before it tugged on the lace of Leopold's boot with its tiny mouth. Then it stepped back and waited. He watched it for a moment before it moved forward and tugged on his lace once more and moved out of his sight.

Leopold followed the stoat away from the dying fire and to Margaret's house. Then it stopped and stared at him before running forward a few steps into the darkness. He heard a breeze once again and then saw the shadowy form of a woman in the darkness. He stepped forward and was met with the woman wrapping her arms around his waist and burying her face in his chest. "Were you hurt?" he heard Megara whisper.

"Meggy?" He laughed, pushing her away and holding her shoulders at arms' length. His heart was beating fast with the relief of seeing her. "There are easier ways to get me to follow you, you know. You're lucky I recognized your stoat friend."

"I didn't want to frighten you. It was easier to find you in the darkness while I was a stoat. They have decent good noses for tracking."

Leopold stared at her for a moment. "That was you?"

"Who did you think it was?"

"That stoat you showed me before."

Megara smiled. "Superus is still asleep on my pillow." She laid her head on his chest once more. The warmth of her cheek slowed the racing in his chest. Leopold knew this was much too intimate, but no one was watching. After the day he'd had, having her near was restorative in a way the healers had not been able to do. He felt her melt into him, and he sighed. "I'm sorry I got angry with you earlier," he whispered into her hair, closing his eyes.

"I'm sorry I won't help you. I heard everything. I know how terrible it was. But I still won't help," she added. "I can't."

"We can't win on our own, Meggy," Leopold breathed. "We will all die. We can't beat them. They outnumber us."

"I'm sorry, Leo," she said, pulling away. "But I can't." She stood in enough darkness that Leopold couldn't see her face. "I wanted to be sure you were..."

"Alive?" Leopold intoned. She didn't respond. "I won't be by the end of this," he intoned. "So, I guess this is goodbye."

He didn't want to guilt her into helping. It tore at his heart to know he was hurting her, but he didn't want her to sit by and watch her people die. He wanted her to realize what her decision meant to them.

He heard her sniffle and move farther from him. "If that's what you believe," she whispered. Then she hesitated. "I hope you fight with courage, Leopold," she said, her voice stronger. "I would hate to lose you to cowardice."

Then he watched her shadow disappear into Margaret's house. He heard the door close, and she was gone. Leopold walked to the fire and sat down to await the end of his watch. He tried to convince his brain to shut down, but words were clawing their way through. He did his best to ignore them, but they crept into his heart. *I love Megara.* He finally allowed the words to form. *I love her more than I love my own life. If it is the last act I perform, I will make sure she survives this and whatever comes next.*

Leopold knew he had no right to think these things. They were not married—not even courting to be married. But he was in love with this woman and he would not allow her to be slaughtered by the likes of Camelot. He vowed to spend the entire remainder of his life defending her. *I love her.*

A Domum knight approached and informed Leopold that he would take over. Leopold made his way to his mother's house in the dark with these secret words echoing in his mind.

What felt like moments later, he felt Jasper shaking his shoulder in their attic. "Come on, little brother," Jasper was saying. "We're gathering the men to strategize for battle." Jasper moved to get dressed when Leopold opened his eyes. *This is the day,* Leopold thought as he yawned and scrubbed his face. *Today I die for the woman I love.* He wasn't scared, he wasn't angry—he was nothing but determined. He would give his life for her if it meant she would maybe see another day. He would not die in vain, even if he was cut down for them to kill her. He would not allow his life to be taken for a lesser cause.

Leopold gathered other men who were prepared to fight and helped shelter those who were still too weak to help. He hid children in cellars or barns and watched as those with magic climbed back to their spots on the roofs, preparing themselves for the darkest day of their lives.

Leopold lost himself again. He didn't allow himself to feel anything as he saw Camelot's army approaching from the forest. Their numbers were significantly less, though they were marching forward with confidence. They still outnumbered Domum, but not by much. Leopold didn't take any reassurance from this. This army had the goal to wipe them out, and they had the resources and skill to do so.

Adina and Jasper stood on either side of him, and he could hear Aldus giving instructions behind them. Jasper patted Leopold's shoulder, and Adina squeezed his wrist once. Her face was set with lethal focus. He felt bolstered with them around him, but he knew things weren't going to end well for them all. Who would he be saying goodbye to at the day's end? Would they be saying goodbye to him?

As Camelot's army stopped at the same point as the day before, Adina and several knights walked forward to Domum's border. Adina shouted loud enough for the army to hear across the great distance.

"Surrender!" The men from the army laughed. "You have sustained many wounds and even deaths. We are still here, whole and ready to fight. Surrender! We'll leave each other in peace."

Leopold heard a voice come across the expanse, but from where he stood, he couldn't hear the words. Adina could, though. "No." She shook her head. "The children will stay where they are."

Leopold's blood boiled and men murmured around him, some calling slurs across the distance. *Did the king of Camelot just tell us to send our children to him? To their deaths?* He twisted his sword in his hand, now very ready to get this day's battle under way. *Let them come,* he thought. *We can take them. We* will *defeat them.* Adina and the knights returned to the people of Domum when the men of Camelot moved forward.

"We fight with honor to defend those we love," Adina shouted with her sword above her head. "We have power they do not understand, and it is clear we have honor they do not possess. Defend our homes with courage, or face the gods with pride." They shouted their agreement, Leopold loudest of them all. This was it, and Leopold would be the most courageous.

The ground force of Domum rushed forward. They took the fight to Camelot, demonstrating their renewed strength. Leopold heard the ground rumble as those with the willpower magic forced it to move. He sidestepped as he ran to avoid long fissures that appeared, sending at least fifty Camelot knights into a deep hole with screams of terror. Camelot's other knights stumbled, but only for a moment before they continued on. Fires flared as troops around him combusted with screams. Wolves leaped for throats, some smaller and presenting as natural wolves rather than shifters, he assumed they were recruited by those with the gift of language.

As Leopold raised his sword to deliver a death blow to the knight in front of him, he felt a burning rip through his middle. He watched the man he'd been about to kill grin and stand, running away. Leopold couldn't move his feet. He looked down and saw something silver protruding from his stomach. The sword was pulled out, and with it, Leopold felt his strength abandon him. He fell to his knees and then sideways, his heart thudding and his breathing coming in gasps. He thought he heard a scream somewhere near him, but his ears were ringing.

His eyesight dimmed, and he began to panic. This wasn't how he was supposed to die. He'd been stabbed from behind. *Stab a man from his front,* Leopold thought. He couldn't see anymore, and the ringing in his head started to fade.

CHAPTER FIFTEEN

A FTER LEOPOLD LEFT, MEGARA stayed awake and watched the sun rise through the window with Superus in her lap. She couldn't sleep. Leopold's words kept replaying in her mind. *"We can't win on our own, Meggy. We will all die."*

"I guess this is goodbye."

The words echoed through her mind all night. She knew he was right. She had heard the battle raging outside while she hid in her mother's house. Megara knew Leopold hadn't meant to say the words with malice. He was trying to protect his home, *their* home, and he knew she would want to as well. She'd been in Domum but a few days, but it was like a dream come true. She had a mother. She had friends. She had a home and a warm bed and plenty of food. It did hurt her when people stared at her or whispered about her—she wasn't unaware of their fear, but it was something she knew would eventually go away. *Not if they're all dead by dinner,* she found herself thinking.

She heard her neighbors begin to move about the village. Her mother left, saying she was going to help hide the children. Superus gazed up at her. She felt heavy. Would he run away too, like Leopold had? Did he know the sort of coward she was being? She spoke the few words that allowed her to speak to her friend in his tongue, but they just stared at each other for a moment.

"Are you going to help?" Superus asked her.

"I am afraid to," she admitted.

"Why are you afraid?"

"If I save them with my magic, will they hate me more?" Tears filled her eyes as she pictured the village people banishing her after she killed the men of Camelot.

"Would you forgive yourself if you do nothing?"

Superus placed his front feet on Megara's collarbone and stared her in the face. "You have to do something, Meggy, or you won't forgive yourself. You know that."

Megara nodded, her tears falling onto his legs and darkening his fur. Though she knew she had to do something, it took her a long time to stand from her chair. She heard the battle cries start and still couldn't bring herself to open the door. It wasn't until she heard his name that she felt the ground move beneath her.

"Leo is down. I was sent to find Anora and take her to the healers. Have you seen her?"

"Get back out there," a man said with a thick voice. "I'll find her."

They were rushing down the road, their voices traveling. Megara's heart stopped in her chest and she found herself throwing open the door and sprinting, Superus chasing after her. *Not Leo*, she thought. *Not now. Not this soon.* Despite his reminders that he was going into battle today, she hadn't thought he'd lie down and let death come.

As she ran to the village center she strained her ears for any other clues, but all she could hear were the screams and shouts from the battle. She tried to remember how to get to the council house, thinking that would be the place for the healers to be.

She ran as fast as she could when she saw Emaline rushing out of the council house and heading in the direction of their home. She was crying. Megara entered the council house, Superus finally catching up to her and clinging to her skirts, and listened to all of the commotion.

The meeting house had changed. The four tables were pushed against the walls, each holding injured bodies. Other injured people littered the floors, healers moving among them. Loud shouts and yelling surrounded her, the scent of blood and noise overwhelming her senses. Her heart pounded and she couldn't catch her breath as she fell against the open door. She wanted to return to her mother's home and cover her ears. *My cellar was never this loud!* she thought as she gritted her teeth and forced her way deeper into the building, letting the chaos consume her as she searched for Leopold.

She stared into every face, blood soaked and otherwise, looking for his familiar russet hair and boyish features. She found him after a young woman Megara recognized from the council stepped away from his cot, her hands soaked in blood. The girl shouted a command to someone else before turning and spotting her. "Megara!" She sighed with relief on her face. "Come over here." She stepped out of the way and indicated that Megara should take her place. Megara complied before the girl spoke. "My name is Stace. I didn't have time to start your lessons, but I need your help if you're able."

Megara studied Leopold and saw that he was very pale, his eyes closed in agony. He was squirming and moaning, his hands pressing on a cloth on his stomach that had already soaked through. She raised her hands and looked at Stace. "What do you need me to do?" Megara set her jaw, knowing she would do anything to save this man's life.

"Edith began teaching you wordless enchantments, yes?" Stace asked. Megara nodded. "How much Latin do you know?"

Megara was surprised by the question. "As well as I could know it, I believe."

"I have no idea how you make the words work, but I'm going to give you a list to try. Translate them and use those if you can." Stace recited several phrases and Megara tried her hardest to find words that matched, her eyes focused on the blood seeping from Leopold's wound. She'd never attempted any healing magic before, so she didn't know what she was doing. She said the words over and over, beginning to worry it wouldn't work and she had found something she couldn't do. Stace was on Leopold's other side doing her own magic. Megara focused as hard as she could and mimicked what Stace was doing with her hands.

Megara cursed when nothing happened, tears welling in her eyes. Superus shifted against her leg. She was shouting now, the rest of the healers quieting as Megara begged Leopold to accept the relief she was trying to offer. She was aware of Stace stepping away when he seemed to fall unconscious. Someone was saying something to Megara, but she ignored them. *This will work,* she told herself as she began the phrases over again. "*Febricitantem,*" she continued, throwing herself into making the words mean something.

The room around her was almost silent when she felt it. The smallest trickle of magic left her body and connected her to Leopold. She laughed in relief when she felt the connection to his warm soul, her tears falling down her cheeks as she clutched to that connection with all of her will. She repeated Stace's list in a much calmer tone, urging the connection to move faster and stronger. She began throwing in other words, bending the language to what she needed it to do. As she worked, she tuned out the whispers around her, ignoring their looks and fear as she focused on Leopold's injury.

After another moment, Megara felt the magic stiffen and sap her energy. Her breathing was coming in rasps. She couldn't tell what her magic was doing for him under the blood-soaked rag covering him, but his face relaxed and his breathing evened out. His face had regained its color by the time Stace took Megara's hands away from him. "Enough, Megara," she whispered. "Don't push yourself too far. Enough."

As Megara relinquished her hold on the magic, she felt her legs give way. She fell to a knee before strong arms wrapped around her and the man lifted her into the air. Superus dropped to the floor. The stranger was gentle as he carried her across the room to an empty cot. Megara kept her eyes squeezed closed so as not to see any of the judgmental faces around her.

The man set her on the bed, and Megara felt a cool cloth wipe across her forehead. She didn't look until she heard the buzz of healers' voices again. When she opened them, she stared at the man next to her. His face was covered with a thick beard, his hair cut close to his head. He had a bloody bandage across his forehead. Despite all of that, he felt familiar. He was avoiding meeting her eyes, but he was the one dabbing her forehead with the cloth. Megara glanced around and saw no one else was looking at her either..

When he could avoid her gaze no longer, the man set the cloth in the bowl. "My name is Aldus," he said in a low voice that seemed to carry the weight of the world. "Leopold is my youngest brother." She understood the familiarity then, the resemblance between them was strong.

"Meggy," she introduced herself, her voice sticking in her throat.

"I know who you are," he said as he sat back in his chair. He folded his arms across his chest and watched her. "I knew your brothers," he said. Megara's held still in surprise. "They were my friends. You need to know, none of us blame you for what happened. How could we? You were nothing but a child. You had no control over what was happening to you. We blame Merlin.

"Many of the people wish they could have done what you did, Meggy," Aldus continued softly, leaning forward and laying his hand on her arm. "So many of these people wanted to see him dead. You did that for them. They're proud of you."

"They're *afraid* of me," she corrected.

"No." Aldus shook his head. "They're proud of you. You're. . . different." Megara scoffed, and he smiled. "You're unique. No one has ever left Domum for as long as you have and returned. You don't do magic the same way. We don't know how to react to you."

Megara thought this over, and as the door slammed open and battle cries filled the air, she was reminded that there was a war going on outside. Anger flared inside her, her body warming and tensing. "What are you doing in here?" she demanded of Aldus. "Hiding from danger?" Her voice was sharper than she intended, and she did not miss his responding expression of disgust and shock.

"Of course not. I'd be out there right now, but the prophets demanded that myself and a few others remain here to protect those recovering."

"Don't you mean dying?" Megara asked.

Aldus's eyes flashed as he leaned forward. "We have lost no one today," he growled. "Everyone has been healed."

Megara glanced around and realized that everyone who had been in the alcove near her now seemed much better and were either sitting upright or had gone out to join in the battle. She sat forward to try to catch a glimpse of Leopold's bed. Stace still stood beside him and had her hand over his stomach, but he was sitting up. Megara attempted to move toward him, but Aldus pushed her shoulder down. "Stace said you need to rest," he argued.

"I need to tell him I'm sorry." She pushed against his hand but couldn't get up. Eventually, she stopped trying and lay down angrily.

"I can't let you leave this bed," he said. "He will come to you when he's ready. I promise."

Megara folded her arms and Aldus seemed to be taking it upon himself to ensure she continued resting. Several minutes passed, and the entire room seemed to empty except for the healers, Leopold, and the guards. Megara stared at the ceiling, straining to hear what Leopold and Stace were whispering about, but she could hear nothing save it be sharp hissing. She heard a man's footsteps moving toward her. She held her breath until losing her patience and tilting her head up to see beyond her personal guard.

Leo stopped a cot away from her. "I thought you said you weren't going to help," he accused.

Megara sat up on her bed, waving a hand dismissively. "I didn't help fight the battle. I healed you. There's a difference."

"Yes," Leopold mused. "I suppose there is."

They stared awkwardly at each other before Megara spoke. "You're going out there again, aren't you?" she asked. Her heart fell into her stomach. All that energy, all that magic to heal him, and he was going to go right out to the front line.

"I have to, Meggy," he said, his eyes begging her to understand. He moved toward her and reached out a hand. "Come with me. Show them we can defend ourselves."

"I won't do it." She shook her head and folded her arms again, keeping her hand from his outstretched palm. She ached to take his hand—either to keep him with her or because she wanted to help, she didn't know. She felt conflicted, and the anger and heat left her body. She sagged on her cot and turned away from him.

You could protect him if you went out there with him.

The voice in her mind was unbidden, unwanted, and it made Megara angry all over again. The fire inside her reignited and straightened her spine. She glared at Leopold, and he lowered his hand. *I cannot use my powers for evil,* she told herself. *I cannot lose myself like that again. Especially not against the same people I hurt last time!*

Leopold shook his head then ran out the door. As it opened, before it slammed shut again, Megara heard the screams and shouts from the battle as it came closer to the village. Stace walked up to Megara, and Aldus offered her his seat. She took it and began checking Megara over. "How are you feeling?" she asked.

"I'm fine," Megara said, still looking at the door that had closed behind the man she'd healed.

This time when he walked away, something had felt different within her. Somehow she knew he'd be okay. He'd returned to her, and that was the important thing. He was coming back to *her*. The fire within her changed. Instead of filling her with anger, it filled her with a warm hope. She needed him to survive this. He was so much more than her friend. She felt as though the connection she had created to heal him hadn't broken altogether, part of it thrummed within her. The pull became more insistent the farther away he got from her. She felt as though she couldn't breathe.

She found herself on her feet, feeling Superus settling himself in her skirts. "Megara?" Stace was asking, but Megara was already halfway across the room. She would not allow Leopold to fight this battle without her. She would not allow him to risk his life. She would not allow him to end up on the cursed table where she'd healed him.

He will survive this day if it is the last thing I do.

Chapter Sixteen

Leopold ran from the council house, snatching his vibrant sword, which had been left by the door. He ran across the bridge into the fray that had entered the village center. He blocked a blow from a man who was cornering a shifter in the form of a familiar clouded leopard, then with a clever riposte brought the foe to his end. The shifter was abruptly human again, his bright red hair blazing in the sunlight. He nodded at him in thanks before shifting back into his leopard form and speeding off again, leaping onto another knight and slashing at his head with powerful paws.

Leopold's body was full of a vigor he had not felt before. It coursed through his veins and revitalized every inch of him.. It was intoxicating as he watched the knights of Camelot raze his home.

Camelot's numbers had fallen throughout the day. Where they had started with more men than Domum, they now appeared to have fewer. The battle was in Domum's favor in numbers, but their militia were still very untrained. For every man leaving the healers, more were taking their place, with heavier wounds as the men of Camelot became desperate. The injuries were becoming more life-threatening. It was almost impossible to get those who needed help to the council house, as they were trampled by the knights moving forward.

Leopold prayed the king of Camelot would draw his men back. *They have to know by now that they won't win*, Leopold thought as he grabbed a knight and plunged his sword into his stomach. *Why are they still here?* There had to be something Leopold wasn't seeing.

He caught up to Jasper and Adina and joined in on their fight, taking up their backs and creating an impenetrable trio. They'd cleared the rest of the platoon they were fighting when Leopold saw a flash of yellow rise above him on the roof across the road. He glanced up, and his heart leaped into his throat when he saw Megara climb up beside Emaline. Emaline's face shone with sweat, but her relief at the assistance was unmistakable. Pride filled him at the sight of Megara's conviction. Her eyes met Leopold's before he blocked a sword coming for his head. Leopold saw something shoot from her hand toward the adversary between Leopold and herself.

Leopold had time to take a breath before he heard the cry. "There she is!" a man near him shouted. "It's the Dragon Woman!"

Half the men around Leopold rushed toward the house to attack Megara, enraging him. He chased them down, Adina and Jasper at his side, tunneling their way to the front so they could protect the girls.

Adina reached the front first and changed her tactic to offensive. She interlaced her slashing with orange magic tossed from her hands. Leopold wasn't paying close attention to what she was doing, but it was leaving burning welts on the skin of the men it touched. He and Jasper joined her and began chopping with renewed vigor.

As more men advanced on the house, more people of Domum joined the trio. It was crowded and confusing in the small area. Leopold's new strength ebbed slightly, leaving his arms heavy and his legs weak. He worried he'd been injured again, but he saw those around him struggling as well. It was too much. Though they were doing well at defending the girls on the roof, the army kept coming. For every man cut down, it seemed two replaced him.

A blast echoed around them, which made the earth tremble. The men covered their ears and fell to the ground as the Camelot knights were tossed backward out of the village limits. Leopold saw that it had happened elsewhere on the battlefield, not just around the house where he was standing. Megara's voice echoed around them all. *"Enough!"* It was as loud as the blast had been, and the men of Camelot came to their feet but did not approach. "Enough of this! Show me your leader, the coward who will send his men forward and hide behind them. Show me the man who will not fight his own battles!"

Angry shouts filled the air until Leopold saw a black horse galloping toward the village center. The man leaped from his horse and raised his sword, despite the distance and forces between him and Megara, and the sword almost blinded Leopold when the sun bounced off it.

"You dare call me a coward?" the man screamed. "I am the king of Camelot! You're nothing but a worthless wretch hidden away by my mentor—until you killed him."

Leopold's blood boiled at the words. Megara responded, "Merlin was the only father I knew, but it was all a lie. He was nothing more than a drunk *coward*." With the last word, the earth shook again, sending the Camelot knights to their knees and causing the king's horse to rear up. The king ducked away from the beast to avoid being trampled. Megara continued, "You were nothing more than a servant months ago. Tell me, oh magnificent king. How did you get to where you are now?"

The murmur from the knights of Camelot could be heard even with the distance. "It was the legend!" King Arthur snapped. "It claimed that the rightful heir would draw the sword from the stone and take possession of the throne. *I* pulled the sword from the stone. *I* am the rightful heir!"

"That was a lie!" Megara screamed. "Merlin fed you that nonsense to manipulate Camelot into accepting you. "

The king removed his helm and threw it to the ground. "You know nothing! I am the king!"

"I know the sword!" Megara retorted, her voice shaking the earth again. "I placed it in that stone! I was there the day Merlin showed it to you. I was *there,* Arthur!"

"I am a *king!* You will address me with respect, witch!"

Leopold could see the knights of Camelot hesitate. He watched them look amongst each other and murmur behind their chieftain's back, lowering their swords. Who did they believe? The Dragon Woman who had claimed to put a sword in a rock, or the peasant who was suddenly their king? Leopold didn't know what he would have believed had it been him in their place.

"Leave. Now," Adina shouted toward the tantruming king. "We will let you leave with more honor than you arrived with Collect your wounded and end this war."

He appeared furious at being addressed by another woman. "We will not leave until we get what we came for," he shouted back. He raised his sword again and screamed, "Death to the Dragon Woman, defense of Camelot, glory in victory!"

The men of Camelot roared their agreement and rushed forward.

Adina gripped Leopold's arm as the men of Domum around them joined the battle. "Cover me! I'm going up with Meggy." He parried an attack aimed at her as she climbed up onto the house. He wasn't sure what she was doing, but he hoped she did it quickly. He forced his combatant away from the house once she found her footing. Camelot's newfound rage against Domum was sapping more and more of that strange vivacity from him, and he wasn't sure how much longer he'd be able to keep fighting this hard. He began praying to every deity he knew, hoping someone would hear him and save their home.

He heard Megara's voice magnified above the din again. "This is your last chance, Arthur!" she cried. "Surrender, and we will let your men live. Continue fighting, and they will each meet the same fate Merlin did!" Her voice cracked as she made the threat. She had not sounded confident enough to make the words daunting.

But the men around him seemed to pause anyway. The knights of Camelot began fighting in the defense, backing away rather than advancing. *They're afraid,* Leopold realized. The "Dragon Woman" had truly terrified them that night. At the risk of betraying their king, they were running from the fight.

Leopold heard screams of pain, different from those he'd been hearing all day. These were tinged with terror. The smell of coppery smoke filled the air, and Leopold risked a moment to glance toward the cries. A man was running away from the troop Leopold was fighting, and he was on fire.

CHAPTER SEVENTEEN

"THAT'S RIGHT, MEGGY," ADINA shouted. "Keep going."

"I don't want to," Megara whimpered as she watched the man run, her hands clenching in front of her. "I can't do it. I can't use the fire again."

"Domum can recover—we can survive your fire. We cannot survive this attack without your magic. Help us, Meggy. Please!"

Megara looked at Adina. Her hair was flying in a mane around her red face, her eyes half crazed. *I have to protect my home.* Megara steeled herself and turned to the men surrounding Leopold. She had learned what had gone wrong in Camelot. Her emotions had been in control the fires. She couldn't do that now, not with so many of Domum so near. Not with Leopold in the middle of it. She focused her energy on the man Leopold was fighting and spoke the words her heart provided. The heat within her spread from her fingertips and launched toward the man, knowing it would miss Leopold.

The heat connected with the man, and she could feel the impact. She could sense it consuming his energy and abandoning her own. She allowed the magic to feed off his fear. He did not have magic, and she knew the fire would not spread from him because she told it not to. The words she spoke broke the connection between her and the man, setting the flames alight.

She ignited the troop near Leopold in the same manner. Their screams caused the nearby knights to break off and run. The people of Domum cheered as the army of Camelot fled into the trees and did not return.

Rather than feeling her energy seep from her to end the magic, Megara felt her magic pulsating through her body as if it were seeking an escape. She searched around for release but didn't know where to turn. Emaline was clutching at Adina, tears streaming down her face before she dismounted from the roof, shouting instructions for how to guide the injured to the healers.

Adina faced Megara, who was staring at her helplessly. "I can't control it," Megara breathed. She put her hand over her chest. "It's still here. I can feel it."

Adina stepped forward slowly, her hands raised. "Let it go, Meggy."

"I don't know how." Megara groaned, the energy pulsating faster. The heat filled her body again.

"You need to let it go," Adina repeated. "Find the source of the energy and let it go."

Megara fell to her knees, clutching her face. Superus made his way out from under her skirts and rested his front paws on her leg, staring at her. She scrambled for purchase in the energy, trying to track it to the end, but it felt like a circle, a ball of magic roiling deep within her.

Adina knelt in front of her and placed her hands on Megara's cheeks. "Give it to me," she said. "Give me the excess."

"I can't," Megara gasped. "It's too much."

"Share it with me, then," Adina commanded. "Let me help you."

Megara opened her eyes and stared into Adina's, greedily reaching for a connection. Her eyes squeezed shut when she found it, tying them together forcefully. Megara tried to moderate the transfer of energy, but the relief was too great. Superus skittered away off the roof.

Their screams combined as Megara tried to siphon the energy and Adina tried to absorb what she was given. Tears streamed down Megara's cheeks as she clutched at it. "I'm sorry!" she cried. "I'm so sorry!"

Adina opened her eyes and stared Megara down. "Find the end," she coughed out. Waves of orange light radiated from Adina. Her back straightened , her voice became stronger. "Find the end, Meggy, and let it go."

Megara reached for the energy within her again. It felt like a tumbling ball of yarn unspooling as it went. While Megara was searching for the furthermost part, she tried to hold on to the strand connecting to Adina, trying to slow it. The energy began moving faster and hotter through her body. Megara screamed once more before she dropped the connection.

Megara shut everything out and focused on the energy. She could feel it roaring, burning her soul. She imagined herself crushing it into a ball, grabbing all of the stray pieces and squishing them together. She pressed it tighter and tighter, feeling the heat increase as she did so, her body beginning to feel coiled and her breathing coming in short gasps.

Adina gripped her shoulders. "Let it go," she said. "You've found it—I know you have. Surrender. Don't try to hold on to it."

Megara's eyes met her friend's steely gaze. She took a deep breath and allowed herself to let go of the ball of magic. As she did, she felt the dam break. She threw her head back and screamed again, feeling waves of power roll off her in blistering swells. Adina held on to her shoulders tightly, a thin wall of orange light across her skin.

As her scream faded, Megara felt the reserve begin to run dry. She fell against Adina, who held her close, the orange light tickling across Megara like a cold rain. The roaring in Megara's head faded. The world seemed to right itself around her. Her breathing evened out. The heat within her ebbed until it stopped. Megara felt serenity within herself.

"Thank you, Meggy," Adina said. "You saved us."

Megara couldn't respond. She couldn't open her eyes. Her mouth felt sewn shut. Her body ached. She felt a single thread of connection still within her, and she knew if she were to follow it to the end it would lead her to Leopold on the ground, wherever he was.

Adina laid Megara on the warm roof and sat beside her, holding her hand. "This will fade," she promised. "This will become easier. We can teach you to manage your energy."

Megara opened her eyes and saw Adina gazing at the forest. People in the village were cheering or shouting instructions. Megara could hear nothing about fire. She had managed to stop it from spreading, and there had been no collateral damage.

As energy slowly began to fill her, Megara studied it. She imagined the ball of yarn again, spooling together light and energy. She closed her eyes and took a deep breath, catching the small imagined ball of yarn in her hands and pressing it to her chest. When she opened her eyes, she felt calmness settle over her. She sat up and squeezed Adina's hand when she realized they were still clasped together.

"Are you going to be all right?" Adina asked. Megara could only nod. Adina squeezed her hand one more time and then left the rooftop.

Megara stayed on the roof and watched the clouds move across the sky. She trembled with the wind. She was aware of the people of Domum repairing damage to their homes and properties with and without magic. She watched them embrace family, kiss loved ones, and cry over bodies. She watched as children ran from their hiding places and were embraced by their parents.

She watched as Leopold approached the house where she was sitting. The string between them pulled tight and began to strengthen once again. He was grinning wider than she'd ever seen him, and he called up to her. When he did so, many of the people around him started to clap or cheer her name. Megara's gaze stayed fixed on Leopold as tears trailed down her cheeks. Aldus's words echoed in her mind.

"They're proud of you."

Megara moved to the edge of the roof and climbed down on unsteady feet. Leopold helped her the last few feet and wrapped his arms around her stomach from behind, lifting her into the air and turning her toward the people of Domum. Megara felt relief and joy fill her heart as she gripped his arms with white fingers. He'd made it through the day—they'd survived. He would live to see another sunrise. When her feet touched the ground, Megara turned and wrapped her arms around his waist, and squeezed him. As she did, she felt that ball of energy within her thrum peacefully.

Megara accompanied Adina to the council house. She had been too weak to assist with cleanup or the transport of bodies—not that anyone would have let her—but she had watched and done what she could. Adina had found her helping with some little children and asked her to follow. When they reached the house, Adina allowed Megara through the door first, then asked to meet with the council without any other people in the room. The other villagers left one by one, all saying thank you to Megara with broad smiles.

Megara was surprised that the room appeared as it had at first. The tables were placed where they belonged. Blood was removed from the floors and walls. The cots had been stored away. It did not resemble the battlefield hospital it had been.

A woman stood from the chair where she was sitting at the head of the room. Megara remembered that Adina's father had sat in that chair. Megara recognized Adina in the woman's face and decided it must be her mother. The woman made to leave the council building at Adina's request for privacy, but Adina reached out and asked her mother to stay.

Once the room was empty of the other villagers, Adina spoke. Megara was impressed by the confidence in her voice. "In the absence of my father," Adina began, "the council will need to choose a new male healer to rule the village."

"We have already asked his successor to take his place," Edith said from her chair at their left. "He is tending to his injured son at the moment but will be joining us soon."

"I wanted to ensure that it had been initiated." Adina nodded. She hesitated before she continued. "I also realize Domum is now in a very vulnerable position. Theoretically, with our magic we could continue to survive as long as we need to without assistance from any other village."

"What are you suggesting?" an old man with a harsh voice demanded from Edith's table.

"I suggest . . ." Adina took a deep breath. "That Domum should close its borders."

The room was silent as the occupants processed what she said.

"*If* we agreed . . ." Edith eyed Adina. "How would we accomplish this? Domum does not have physical borders like other villages and kingdoms. Do you propose we build some?"

Adina took Megara's hand, pulling her forward. "Meggy has a way with magic that we don't understand. She has learned how to use it differently. If we get her the resources she needs, I believe she could find a way to mask Domum from outsiders."

Edith considered them for a moment, then looked around the room. "What are the thoughts of the council?"

Adina's mother spoke from beside Adina. "Do you believe you could do this, child?"

Megara faced each member of the council as she thought about it. "I'm sure that if I have the right words, I can do anything."

Edith smiled at Megara. "I believe you are right. We will begin to research it, and we will consult with Megara about what her requirements will be. Thank you for the suggestion, Adina."

Megara and Adina made to leave, but Ibb spoke behind them. "Megara, would you wait? We have something else to discuss with you."

Megara shot Adina an expression of surprise, but the woman looked equally shocked. Ibb continued, "This is, for the moment, meant to be a private conversation between the council and Megara." This dismissed Adina and her mother.

They left and closed the door behind themselves before Ibb spoke again. Megara addressed the young girl at the second table. "Megara, Judd and I are the council prophets. We are able to observe the future and see what is to come. We've been meditating extra hard the last few weeks regarding you, as you know, and there are some things we think we should tell you.

"First, I want you to know you will find comfort in Domum. You are going to be welcomed with open arms."

Megara felt a tingle run down her spine.

The man named Judd spoke next from the final seat on Edith's table. He seemed to be Leopold's age and was built much like him, with a slim body and muscular arms and shoulders. He had a more prominent jaw and kept his hair longer, and with the frown lines on his face, it seemed as though he'd seen too much. "However," he interrupted, "though you will be happy here, and you will find love, we . . ." He glanced at Ibb on his left, then to Megara. "We feel it is our duty to tell you what we see in your future. It is for you alone, do you understand?" He stared at Megara. "Though it involves others, you must not repeat it to anyone. Knowing one's future is a terrible fate, and we do not take sharing yours lightly. Do you understand this?"

Megara was frightened by his serious tone, but she nodded. *If it's so terrible to know your future, why are you telling me mine?* She wanted to scream this at him and cover her ears so she wouldn't hear what he had to say. She shifted on her feet and bit her lip.

"In a short while, you will enter an arranged marriage, as is custom in our village," Judd continued. "The council will choose a husband for you. You will accept this and be happy and in love." He sounded annoyed with that last word. "You must pass some trials of your own before this comes to pass. We see rocky waters blocking you from that happiness. We have seen you experience tribulation on behalf of Domum—your loyalties will be tested. A dark force will arrive in Domum, despite your best efforts." Megara saw Judd's eyes flit around the room. She was suddenly aware that he was censoring her future he so bluntly wanted to tell her. She felt a sharp irritation at his dramatics. "You must depend on and trust the magic you hold within yourself. *Things* will happen that we will have to learn to endure.

"The reign of the black widow and the lion shall cease with the rise of the dragon bringing peace. We have seen this, and we know it will come to pass. We don't know when. Your future is your own to make as you will, but we will be watching and seeing how your choices move you toward the end we have seen."

Megara stared at Judd, her mouth open. *What does that even mean? Am I supposed to remember it?*

Edith broke the awkwardness when no one else would. "You may leave now, Megara. I think the council has said its piece."

Megara left, not sure what to make of what she'd heard and not sure she wanted to understand. She tried to go over the promise mentally, commit the words to memory. *They must have thought it was important to tell me all that. I'll protect Domum like Adina wanted, but what does that mean? I agreed to it, but I have no idea how to do it. They said I'll get married, but the council will choose who I marry. How is that fair?*

The reign of the black widow and the lion shall cease with the rise of the dragon bringing peace.

After leaving the council building, she followed the strange seam between them and found Leopold with other men, lifting some heavy things into a cart in the village center. Megara recognized Aldus in the group of men. She watched them for several moments, exploring the string of magic which had appeared after she healed Leopold. She wasn't sure if it was normal to have this lingering connection after mending a person. It didn't quite feel like the same conjunction she'd relied on during the treatment. It felt knitted to her magic, but it wasn't resonating with the same energy. She couldn't quite describe it. When the men noticed her, a few cheered her name and grinned at her.

Leopold's brow was dripping with sweat. "Hello, Meggy," he called. She felt drawn to his side, almost as if he were tugging on that string of energy within her. "Give me a few more minutes here," he said before returning to work. When he was done, he sat down with her in the grass. "How are you?" he asked.

"The council had a lot to say to me today," she said.

"They aren't upset with you, are they?" He seemed concerned and glanced across the river then back.

Megara shook her head. She wanted to tell him about the strange prophecy, but she remembered her promise not to share what they said. "Adina had an idea for how to protect the village," she said, watching the people of Domum. "They're going to use my magic to separate the village from everywhere else."

"What does that mean?" he asked, surprised and worried.

Megara shrugged and wrapped her arms around her legs. "I don't really know," she admitted. "I know it's going to happen. But. . ." She hesitated, then continued. "But I don't know how well it will work. No matter how hard I try, things can always go wrong."

"Things can go wrong with every part of our lives," Leopold pointed out with a laugh. "Someone could get trampled by a cattle stampede. Someone else could get sick and die, making everyone fearful of contamination. We could get a massive weather storm that wipes out all our crops. The prophets can try to warn us, but they always say the future is not set in stone. We are able to pick our own paths."

It doesn't sound like I can, she groused. They sat together in the grass as the people around them worked. It was a calm silence, a peaceful one. There was no more rush, no more insistent need to move. They were home together at last. Megara liked the feeling she felt sitting beside him.

"You saved Domum," he said.

Megara's heart fell as she thought about the men she had burned. The reason they had surrendered was because of their fear of her. "Yes, but at what cost?"

He stared at her with a confused expression dragging his eyebrows together. "What do you mean?"

"How many people died over the last few days?" she asked.

He hesitated but said, "It's not as if you haven't killed before, Meggy."

Megara felt fury explode within her, straightening her spine and filling her head as she glared at him. Her magic spooled tighter within her. "You don't understand," she spat. "You didn't do it."

"I killed people too, you know," he responded, his voice rising. "I killed men this week too."

"You don't have to watch people try to run from you when you know it'll do no good," she argued. "You fight with your hands, with a sword. I fought with *magic*." She felt her hands begin to shake. "I fought in a way that did not *allow* them to escape. I burned them as they ran away from me. How many of them had families? Mothers, fathers, children, wives, people who were counting on them returning home? How many families did I destroy to protect my own?"

Leopold watched her for a moment before turning to face her and taking her hand. "Meggy, I can't promise you this will never happen again. I certainly can't promise that you'll never use your powers against anyone again. But what I can promise is that you will never have to do it alone. Ever. I swear to you on my life—"

"Don't say that," Megara gasped.

"I mean it, Megara." His voice hardened into a frightening surety, and he stared at her. "I swear on my life that I will never allow you to go through this life alone. I know that eventually, the council will choose a husband for you. I know I will have to relinquish a part of my vow when that happens. You are so precious to Domum, to me. You cannot understand the enormity of your contribution. You are Domum's savior, and you are also my friend. And I will be with you every step of the way."

Megara held their fingers to her cheek hesitantly, and stared into his eyes. "I accept your promise," she said. "I hope I'll never have to call you on it." As she finished speaking she felt the invisible link between them hum and root more solidly within her.

CHAPTER EIGHTEEN

LATER THAT NIGHT, LEOPOLD stood behind his mother's house and finished washing his face before heading down the dark roads to the village center. He heard the celebrations well underway, though much quieter than he felt they were under normal circumstances. The people were still mourning those they'd lost, but it wasn't as sad as it could be. The people all knew their loved ones had died in defense of their homes. It would disgrace their deaths in the eyes of the gods if they did not celebrate the victory and their sacrifice.

He found Jasper leaning against a wall, watching Adina as she spoke with her mother at the far end of the village center. "How are you feeling, brother?" Jasper asked when Leopold approached. "Have you recovered well?"

"Good as new." Leopold smiled.

Jasper nodded. "Good. Aldus told me it was Megara who saved you, not the other healers. I'm glad she has enough control over her power to help you."

"Megara has more control over her magic than I think anyone gives her credit for," Leopold said, his voice bordering on defensive.

"Well, if she does, I hope she is willing to help our friends learn theirs to the same level."

Leopold didn't respond. He'd seen Megara and Margaret approach the center. Megara's hair was braided again, and she was wearing a beautifully simple dress of pale pink. Jasper chuckled next to him. "Looks like we've finally found a woman to catch your eye," he murmured for Leopold to hear.

Leopold didn't care enough to deny it. He couldn't lie to himself. The woman was beautiful and powerful and yet still meek and unsure, and somehow all of those qualities were so balanced that when he gazed at her, he could only see a woman he admired. He'd never felt so drawn to anyone before. He loved the way the firelight danced across her collarbone, the way the breeze played with the loose around her face, the way her voice rang like a bell or shook his earth like thunder. He loved it all, and detested himself for it. A woman like Megara was certain to be arranged in a powerful nuptial tie with a man of strong magic to match her own. Katherine and Edith would have concerns for her treatment and safety, as did Leopold. He would respect whomever the council chose, no matter their decision. However, he also intended to keep his promise to Megara. She deserved a friend, a true friend, who would stay by her side throughout her life. He was determined to be that person.

"What about you,? Leopold asked to change the subject. "Have you moved on from Adina?"

Jasper sighed and deflated, Leopold wanted to take the question back. "Almost," Jasper said, catching Leopold off guard.

"Almost?" he asked. "You, the man who has been pining after her since the day I was assigned to serve with her?"

"With her father, I felt I had a chance and could argue my case. I have come to realize that a man of my status can never gain enough favor with the council—or Katherine—to have a chance with her daughter. So, I will serve beside her and pine no longer. I'll become like Aldus. He seems to have his life figured out."

Leopold looked toward their elder brother. He was sitting alone on the edge of the light, staring at the fire. He was deep in thought, his jaw clenching and unclenching. He appeared deaf to the world. But for the first time, Leopold noticed the many young women who were watching him. They'd whisper to their friends and giggle with red faces behind their hands. Leopold had always admired his eldest brother. He was confident and honorable. Leopold had never questioned Aldus's intentions not to marry before, but he realized his brother was missing the point. Marriage wasn't a selfish desire to abstain from—it was a selfless one, to cherish another person for the remainder of your days. *He always says he's content to care for Mother the rest of his life, but what happens when she's gone? What will his purpose be then?* Leopold wondered. *Who will carry on his name—who will he teach and care for?* He hoped that with Aldus's status, he would either find a young woman on his own, or the council would choose a woman for him deserving of his dedication.

"I will see you at home tonight, little brother," Jasper said as he moved away from the wall and wandered over to some men near the food tables.

Leopold was about to head toward Aldus when Emaline and Adina approached him. "Have you heard the news?" Adina asked him with a smile.

"What news would that be?"

"Edith is going to announce the plan for Domum tonight," Adina said. "They're asking Megara to do something unheard of."

"She did mention something to me earlier." Leopold nodded. "Something about hiding Domum away from the rest of the world?"

Adina nodded, and Emaline gasped. "What does that mean?" she asked. "Will we still be able to leave? Or return?"

"I hope so," Adina said, taking her hand. "I'd still appreciate the ability to wander! I'm not done exploring yet."

"Have you not had enough excitement this week?" Emaline teased.

Adina laughed. "No, not yet. I have room for more."

Edith called the crowd to her near the bonfire. The council filled in the space around her. The old man replacing Adina's father was led to a chair beside her, his frail body guided into it. "My friends," Edith said, "the council has been discussing what is best for the village." She held out her hand and gestured for Megara to join her. Once she did, Edith wrapped her arm around Megara's shoulders. "Our friend Megara has agreed to help us with a new venture. We do not know how long it will take or what it will entail, but she will help us hide Domum from the view of outsiders." A rumble of nervous chatter went among the people. Edith allowed it for a moment before continuing. "It is a frightening prospect, but we are in frightening times. We do not wish for another war like the one we've just experienced, and we also do not wish for our unique magic and teachings to be spoiled or manipulated. We will continue to discuss this option in detail, and if any of you have suggestions or concerns, please come forward. We will listen to any advice you may have. We are doing this to protect all of us, so of course we seek your input.

"We have all suffered," she said, her voice gentler. "We all must use this opportunity to care for one another. Check in on your neighbors. We are a strong community, but we must come together now more than ever." Edith smiled broadly. "We also must remember to celebrate life. Our lost daughter has returned to us! And she has offered us a new perspective on our magic. Allow her to heal your hearts. Now, let us continue the commemoration. Feast with us, and enjoy the new day."

The people were laughing and telling stories until the sun rose the next morning, as tradition called for. It was time used to appreciate the days past with their deceased loved ones and start the new day with hope. Leopold laughed with Adina and Megara until his face ached, relishing the joy he felt. It had been so long since he'd felt so at ease in this place, and he was relieved to feel content. He looked around at his neighbors and realized he had underappreciated them before. They each had their own worries, fears, and anguishes, but they'd come together when they were needed because they were all full of loyalty. Now that he'd found purpose in his life, he hoped to be able to love those around him, as Edith had requested. He owed it to them, to himself. He wasn't going to sit and feel angry at the simpleness of his life anymore; he planned to reap the benefits of the straightforwardness of his home.

Anora approached, took Megara's hands in her own, and held them. "I am so happy you are home," Anora said. "And I am so grateful to know Margaret has some of her family back. Your mother adores you, and your father and brothers can rest in peace now. Welcome home, Meggy."

Tears slid down Megara's cheeks at the mention of her father and brothers. "I am sorry about your husband," she whispered.

Anora shook her head and wiped Megara's tear away with her thumb. "Oh, sweet girl," she cooed. "My husband was a brave man, and he died honorably. He was such good friends with your father, and if his life had to be taken in defense of the people he cared deeply for, he wouldn't have wanted it any other way."

Leopold had not been aware of the friendship between his father and Megara's. *Why has she never mentioned that before? That seems like a pretty big detail to gloss over. I've told Meggy it's not her fault he died, but in a way it was—he died trying to protect his friend's daughter. Meggy didn't cause his death, but she was the reason for it.* He also admitted to himself that he had made the same vow—he would willingly lay his life down for Megara and his loved ones, as his father had done.

Later that night when Emaline took Megara and Adina to dance beside the fire, Leopold broached the subject with Anora. "I didn't know that Father was friendly with Megara's family."

Anora nodded. "Aldus befriended Megara's brothers during lessons, and then your father introduced himself to her family. They were very close after that. That's why he went to help." Anora sighed. "He couldn't sit by and watch his friend's child be taken He knew what he was doing.."

Leopold had heard of Aldus's friendship with Megara's brothers once or twice. It hadn't been talked about much after their celebration of life had passed. Leopold had assumed Aldus had become stoic to support their mother after their father had been killed, but perhaps it was the loss of his friends and their fathers all at once that toughened Aldus.

Leopold studied the faces of the villagers until he found Margaret. She was assisting with food distribution and laughing with Edith and another woman Leopold didn't know. He tried to put himself in her shoes for what felt like the hundredth time. To lose all of your children and your spouse in the same night? Leopold knew he couldn't truly understand the pain of losing one child, let alone three, but he tried to imagine what it would be like if his siblings didn't come home. Having to adapt to a new life where they weren't there. He couldn't do it. And when he tried to imagine what it would be like to lose a spouse his mind froze on Megara. Now that she was so intwined in his life, could he imagine going a day without her by his side? He was sure he would survive a loss like that, he'd have to, but it wouldn't be much of a life. *Margaret is the perfect example of long suffering*, he thought.

As the hours passed, Leopold danced with many of the girls their age, including Philipa. He danced with her to compare what he had once felt for her to what he felt for Megara, more than any other reason. She was a beautiful and kind young woman. *But she is a candle while Megara is the sun.*

Adina, Jasper, and Leopold taught Megara the village dances with Emaline's help. Stories were shared of the dead, and hopes for the future were cried out. As the fire died down and the villagers said goodnight, Leopold felt his heart lifted higher than he'd experienced in a very long time.

Part IV

CHAPER NINETEEN

MEGARA SAT IN THE town center watching over the people as they fell back into their daily routines. Since she didn't have a job yet other than her studies, she didn't have any place to be. Later she would meet with the council to discuss a plan to shield Domum, but that wasn't until the sun began to set. Adina and Leopold were off doing whatever they did during their days and Emaline was working with her mother, so Megara was left to her thoughts.

Weeks before, Megara had been hiding in a cellar. She had spoken to no one and had been obedient and waited for Merlin to arrive home, after a day of doing who knew what. She read her books all day every day, eating very meager meals. Now she could sit and look at fields and people and wide-open spaces. She had eaten her fill at breakfast and would eat a modest lunch before meeting with the council of Domum, a collection of people who were powerful and knowledgeable and the protectors of the village. She was revered as a hero. She had a mother who doted on her, making her new dresses and styling her hair in beautiful designs every day. She had friends who loved her. Real friends, not just her animal friend Superus, who now dozed beside her on the bench. She could go where she pleased and do wonderful things that didn't need to be in secret. She felt alive for the first time in her life.

As she thought about all of this, a smile spread across her lips. She was becoming proud of who she was. She was not Merlin's secret anymore. She possessed her own beautiful secret, a home that was full of people devoted to each other.

"Now, Meggy," Merlin said as Megara put her book away before bed. "Sometimes people don't know they need saving. Just like the people of Camelot. You're going to save them, though, Meggy. When you're bigger and stronger, you're going to show them a higher way of living."

Megara remembered thinking that the mouse stealing from the ants was what Merlin meant by a "higher way of living," but she realized now she was wrong. It meant living for someone else, living to protect and serve another person beside yourself. She was grateful she'd learned this now.

Megara pondered on the task ahead of her. The council had asked her to hide Domum. She understood their reasoning. The rest of the world felt threatened by their magic. It was dangerous, and Megara knew the king of Camelot wouldn't be so easily scared away. He would be back, and because he now knew what to expect from her, he would be even more dangerous. She had to hide Domum, but she would be lying to herself if the thought didn't make her heart beat faster with fear—the thought of hiding this beautiful home away, the thought of becoming secret again. She might have more space to roam and more people hiding with her, but now that she had known what it was to be free, how could she bring herself to remove that freedom not just from herself but these people around her?

After her lunch, which was shared with Margaret on her break, Megara began her walk along the road toward the council house with Superus skittering at her side. She could hear the children laughing and smell the wonderful scents on the air. She felt the sun beating on her skin and the wind blowing through her hair. It wasn't quite time for her lessons, so she wasn't rushing. She was allowing herself to experience this new life.

She was on the bridge when she came upon Katherine walking with her younger daughter. They smiled at her, and Adina's sister walked up and hugged her. "Thank you, Megara!" she whispered in her ear.

"My name is Meggy," she corrected with a stiff smile. She knew the village had her full name committed to memory but she had always just been Meggy. Hearing the name Megara felt foreign. When she was already trying to accept and live in a new reality, she wanted something of her past life to stay. She felt Superus hide beneath her skirt.

"Mine is Leah," the girl said. Megara guessed they were near the same age.

Katherine smiled for a moment before it slipped from her face. Her eyes seemed sad. "Megara, are you happy?"

Megara bristled at the insistent use of her full name. She had just corrected Leah, and Katherine hadn't seemed to care. She decided not to correct Katherine, though. "I am happy to be home. I'm happy we're all safe."

"But you are lonely," she perceived.

"I'm less lonely than I was!" Megara insisted. "I have never had so many friends before."

Katherine smiled. "All right," she said. "Go on your way, then."

After Katherine and Leah passed her, Megara reached down and picked up Superus, holding him in her arms as she continued across the bridge. She reached the council house and walked through the door with Ibb, then sat on the chair they'd left for her in the middle of the room. She felt a bit on display and it made her uncomfortable.

"Are you ready to begin?" Edith asked.

"I think so," she said, stroking Superus as he got circled on her lap then settled down.

"Megara," the woman to her right said, "my name is Gloriana. I shape shift. I hear you can do this as well?"

"I've only tried two animals," Megara explained. "When I tried the mouse, it didn't go the way I planned." Gloriana and the man next to her chuckled at that. "But I have been a stoat a couple of times, like my friend Superus." She gestured to the creature in her lap. He hadn't left her side since she found him and she hadn't found a way to thank him for that, or to tell him what it meant to her. Even when she had left her mother's house to heal Leopold and during the battle.

The old man sitting at the other end of Glorianna's table stood and began hissing and squeaking toward Superus. The stoat responded with similar noises.

The old man looked shocked. "Your power never ceases to surprise me, Megara," he said with a sigh. "Not only can you shape shift, but you can speak to him in your human shape as well?"

Megara nodded. "I found the charm the day Merlin . . . the day I . . ."

The old man nodded and relaxed in his chair. "Well. You are very talented," he grumbled.

Superus fell asleep as the rest of the council continued to ask her questions about how Merlin had taught her. They asked about the books she read, the language she had learned, and what Merlin had taught her versus what she had taught herself.

"When you learned Latin, was it a lengthy process, or were you able to pick up on it quickly?" Gavin, the man who had spoken to Superus, asked.

"It was difficult," Megara said. "I learned to read in our tongue much faster than I learned to read in Latin. It was complicated and hard for me to understand."

"And yet you could speak to the stoat with a spell?" he asked.

"I don't know how to explain it." Megara shrugged. "I know that I cast the spell and was able to speak to him."

The man beside Edith to Megara's left, Lief, asked Megara how she phrased her spells. He was the male creation member. He had Megara demonstrate a spell. She thought hard about what she wanted to do. They already knew she could shape shift and create fire, so both of those seemed pointless to demonstrate. She whispered, "*Pulchra papilio,*" and from her hand flew a small multi-colored butterfly.

Gavin and a woman with curly brown hair both chuckled at the top of the room and spoke to each other in a tongue Megara didn't recognize. The woman spoke to her. "*Mihi nomen est Olympia. Verba tua magica non sunt. Expediam.*"

Megara stared at her—at Olympia. She'd understood what had been said—not because of her magic, but because she had spoken Latin. She had said her name was Olympia, and she told Megara she wasn't speaking any magic words. Megara had felt no drain on her energy—the ball within her had not even shifted.

"You understood me without magic because you understand Latin," Olympia said so the others could understand. "But you could not understand anything I said to Gavin in the other language, could you?" Megara shook her head and Olympia nodded, addressing the rest of the council. "Though she is very talented, she does not have the innate power of language. I'm not sure how much help Gavin and I will be in this endeavor."

"You'll be helpful if we need to communicate with those outside Domum to obtain books," Edith corrected. "And to translate the books if she cannot read them."

Gavin and Olympia nodded but sat back in their seats, not offering anything more to the conversation. Megara wanted to say she hadn't been trying to use her magic when they had spoken in their aside as their brief conversation hadn't lasted long enough for her to cast a spell. The rest of the council continued to interrogate Megara for another hour. As the crickets began to sing outside the door, the council decided they needed to ruminate on what she had told them. Edith dismissed Megara.

She nodded and stood to leave, Superus curled in her arms. As she walked through the door of the council house, she watched many people cross the bridge. An excited young girl Megara somewhat recognized approached with a broad grin. "Katherine has an announcement to make in the village center!" she squealed, looping her arm through Megara's.

"What kind of announcement?" Megara asked.

"They say she has the name of the next couple to be married!"

"I've heard Domum arranges marriages, but I don't know what that means."

"Well," the girl said, her face lighting up. "In Domum, usually it's the council leader who makes the matches, but because he . . . because he's not here . . ." She shifted with discomfort but shook her head and continued. "Katherine is going to announce a couple chosen by the prophets because they will be happy together. The council arranges partnerships if they think it's best for the village and the couple."

"It sounds terrible," Megara said out loud, feeling nauseated. *The council is taking away our agency,* she thought. *The people can't even choose who to love?*

"It's not, Meggy," the girl said. Her eyes were wide. "Think about it. Wouldn't you want to know who you will marry, who will make you the most happy? Wouldn't you want to know your fate?"

The reign of the black widow and the lion shall cease with the rise of the dragon bringing peace.

"No." Megara shook her head, dread filling her stomach. "I don't want to know my fate."

The girl looked annoyed that Megara didn't appreciate the excitement of the moment. She let go of Megara's arm and moved ahead of her. "Well, I doubt your name will be called," she called as if it were an insult and then hurried on with some other young women. Megara hoped she was right.

When Megara arrived at the village center, she stayed at the perimeter of the crowd, hoping to avoid attention and that hiding would mitigate the possibility of her name being announced. She knew it was illogical, but it felt like the safest option. Superus wriggled out of her arms and crawled under her skirt to hide, allowing her to keep her arms free.

Megara saw Katherine walk to the front of the bonfire, turning to face everyone with a broad smile she had not possessed earlier that afternoon. "My people," she called with joy in her voice. "While I have watched the repair of our home, it has come to my attention that our spirits could still use some healing. For this reason, I have asked the council to introduce a new couple to Domum.

"It is usually the council leader who takes this honor upon himself. He works with the prophets to find those they believe will create the happiest union, and he has always—" She broke off for a moment before correcting herself. "He *did* do very well with this task, but I have asked to deliver the announcement in his place. As I searched for a young couple who was most deserving, this choice became clear to me. The prophets agreed! No other man has given so much of himself for so little in return. He has set high goals and made plans for his life that we honor and congratulate, and we know he will accomplish them. I also have come to believe he will be the best mate for my daughter. For this purpose, the prophets have chosen Aldus, son of Dain and Anora and our most honorable border patrolman, to wed my daughter Leah."

Excited gasps filled the circle as everyone turned to speak to each other.

Why would they marry Leah off before Adina?

Has this ever happened before?

Megara glanced around in surprise for Leopold's brother. She wasn't sure why the villagers were so shocked at this announcement. She wanted to see how he was responding. Aldus stepped toward Katherine with his shoulders back, his gait confident as he joined her beside the bonfire. Leah's chin was lifted with dignity as she joined them, her eyes wide and her cheeks flushed.

Katherine took each of their hands and raised them, speaking louder to the crowd. "If they agree to this union, their ceremony shall take place in three months on the solstice." Katherine lowered their hands and looked between them. "Aldus, do you agree to take my daughter as your own and protect her with the same determination with which you care for your family?"

"I will," he promised, his deep voice heavy and serious.

"And Leah, will you accept this arrangement with courage and pride?" Katherine's voice was almost harsh as she stared at her youngest daughter.

"I—I will, Mother," Leah stuttered.

Katherine addressed the village people again. "Then it is settled. We will begin preparations immediately."

CHAPTER TWENTY

LEOPOLD AND JASPER STARED open-mouthed at their brother as cheers erupted around them. They'd heard someone was being betrothed that day, but of all the people in the village who were praying they'd be chosen, their brother—who had always told them he wasn't interested in love—was chosen, and he had been chosen to marry Leah. *Before* her older sister was married. *What is Katherine doing?* Leopold thought as he and the rest of his family surrounded Aldus after the rest of the village wandered away.

"Did you know about this, Aldus?" Anora asked, her voice and body stiff as she clutched his hand.

Aldus shook his head. "We should speak in private," he said loud enough for them to hear.

"Come," Anora said. "Let's go home."

As soon as the door was closed, Jasper lit the lamps while the others gathered in the kitchen. Jasper placed a lamp on the kitchen table, and they all sat.

"What did you know?" Emaline asked.

"At the celebration of life, Judd approached me," Aldus admitted. "He told me things were to change, and that I wasn't to speak of it to anyone. He told me to be aware, that my name was being mentioned within the council. I didn't know it was about this. I thought I would be sent on a quest, like Leopold was."

"What does this mean?" Jasper asked. "Has this ever happened before? Why wasn't Adina married first?" It was customary for the eldest daughter in a family to marry before her sisters, even if that marriage came within days of the younger daughter's.

"Do you think Katherine would sabotage Adina like this on purpose?" Emaline whispered.

Jasper turned to her. "Sabotage her?"

""You men may not understand this, but for women, this order is very important," Anora explained. "It determines how much financial support each young woman will be given. By marrying first, Leah will receive more support from her family's fortune."

"Why would Katherine do that to her own daughter?" Jasper demanded. His feelings for Adina were obvious, though he'd told Leopold he had abandoned his feelings for her.

Anora shook her head—she had no answer. No one spoke for several moments before Leopold stood and headed toward the door. "Where are you going?" Jasper asked, his voice still stony.

"I need to find Meggy," Leopold said. "I want to know if she has any idea what's going on. The council may have told her something."

"If they did, they probably would tell her not to share it," Anora warned him.

"I have to try," he insisted before he closed the door behind him.

It didn't take Leopold long to find her—she was on the bridge. It seemed she was coming to find him as well. She was in a hurry, her eyes wide. He took her arm and led her behind a nearby house. "Do you know what's going on?" he asked under his breath, glancing around for anyone listening.

Megara shook her head. "I'm hearing so many things, though," she whispered. "So many people are confused. Is it really this big of a deal?"

He nodded. "According to my mother, Adina should have been married before Leah. Something is going on, and I don't know what it is. Did the council tell you anything?"

Megara froze, and he looked at her. "Not about this, no."

"Meggy, what do you know?" He gripped both of her arms. "Please—if it involves my family, tell me."

Megara stared at him, something flickering in her eyes. He could sense her mind working quickly. "I—I can't. I'm sorry, Leo. They made me promise not to."

"Is my family in danger?" he asked, his throat tight. "Just nod yes or no." Megara's eyes were distant. She wasn't listening to him. He shook her, dragging her back to him. "Meggy, what is it?"

"I can't tell you," she croaked. "I don't think it involves your family, but I can't tell you any more. I don't know what is going on, but there is a lot changing." She shuddered and wrapped her arms around his waist, burying her head in his chest. "Something big is happening. I'm scared, Leo. I don't understand what's happening."

Leopold wrapped his arms around her shoulders. "I swore to you I'd stand by you," he reminded her. "I will. I just have to protect my family too."

"I'll help." She stepped away from him, her jaw set. Her eyes flashed in the moonlight. "I will do whatever I can. Your family, my family . . ." She cleared her throat, staring him in the eye as she straightened her shoulders. "They are one and the same. Whatever happens, we'll make it through together."

Leopold had to stop his mouth from betraying him. He wanted to tell her how much that meant to him. He wanted to tell her he wished he could make her words true. He wanted their families to truly be one and the same. He wanted that 'together' to be recognized by everyone in Domum.

He wanted to marry her. But he couldn't tell her. Not yet.

"Together," he said instead. "We'll protect them together."

CHAPTER
TWENTY-ONE

URING HER LESSON WITH Edith weeks after the battle,
Megara had asked her about Merlin. She didn't dare ask anyone else—she was still worried they would all hate her because of Merlin's attack—but she needed to know. She needed to fit all of the pieces
together with the man the village knew as a monster and the man
Megara knew as a father. Edith was kind and unquestioning when she
answered Megara's questions and never made her feel foolish.

"Merlin was the first visitor Domum had received in a decade,"
Edith said. "Over the years, we had seen members of our community
leave on their own. Some returned and some brought lovers to visit
their families, but we had not had a stranger come to us in a very long
time.

"He said he had heard about us from a Domum native who was
passing through his village. He never told us where he was from, or
if he did, I do not remember. But it wasn't Camelot—that I know

for certain. He told us his village also had magic, but much less than Domum. His own family had some magic in their blood. He said his younger sister had been born with magic, but he and his brothers and parents had not been blessed with any.

"Merlin told us he wanted to learn more about magic, to come to a place that used it more prevalently. Maybe that would coax his own magic out. He stayed with us for several months. He would sit at the bonfire and tell stories to eager children of his travels across the land. He flirted with many of the women. He was loved by so many in our community and welcomed with open arms." Edith frowned. "Then one day . . . something changed. We have studied journals and discussed memories trying to understand what had happened, but we have no answers.

"One night, Merlin decided to take you. He must have seen something in you. It was days after you began walking around town. Before then, your mother had carried you in a wrap when she visited the shops. Merlin broke into your parents' home and took you from your bed. Your father caught him on the way out the door, and Merlin attacked. Your mother's screams awoke the neighbors. Your father was surprised and went down. You were crying." Edith's eyes were haunted. "Your brothers, your sweet brothers were so young. But they saw their mother's fear and they saw their father fall, and they tried to attack as well.

"Merlin had a pouch of some kind of powder, and when he threw some of it at your brothers . . ." Edith shivered as she remembered. "Their skin began to blister. When the neighbors tried to use water to soothe the skin, it made the effects so much worse. Merlin escaped amidst the panic.

"Your brothers passed away from the pain. Merlin was very skilled with various sorts of weapons, and so very clever. These were facts none of us had thought twice about during his stories."

Though the words Edith was saying were chilling, Megara could easily picture her surrogate father within them. She remembered the night he had died, how cruel he had been. And she'd come to admit to herself that it hadn't been the first time he had been cruel. It had caught her off guard because of the subject. He had never hinted that he had not been her family. She still wasn't sure what had made him say those terrible things that night, but he had. And she could picture him in Edith's story.

She knew whatever that powder was he had used against her brothers, it hadn't been magic. She said as much to Edith. "Merlin didn't have any magic," she explained. "Not once in all my life did he use magic. He made me do everything. I studied from the books he provided. He worked through the problems with me when I couldn't understand what I was reading. But he couldn't do magic himself."

Edith nodded. "I think we had been convinced he could have a touch of the magic deep within him. Maybe we were beguiled into believing there was more to him. But I believe, now, there was no chance of that."

On the eve of the winter solstice Megara brushed her hair as she gazed into the mirror on her wall. She marveled at the woman reflected back at her. It had been months since she had arrived in Domum, and her reflection was very different from who she had first seen in Camelot. Her eyes were brighter, her hair shinier. Her cheeks had filled out, and her skin had a warm tint to it. Her freckles had darkened, too. Megara knew the changes had spread beyond the skin as well. Once she had eaten well for a couple of weeks, her body had begun to catch up to normal. She experienced her first woman's cycle within a few weeks of being home. She chuckled now to remember how frightened she had been of the blood. She didn't know what was happening to her. Her mother had been very patient with her while explaining what her body was doing. The next month, her cycle wasn't as frightening.

Megara tied her hair with a ribbon and turned to the dress her mother had laid out. Today was the day of the celebration for Aldus and Leah. Their marriage had been finalized within two weeks of Katherine's announcement—Leopold had said this was also part of their strange traditions—but the celebration was slated to take place on winter's solstice, which was tonight. It had been fascinating for Megara to watch the nuptials. It had been very simple. They had taken place at the bonfire in the village center. Aldus and his brothers stood at the bonfire, and Leah was brought forward in a beautiful cream-colored dress. Katherine had presented her to her groom. If Adina had been married, she would have escorted her sister.

Zaccharia, the ancient male healer who had replaced Adina's father when he was murdered, had been the one to seal the union and dedicate it to the gods. After the speech, Jasper had taken Leah's hand from her mother and handed it to Aldus, and their coupling was complete.

Emaline had told Megara that the couple would be gifted a freshly built cabin at the edge of the village. It was a simple one-bedroom cabin, like Margaret and Megara's, and it would be their home until they had a child. Tradition stated that the couple was expected to have a child within the first year of their marriage or the union would be dissolved, but Emaline had whispered to Megara that Aldus had not been intending to follow that tradition. "He doesn't feel right marrying Leah without courting her so he intends to court her after their ceremony. Then he will give her that first year to decide if she would like to continue their marriage or allow it to be dissolved."

"Would he get in trouble for doing that?" Megara asked her.

Emaline shook her head. "It's tradition to do it the other way, but not law."

As the months passed, Megara had watched the couple go from being awkward neighbors to comfortable friends. Aldus was home from border patrol a lot more than he had been before, and they were seen around the village quite a bit. Leah had appeared uncomfortable with the arrangement at first. Megara was curious whether there had been a fight about Aldus's plans for their relationship. Now the couple seemed inseparable. They were always holding hands, and Aldus didn't appear quite so serious anymore.

When she had been watching their relationship blossom she'd been fascinated. She wasn't privy to their interactions every day of course, sometimes it would be weeks before she saw them together. But knowing where they had started and seeing where they were heading was interesting to her. She still wasn't sure she liked the idea of the council arranging the bonds, but she decided they made it seem like it was working. For them, at least.

Tonight being winter solstice meant the village was to celebrate the marriage of Aldus and Leah, and of the five other couples who had also been married during the fall season. Leopold had told Megara the village did this to preserve resources, holding a celebration every summer and winter solstice for the couples wed in between times. The couples would be dressed in black this evening, and everyone else would be in their finest colors. Megara would wear a pale purple, which she had decided was her favorite color.

Once Megara was dressed, she walked into the kitchen, where her mother was sipping some tea while she waited. Margaret smiled at her daughter and stood from the table. "Are you ready?"

"Nearly," Megara said as she sat in the chair next to the fire. She pulled on her warmest boots and took the shawl from the stand beside the hearth where she had been warming it. It had snowed the day before. She had been familiar with the cold, very familiar, but seeing the snow had been a new experience. Merlin had never allowed her to see it before. Megara thought it was beautiful. It quieted the world, as if covering it in a blanket. She had been expecting to endure another season of freezing under a thin blanket, but Margaret had opened a chest full of thick quilts and warm boots and socks and jackets. Megara had chosen the shawl for this evening—it was the shade of purple she had come to love, and she adored the stitched pattern on it that reminded her of the snowflakes all around her.

Margaret met Megara at the door, and they left arm in arm and walked toward the village center. The bonfire was already roaring. The couples were seated around it, and empty chairs spread behind them. Their families sat closest to them and then friends and neighbors filled in behind them. Between each couple were placed tables with food piled on them. Once the celebrations were underway, the couples would dish up the meals for their families and friends.

Margaret and Megara sat several rows behind Aldus and Leah. Megara did not recognize any of the other couples, and Margaret was content to sit wherever Megara wanted to. Once all of the chairs had been filled, Zaccharia stood before the crowd.

"Thank you for joining us," he wheezed, "as we celebrate the union of so many of our friends. We are grateful to them for being willing to expand our family. Tonight we feast in their honor, and we celebrate what the new season will bring."

The couples all stood from their chairs and faced each other, holding hands. Zaccharia walked to each of them in turn, and they exchanged private vows that could not be heard by the audience. Once they had exchanged their vows, Zaccharia presented them with matching rings to symbolize their union. One by one, the couples took their places behind the tables where they would dish up the meal. Their guests stood and walked to the tables. Valeriana and Roland, the council psychokinetic members, moved the chairs with magic, arranging them around tables where everyone could eat and turning the space into a dining area.

Once Megara and Margaret could approach Aldus and Leah, they were met with smiling faces. Leah grinned and held a plate out to Megara. "Thank you for being here, Meggy," she said. "grateful for what you've done to protect our home."

Megara smiled and glanced at Aldus. The man in front of her seemed a far cry from the one who had sat beside her during the battle. His eyes were softened, and his smile was easy. She had even heard him laugh at something Jasper had said once the meal was presented. Aldus and Leah may have started their relationship with uncertainty, but they seemed to have grown into it as the months passed.

Aldus gestured that Megara and Margaret should join his family at the front of their section. Margaret thanked him, and they took two of the empty seats. Megara ended up beside Leopold with her mother on her other side. She smiled at him and he grinned back and pulled her chair out for her.

Leopold had been rather busy since the battle had ended so they hadn't seen much of each other. Adina had asked him to be of assistance to Margaret and Megara when he could, but he was kept busy with the patrol as well. The watches had become more staffed as everyone anticipated a possible retaliation from King Arthur and Camelot. The council was helping Megara search for a solution, but the village wanted to be prepared just in case. When Leopold wasn't on watch or with Megara, he was helping Adina train the village people in combat.. The younger men were drafting themselves into the patrol and taking shifts whenever their other duties would allow. The fathers were learning to fight when they could as well. Even the women were joining in when their chores were completed. Some of the younger women joined combat while most joined the healers to learn from them. Those with magic were stepping up their studies as well. The battle had left an impact. Megara preferred not to think of those horrible days.

"How are you feeling?" Anora asked Megara when the conversations around them began.

Megara smiled. "Never better," she said.

Anora studied her face. "You know you don't need to put on a brave face if that isn't the case, right? You are welcome to speak your mind."

"It has been different to be out in society and be able to speak freely, but truly, I am doing better than I ever had been before."

"That's good," Anora said. "I am glad you are finding your way."

Megara felt Leopold bump her knee with his own under the table while he continued speaking to his brother. When Megara glanced at him he winked before returning to his conversation. She felt a strange feeling in her stomach, like the wings of Adina's famous butterflies were skittering inside her. The tension between them which had appeared after she healed Leopold had never weakened. She could always feel a general tug to him—wherever he was in the village. It never waned. When he winked at her she felt the connection thrum.

Megara tried to think about anything else, to settle her stomach. She remembered what it had been like when she first came to Domum. There was so much food to be had and so many names to learn. Now, though, she could remember the names of all of the people she associated with. She could eat a full plate of food without feeling as though she needed to sleep for a week to digest it all. The colors and sunlight didn't burn her eyes anymore. Even Superus had felt more at home and would venture out for a few hours at a time. Megara felt comfortable in her own skin. It was amazing how quickly she had adjusted.

Thinking about all of the differences was calming, specifically because of the strength she had found. It was true, what she had told Anora. At first it had been overwhelming and difficult to find the words she needed to use to communicate with these strangers. Now she felt secure in her own skin.

As the evening came to a close, Margaret and Megara said their goodbyes to Leopold's family and left the town center. They held hands as they walked home in silence. Megara was lost in her own mind. Margaret was used to this and let her stew for as long as she needed to

Margaret had asked her once if she remembered anything from before Camelot. Megara had tried, really tried, to remember. The only thing she knew for certain was that her heart sang whenever her mother was near. She had never once doubted Margaret being her mother. Even if they hadn't resembled each other, Megara felt her soul recognized her mother's. Margaret had conceded that Megara had been too young to have any real memories of Domum.

As Megara dressed for bed after the celebration, she thought about what Edith had said before about the night Merlin had taken her. She could imagine young Merlin. She knew how charming he could be. She ached to ask her mother what she remembered of the cod, but knew it was too late in the evening to bring up the pains of losing her husband and sons. Merlin always knew the right words to draw a person in, a trait Megara had often wished she had inherited—though now she knew she'd never have been able to inherit anything from him at all. She remembered so many stories by the fire upon his knee. So many times she had thought Merlin hung the moon and the people of Camelot should bow to his greatness. She had come to realize Merlin was the age of Aldus when he had arrived in Domum, and what Edith had said about Merlin's family mirrored Leopold's. Megara thought about that quite a bit and wondered what would make a man like him so desperate for magic.

Megara lay in bed, pulled the quilt to her chin, and closed her eyes, listening to her mother's soft breathing in the darkness. Superus skittered into bed and crawled up next to Megara's chest. He snuggled into her chin and chittered softly. Megara focused until her head ached but managed to cast the language spell without using her words. She felt connected to Superus and opened her eyes to see him. His fur had changed to match the snow outside and he all but glowed in the dim moonlight. "Goodnight, Superus," she whispered in his tongue.

"I wanted to know how the tradition went," he said impatiently.

Megara smiled. "It went well," she said.

"You know better than to leave it at that." Superus nipped her chin and she stifled a chuckle in his head.

"It was beautiful," she finally sighed. "There is a different sort of magic in their traditions. It's not a real magic like what I'm used to. It's like . . ." she struggled to find the words. "It made my heart feel warm and happy."

"When will it be your turn?" he asked her.

"I don't know," she said honestly. "The council told me they know I will marry someone they choose. I don't know when that will happen though. Maybe after I save Domum they will find me worthy."

"You told those girls that you don't like the idea of an arranged marriage. Have you changed your mind on that?"

Leopold's face flashed in her mind, but she forced herself to remember how happy Aldus and Leah had looked this evening. "I want to follow Domum's traditions," she finally said. "I want to feel more like one of them. Maybe following all of their traditions is how I can do that."

Superus laid his warm body across her neck and hummed. He didn't say anything more and she soon felt his breathing change in his sleep. She stroked his fur until she followed soon after, letting the magic connection fade with her consciousness.

CHAPTER
TWENTY-TWO

Leopold helped Jasper move the final platter of food into Aldus's cart to take home. As a wedding gift, Adina had created a cooling crate for her sister where they would be able to store their leftover meal for a few days until they finished it.

Jasper patted the horse pulling the cart once more before nodding toward the bridge in a silent request for Leopold to follow. Once they crossed the bridge, Jasper spoke. "How is training going?"

"We've seen a lot of success," Leopold began. "And a lot of people have strengthened themselves. We've also seen how much we've been lacking, though. We shouldn't have let our village become so lax in training. We've been too reliant on peace."

Jasper nodded and then pulled Leopold to a stop and faced him. "How is Megara's training going?"

"She seems more confident now. I haven't spent much time with her lately—been busy with my other tasks—but she doesn't seem like she'll blow over in the wind anymore."

"Has the council discussed giving her any kind of physical training?"

"What do you mean?"

Jasper stared at the moon for a moment before looking to Leopold. "She is a target. Until she can teach others how to use magic like she does, she's a liability. Talk to the council and get approval to start teaching her combat. She'll need to be able to protect herself."

"She's the most dangerous person here," Leopold argued. "She doesn't need a sword to do that."

"We don't know what her limits are," Jasper shook his head. "Every other person in this village has a limit on their magic before they burn out. She hasn't shown that yet. Or talked about it to anyone."

"That you know of."

"What's that supposed to mean?"

"I'm just saying, Megara doesn't have the same understanding of her magic. It's possible she does have a limit and hasn't been able to express that to us because she doesn't know how to."

"We've been assuming it doesn't exist because she hasn't told us. We can't know what we don't know," Jasper said.

"Thinking like that got Dad killed." Leopold and Jasper stared at each other for long moments before Leopold continued. "Everyone thought Merlin was a good guy because he never said otherwise. We need to assume there is more to the story than we're being told."

"Then make her tell it," Jasper ground out. "We need this knowledge. We need to know what he taught her. And she needs to learn to protect herself while she's trying to protect us."

"That's so much to put on her," Leopold said.

"Domum works because the villagers are unselfish," Jasper said. "She needs to decide if she belongs here or not." He walked toward home.

Leopold huffed a breath and swayed to the shoulder of the bridge. From his spot next to the trees, he couldn't see her house, but he gazed across the river toward it as if he could. He knew Jasper was saying these things out of concern for Domum, but Leopold's concern was for the girl herself. He had seen the way she had adjusted and he wished he could explain the changes to Jasper so he'd understand. She wasn't as jumpy. She seldom got angry like she used to, so he didn't feel like he was walking on thin ice with her. She held herself with more confidence. Her clothing didn't look like they were draped on her like old rags. She seemed healthy on the outside, but Leopold knew she still had a long way to go on the inside. Eighteen years of living with Merlin was not going to go away in a matter of months.

Emaline came across the bridge then. "Waiting for me, big brother?" she called. "You shouldn't have."

Leopold held his hand up and gestured toward their house. "I have to make sure my little sister gets home safely."

Emaline grinned and skipped to him, wrapping her hand around his offered arm. "I thank you, good sir," she teased.

Leopold nodded regally.

Leopold couldn't focus on Emaline's presence as they walked. His mind was replaying the conversation with Jasper and trying to picture

Megara with a sword. "Do you think Aldus will be happy?" Emaline asked.

Leopold looked at her. "What?"

She rolled her eyes. "Do you think he will be happy with Leah? He seems like he's coming around to the idea."

Leopold nodded. "He does seem to be easing into married life."

"Do you think about getting married?" Emaline asked. "I do sometimes, but I don't know if I would want to be in an arranged marriage. Although, knowing it's the best option for you and having that endorsed by the council would be nice."

"I imagine you could make any man bow to your expectations," Leopold chaffed.

Emaline jabbed her elbow into his ribs. "And what about you? Do you want to be married soon?"

Leopold shrugged. "I have a lot of life to live. I don't think a wife would improve anything right now, so why rush?"

Emaline pulled him to a halt outside their door. "What about Meggy?"

"What about her?"

"Some of the girls have whispered that Meggy is against the coupling traditions here. Do you think she will be okay when the council decides to choose her match?"

"Meggy is learning about our traditions for the first time," Leopold reminded her. "They're bound to be strange, being different from how she expected her life to go." *I don't even know if she ever considered being married. Would Merlin have ever allowed that? Or would she have rotted in that room for the rest of her days?*

Emaline glanced around and lowered her voice. "Would you want to marry her?"

Leopold weighed his response. "I would," he said. "I promised her I would never let her be alone. I told her I would not abandon her when she was married, either. It would be easier to keep that promise if we were married."

Emaline smiled. "I'm no council seer," she said, "but I think you two would be a magical pairing." She hugged him before stepping through their front door. Leopold stared toward Margaret's house one more time before following his sister.

He could hear Jasper and his mother speaking in the sitting room. He went up the stairs without a word. As he dressed himself for sleep, he thought again on Jasper's opinions, and about his promise to Megara. He couldn't deny he liked the idea of Megara being able to protect herself with a sword, but he knew she was much more dangerous with her magic. He decided he would discuss the idea with Adina and see what she thought.

The next morning, Leopold found himself alone at the family table eating breakfast with his mother. Emaline had already left for her lessons with the council. Jasper had returned to his border duties. Leopold chewed his food slowly.

Anora cleared her throat. "I appreciate your help cleaning up last night," she said.

Leopold nodded and focused on his breakfast. His mind felt like it was still catching up to his body being awake.

"I'm glad Aldus invited Margaret and Megara to sit at our table."

Leopold swallowed a bite. "It's been good to have her join the village."

"I think you should spend more time with her." Anora said it as if it had been on her mind for a while. Leopold blinked at her.

"I already see her whenever I can," he reminded her. He tried to force his head into the conversation.

Anora pulled his plate from in front of him and set it aside, then took his hand. "The girl needs more than someone from the border patrol checking in on her. I know your duties are important and that Adina has you running her errands." Anora made a face at that. "But you need to be there for Megara, too. You and Adina and Emaline are likely her only friends. She cannot learn how to fit into the village culture if her friends are constantly busy themselves."

"I don't know what to do," Leopold admitted. "I don't know what more I'm able to show her."

"Be her friend," Anora prodded. "Invite her to events and spend your free time with her. She will pick up on things if you are there for her."

Leopold eyed her suspiciously. "Is this about what Emaline said last night?"

"What did she say last night?" Anora spoke the words, but she wouldn't meet his eyes. He knew she had heard every word.

"Emaline said girls in the town are talking about Megara not agreeing with the traditions."

"I had heard that." Anora busied herself with stirring the tea in the pot.

"Mother, I cannot force her to like our traditions." *Even if she accepted the arrangements, I doubt she'd want to hear about it from me.*

"I'm not asking you to." She took his hands again. "I'm asking you to be around her more. Have her in the village more. Let people see her more."

"She's adjusted a lot for the short time she's been here."

"She has," Anora agreed. "But her being involved in the community would make her less of a target for dangerous gossip. She won't be as exciting to talk about if everyone sees her around regularly."

"I don't want to smother her," Leopold said. "And I don't know what I'm doing."

"I have never been in your situation before," Anora said. "But I'm sure you'll figure it out."

"I don't want anyone getting the wrong idea."

"What wrong idea?"

Leopold sighed and squeezed his mother's hands before letting go. The words he wanted to say, to tell his mother how deeply he'd fallen for Megara and how quickly, they wouldn't come. "Emaline has already asked me if I want to marry Meggy. I don't want to appear as though I'm courting her. She has so much going on right now, and such important work. Courting and the like should be the last thing on her mind."

"Have you asked her about the work she's doing?" Anora asked.

Leopold hesitated. "You know I don't understand magic. I prefer to stay away from all of that. I don't like seeming the fool when I can't keep up."

"Start there," Anora encouraged. "Ask her about her work. Forget the rest of the villagers."

"But you just said—"

"The gossip is problematic, yes," Anora interrupted. "But we want Meggy to feel at home. She will do better in her studies if she feels supported."

Leopold sighed. "I'll see if Adina will allow me to adjust my schedule." He had no qualms about spending more time with Megara. It was the thought of denying his affection that often which concerned him.

Anora patted his hand and pushed his plate toward him. "Good man."

Leopold left his empty plate with his mother before heading to the council building. He passed by Adina's house on the way. The new council leader had chosen not to move into the official residence. He stated he was too old and didn't want to make a big move like that, so Adina and her mother now shared the upper floor of the large home between the two of them. Katherine allowed the council to continue using the bottom floor for training with Zaccharia.

He saw his friend walking toward the council building. He sped up and matched her pace. "Good morning," he said.

Adina grinned at him. "Good morning!"

"Do you have time to discuss a change in my schedule with the council?"

Adina looked concerned and slowed to a stop, touching his arm. "Is everything okay?"

Leopold nodded and casually shifted her hand away from him. "Yes. I am just going to ask for some more personal time."

The council kept a strict eye on their schedules; they were soldiers and were intended to be doing work for Domum, but how they spent their leave could be up for debate. Leopold hoped he could ask if part of his shifts serving Domum could be with Megara. Maybe they would increase the space in his day he was assigned to assist her.

"I am heading to speak with Leif right now about my training this morning. Are you going to speak with them now?"

"I am. I wanted to give you that heads up."

"I appreciate that."

They entered the council building together and found the council already gathered. The missing members were the healers Zaccharia and Stace and the prophet Ibb.

"Welcome." Leif smiled. The greeting quieted the rest of the council.

"Good morning," Adina responded. "We wondered if we could have a moment of your time."

"We were going to send for you ourselves," Edith told her. "We had some things to discuss as well."

The young page boy assigned to the council brought forward two stools and set them on the large rug in the center. Adina and Leopold took their seats.

Valeriana, the psychokinetic representative, spoke first. "As you know, we have been working with Megara to strengthen her powers and find a solution to protect Domum. She is doing well in her studies, and we have learned much from her. Olympia and Gavin have found some scrolls to reference." She indicated the two language representatives. "We believe we are getting closer to our goal. However, Judd has foreseen the need to change some of our plans."

Judd glared at Leopold. They had never gotten along. Leopold had always felt like Judd was angry at him but could never understand why. "You will be relieved of patrol duties."

Leopold blinked in surprise, his stomach dropping. "What does that mean?"

"You will no longer be in service to the patrol."

Leopold heard Adina's breath catch. The words didn't make sense to him. "What does that mean?" he asked again.

Judd's typical glare made its appearance, and he rolled his eyes. "Due to the things Ibb and I have seen, you will no longer be needed on the patrol. So, you are being removed." Judd seemed even more annoyed to need to reference the child prophet.

Leopold cleared his throat. "Then . . . what will I be doing?" He felt as though his heart would explode, it was beating so fast. All he had known for half his life had been training with the patrolmen. He had assumed that would never change.

Edith broke in. "You're beating around the bush," she chided Judd before turning to Leopold. "Leo, you have performed your duties well. You have served your purpose in the guard. We are releasing you from those duties and giving you a new assignment. The prophets have seen that things aren't going to go quite the way we had hoped. We need to reassign you to protection duties over Meggy. You will command your own squad." Edith turned to Adina. "You, Adina, will be serving in this squad under Leo. We are also reassigning Jasper to serve with you as well, along with Faust and Quentin from Jasper's current team."

Leopold shook his head. His head felt like it was floating off his shoulders. "Why me?"

"You're the one she will trust the most," Olympia said from the top of the room. "We needed someone she would respect and obey. You're the best option for that."

Adina's face was empty of emotion. Leopold faced the council. "Why the changes?" he asked. "What have you seen—why is it so important for her to be protected now?" He reminisced on Jasper's insistence on the bridge the night before. What did he know?

"She needs to travel to Merlin's village," Judd sighed. "The information we need is there."

No one spoke as he tried to process this. "She has to return to Camelot?" Leopold asked.

"No." Edith shook her head. "Merlin's home village. Where he was before he came here."

"We don't know where that is," Leopold stated.

"We do now," Edith corrected. "The scrolls that were found detail another village like Domum, and the answers will be there. But she needs to be protected when she arrives."

Leopold waited for more to be said. When he realized there wouldn't be anything else, he asked, "When does this happen? When do we leave?"

"We will have that information by the end of the week," Edith promised. "But you are relieved of patrol duties as of today. Leo, I will ask that you inform Margaret and Meggy today about upcoming travel."

Leopold nodded, feeling numb. Being told his purpose was changing felt like too much to comprehend.

"We have more to discuss with Adina," Leif said. "You are excused, Leo."

Leo stood and walked away. He wasn't conscious of leaving the council building, but he made it to the bridge before his mind cleared. He sat on the ground beside the bridge and waited for Adina to exit.

He had worked been in training to be a soldier for the border patrol for a dozen years. Jasper had joined training a few years after that, so Leopold supposed it made sense that he would outrank his older brother. The shifter Faust—who had been the leopard Leopold had assisted in the battle—was close with Jasper and was known for messing around both on duty and with the women in town. Leopold didn't know much about Quentin other than he had psychokinetic powers and was very quiet. *Did Jasper know about all this last night, was that why he wanted Meggy to learn to fight?* Leopold wondered. *No, he couldn't have. They would have told the squad leader before the squad, right?*

When Adina exited the building, she seemed about as stunned as Leopold felt. Leopold got to his feet. "Is everything okay?" he asked, mentally acknowledging the role reversal.

Adina faced him but seemed a million miles away. "I guess so," she said.

"What did they tell you?"

She shook her head, clearing her expression of the shock and replacing it with a stubborn set of her jaw. "Nothing you need to be concerned about I. . . Well, I have a . . ." She shook her head again. "Let's go find Meggy."

She marched across the bridge, leaving Leopold to follow. As they came to the village center, they started by going to the tailor shop where Margaret worked. Megara often joined her mother in the mornings and was learning to sew. She said Merlin hadn't let her learn any physical skills because he expected her to use magic. Now she was making her rounds through all of the manual trades in the mornings before her afternoons with the council.

Leopold held the door open for Adina when they reached the shop. She walked in with a smile on her face and greeted everyone loudly. Leopold followed and tried to appear as optimistic as she did. He didn't feel very convincing.

His eyes caught Megara's in the rear of the room. "We need to borrow her for a few moments," Adina told Margaret. "To explain the council's new wishes."

"Why didn't they plan to tell her when she goes there this afternoon?" Margaret asked hesitantly.

"They wanted to reserve this afternoon for lecture and practice," Adina replied with ease. "They asked us to deliver the news beforehand so if she has any questions, they can get through them with little distraction from her lessons."

"I suppose . . ." Margaret turned to Megara, who had reached her side, and took her hand. "Just come back when you're finished," Margaret said to her. Megara smiled and gestured for Leopold and Adina to lead the way.

Leopold followed both women out the door and swallowed his discomfort the best he could. He was nervous. He didn't understand why his stomach felt like it was rolling over and over. He couldn't meet Megara's eyes. He noticed Superus, his fur now white for the winter, peaking out from under Megara's skirts. Adina began to explain. "We met with the council this morning." Leopold could feel Megara tense up with that sentence. "They've given us new assignments."

"You're not on the border patrol anymore?"

Leopold waited a heartbeat before looking up and realized Megara and Adina were both staring at him. Leopold cleared his throat. "Uh, no. No, I am not. They've decided to use my skills differently."

Leopold cleared his throat again. *Why is this so hard?* "They've decided to give you a personal safety squad, and I'm to lead it."

Megara's eyes narrowed. "Why do I need a safety squad?"

"The council is going to ask us to take a journey," Leopold explained. "And they want to make sure you are protected when we do so."

"I'm assuming the squad isn't just you two?"

Leopold shook his head. "It's myself, Adina, Jasper, and two other border patrolmen. Faust, who is a shifter, and Quinten, who uses psychokinesis."

Megara studied Leopold's face. "I understand the other three," she said. "But what is your place in this?"

Leopold's mouth went dry. "I'm the leader," he choked out. "I'm the leader of the squad. They . . . well, the council said I was the best choice."

The council said you wouldn't listen to anyone else.

Megara turned to Adina, releasing Leopold from her gaze. "When do we leave?"

"We don't know yet," Adina said. "We're waiting to be told. But they said we are going to go find another village with magic."

Leopold looked at Adina in question. *Why not say it's Merlin's village?*

"What are we searching for there?" Megara asked.

"Knowledge. Information on how to better protect Domum."

When Megara glanced at Leopold, he had to force himself to match her gaze. It was hard. She was angry. He recognized the stiffening of her spine and the ice in her eyes. "And you're okay being assigned to protect me?" she asked.

Leopold set his jaw and stared her down. "I told you I wouldn't let you be alone," he reminded her. He was grateful his voice sounded much more steady than it had before. "That hasn't changed. I'm with you to the end."

Something flashed across Megara's face and was gone before Leopold could identify it. She looked toward the village. "I just got here," she sighed. Leopold watched her spine melt. The wind blew a fresh chill toward them and she wrapped her arms around herself. "I don't want to leave again." Leopold's eye was caught by Superus who chose that moment to climb up Megara's skirts. She held him in her arms with little reaction.

Adina touched her hand. "It's not forever," she reminded her. "Think of it as an adventure. We'll be with you, and we'll bring you home."

Megara met Leopold's eyes again. They were softer now. "Thank you for accepting the new position," she said. "I'm sorry your skills are being wasted on me."

"They're not being wasted," Leopold insisted. He wanted to take her into his arms and reassure her that he wasn't disappointed with the task or even fearful of it, but the uncomfortable creature stirring deep in his gut wouldn't let him. "I don't know what the journey will entail, but I know my skills aren't being wasted. The council prophets have created this team for you. We'll all be necessary for whatever comes."

Megara's eyes filled with tears. "Leo, will you help me tell my mother?"

The twisting in Leopold's gut settled. He took a step toward her and placed his hand on her back. "Of course," he said. "Whatever you need."

CHAPTER
TWENTY-THREE

M EGARA TOOK A STEADYING breath before nodding. "When should we tell her?" she asked.

"I would recommend telling her when we have more information," Adina said. "We don't want to worry her and not have answers to give her."

Megara's magic was shivering within her, as her arms were in the cold air. Throughout the last several months, she had been able to understand the ball of magic better. She could picture it in her mind more now. It wasn't quite a ball of yarn, but more like a sun. Some days it was dim, as though there were a cloud covering it. Others, it was bright enough to blind her. When she needed to use her magic, she imagined a beam of light bursting from her. It wasn't as tangible as the string had been, but it was malleable and could be reflected rather than just draining her. Now the ball of light within her seemed to roar brighter.

Megara knew something was wrong. He was struggling to look at her. He was shuffling his feet as though he were uncomfortable. He kept flexing his fists. She had never seen him act like this before. He was always the perfect picture of calm. Megara felt as though he were angry; either at her or the council for the new job. As her magic seemed to reach for him, she took a step back.

"I should get back to work," Megara said. "I have a short time before my lessons begin."

"We will keep you updated," Adina said. She seemed off as well. "We'll get through this together." Her smile didn't touch her eyes as it usually did. Her hand had trembled when she'd touched Megara's.

The way her friends were reacting to this new assignment was putting Megara on edge. She knew they weren't telling her everything. She didn't know if they thought they were protecting her or if they didn't trust her, but something about this assignment did not feel right.

"I guess I'll see you later," she said walked away.

As Megara was walking to the shop, vaguely aware of Leopold walking a few steps behind her, she heard someone call her name.

"Meggy!" When Megara looked around, she saw Katherine smiling at her from one of the side streets. "Do you have a moment?"

Superus leaped from her arms and scurried under her skirts. Megara dropped her hands to her sides and straightened. She still felt off-balance with the way her friends had spoken to her, so she relied on the steady thrum of the magic within her to keep her calm. "Good morning, Katherine," Megara said. "What can I do for you?"

Katherine smiled at her. "I was hoping to speak with you in private." She glanced at her daughter, who Megara hadn't realized was still behind her. "I will see you at home tonight." To Leopold, she said, "You are dismissed."

Megara bristled at the abrupt ousting of her friends. Megara could hear the audible clack of his jaw as Leopold's mouth clamped shut. He nodded once before walking past them, continuing the path they'd been traveling. Adina left in the opposite direction. Megara faced Katherine.

"Let us take a walk." Katherine wrapped her arm through Megara's and walked her away from the tailor's shop, down the side alley she'd been in. They followed the common footpaths to avoid the deeper snow. "Have I ever told you I knew your father?" Before Megara could respond, Katherine continued. "Of course not. We haven't had a chance to speak, have we? I want to know how your training is going. I want to hear all about your progress."

Megara swallowed. She felt uncertain about sharing her progress with anyone. She didn't know how to put into words what she was learning and how she was growing. She hadn't been able to explain her magical sunshine. When she'd tried to explain it to Judd, he had stared at her like she had two heads. "A lot of what I have learned has been a reframing of how I understand magic," Megara responded. "Instead of connecting the magic to words, I'm learning how to feel the magic within myself. I've been taught that the magic is a part of me, not just something I can use."

"What about being able to use multiple classes of magic?" Katherine asked. "Have they figured out how you can do that?"

Megara shrugged. "Not really. Henry, the shapeshifter, has some theories. It goes back to my thinking that I was drawing from external magic rather than pulling from within myself. He thinks that everyone else is so in tune with one type of magic because they've been told all their lives that's all they can do. He thinks everyone might be able to channel the other classes if they try to picture it like I do."

"And how do you picture it?"

Megara's magic rumbled in her middle. She felt her mouth moving before she could think of an answer. "I used to picture it coming from the world around me. I read the words and used the words to tell the magic how to interact with the world. Now . . . it's like I have this essence inside me that is constantly trying to be set free. I have been learning to take pieces of that magic—without words—and apply it outside of myself."

Megara blinked. That had not occurred to her before she'd spoken the words.

Katherine hummed. "It's a shame Merlin did not explain to you what exactly he was teaching you."

In Megara's mind she pictured the book she had stolen from Merlin's home during her escape from Camelot. She hadn't cracked the cover since she'd arrived in Domum, and she wondered if it might have some answers for her now that she had a new understanding of magic. She stopped Katherine as they reached the bridge. They'd gotten all turned around in their trek. She felt uncomfortable—Katherine's words were not sitting still in her mind. "I need to get back to the shop," Megara said. She nodded to Katherine. "Thank you for the walk."

"I anticipate many more." Katherine smiled at her. "Have a good day!"

As Katherine walked across the bridge, Megara made her way to the shop. She wasn't sure where Adina had gone, but as she looked ahead, she saw Leopold leaning against the front of the building she was approaching. He pushed himself off the wall and straightened as she came closer.

"Was there something else you wanted to tell me?" Megara asked.

"There is a dance in the old town tonight," Leopold rushed out.

Megara waited for him to continue. When he didn't, she prompted him, "And that means . . .?"

"That means . . ." Leopold smiled. "I would like you to come with me."

Megara blinked at him. "To a dance?"

"Unless you don't want to."

"I don't know how to dance," Megara admitted.

"Let me teach you."

Megara examined him. He seemed to have gotten over whatever had been plaguing him five minutes ago. "Why were you so angry?" she asked instead of answering. "You didn't seem very excited to be assigned to me."

Leopold's smile faltered. "I felt blindsided by the council, but I wasn't angry. Especially not about spending more time with you. I feel like I'm missing something important."

"I can relate to that." Megara brushed her hair behind her ear. "So, this dance. Am I supposed to wear something specific?"

"No. You can stay in that dress if you would like. I'll come to your home this evening and escort you."

"All right," Megara assented . "I guess I will be seeing you this evening." Leopold nodded and walked away, waving a greeting to a red headed man as he walked down the path.

Megara entered the shop, grateful for the warmth from the small fire in the rear of the room. The other seamstress women glanced up at the tinkle of the store bell and then returned to their work. Margaret kept her gaze and patted the bench beside her.

When Megara sat, her mother grabbed her hands. "What is it?" she asked in a whisper.

"The council asked me to meet with them a little earlier today," Megara lied. She changed the subject when she saw that her mother didn't believe her. "Leo invited me to go to a dance in the old town with him tonight. He said he will come pick me up tonight."

Margaret's eyes went wide. "That is fun!" she said with excitement before standing and walking to the nearest woman. "I need to leave for the rest of the morning," Margaret said. "I will return this afternoon." The woman nodded without looking up, and Margaret returned to Megara. "Come," she said. "Let's go home and find you something to wear to the dance."

"But Leo said I didn't need to wear anything special. He said I could wear this."

Margaret rolled her eyes and pulled Megara to her feet. "He would say that," she said. "Men don't think about fashion. Come. We have plenty of options at home."

As Margaret led her daughter through the streets, Megara thought to what Adina had said. *Think of it as an adventure. We'll be with you, and we'll bring you home.* Megara didn't feel as though she wanted an adventure. She wanted to stay in Domum. She enjoyed learning magic with the council. She loved having a mother who doted on her. She was feeling like she could be normal. Was she ready to walk away from all of that?

Once they arrived Margaret went straight to a trunk in their room and laid out several warm options for the dance for Megara to choose from. After a decision had been made on a new dress Margaret played with Megara's hair. Before Megara had time to feel uncomfortable with it all, it was lunchtime, and Margaret granted her a break to eat before going to her lessons.

Megara bundled up, as she wasn't sure if her lessons would be inside or outside for the day. She walked the back roads to the bridge at a swift pace, not wanting to run into anyone who could make her any later. She reached the bridge that led to the old town with no interruptions. As she crossed it, the wind blew against her. She turned to stare down the river instinctually, turning her face from the wind, and stopped walking. She squinted and moved toward the railing, facing the west. She thought she had seen movement at the mouth of the river. She shook her head, deciding it was a trick of the light before she continued across walkway to the council building.

As she approached the building, Katherine exited, calling over her shoulder, "Thank you for meeting with me, Zaccharia. I look forward to next time." Katherine stopped, seeing Megara in front of her. Something about her expression made Megara uncomfortable. "Enjoy your lesson, dear," she said. She stepped out of the doorway and gestured inside. "Come, come, out of the cold."

Katherine stepped aside and allowed Megara to pass before closing the door behind her. It took Megara a moment to adjust to the low light. The warm air smelled of something she couldn't place, but it was comforting. As her eyes adjusted and her muscles loosened, she gazed around the room. The only occupant was indeed Zaccharia, sitting in his chair at the head of the room at the farthest table.

"Come, child," he said in his raspy voice. He pointed to the stool positioned opposite himself. Megara stepped forward, placing her cloak on the sideboard to the right as she passed. She took her seat and smiled at the old man.

"Good afternoon, Zaccharia," she said.

He smiled weakly at her. He seemed distracted for a moment before he relaxed and pulled a scroll in front of him. "I trust Leo and Adina found you this morning and discussed your new task?"

"Briefly." Megara sighed. "I don't know if I want to do it."

Zaccharia was the oldest member of the council, but Megara had felt the most comfortable with him and with Edith the last several months. She liked the way his voice calmed her and the way he always knew what to say. She felt he was the best at not expecting too much from her.

"That is understandable," Zaccharia said. "It is hard to find the desire to leave home at times."

"I don't know if I'm the right person," Megara said. "I am just now coming to understand my magic in the first place. Am I the right one to go speak with another village on the subject?"

He interlaced his fingers across his rounded belly. "My child, what are you imagining this journey to be?"

Megara shrugged. "Adina said we were traveling to another village to ask them to help us protect Domum," she said. "But they didn't say where, and I guess they didn't say why, either."

"We don't have much insight," he said. "The prophets are trying to understand more about your journey, but it is becoming difficult. They described a veil being placed over the traveling party once you leave Domum. They can't look through it."

"Then maybe we shouldn't go," Megara suggested. "Maybe it's the wrong path and we shouldn't be on it."

He sat forward, touching the scroll again. "Perhaps." He tilted his head to the side. "Perhaps there is another explanation."

"Of course." Megara lowered her head in respect. "I'm sorry. I didn't mean to speak when I wasn't invited."

He reached forward and tipped her chin up. "Do not apologize," he instructed. "Speculation is half of what the council does when they converse, especially when it comes to blurry predictions by prophets half their age." He smiled. "It is all right to question things, Meggy."

"I don't want to leave," Megara whispered. "I was gone for so long already. I have missed out on so much. Why do I have to be the one to leave?"

"It is not forever," Zaccharia responded, matching her volume. "We feel sending you is right because you have a different understanding of magic that none of us have ever possessed."

"I'm tired of being special," Megara said, her voice harsher than she intended. "I want to be normal."

"Merlin took that choice away from you the day he took you," he said. "And because we still don't know *why* he took you, we have no choice but to accept the fate he placed on your shoulders."

Megara slumped. "I understand."

Zaccharria smiled once more before straightening in his own chair. "Let us begin today's lesson," he said. "You've described your magic to me in the past as a force within you that you manipulate with intentional phrasing, yes?"

Megara nodded. "Essentially."

He pushed the scroll forward. "This is the first explanation we give young ones when they are learning to harness their magic."

The council members had explained to Megara before that they didn't want to treat her as a young magic user because she'd had control over her magic for more than a decade. Most young magic users were not able to manage their magic for several years and ended up causing mayhem while they tried. Megara had expressed never experiencing anything like that. This was the first time she was being introduced to the children's lessons.

Megara pulled the scroll toward her eagerly. She stared at it. There were no words to read. In the middle of the scroll was a charcoal drawing of a woman. Her eyes were closed, her hair floating around her, and her hands steepled in front of her chest.

"Who is this?" Megara asked.

"She is the Nameless Goddess," Zaccharia explained. "She is one of the gods who gave us her magic."

"A god gave you magic?"

"And you," he said. "In Domum, we believe all of our magic was gifted to us by the gods. The Nameless Goddess gifted us creation and shapeshifting. Raphael gifted us the gift of healing. Bridget gave us prophecy. Prudentia gave us psychokinesis, which young children refer to as willpower. And Ohad offers us our various workmanship skills and the power of language."

"Why is the Nameless Goddess . . . nameless?" Megara asked.

"There is no record of a name," Zaccharia said. "No one knows what it was or if she even had one. Considering her powers of creation and shapeshifting, I'm not even certain she is female. This is how she is represented, though." He gestured to the scroll in front of them. "She presides over all of our other gods. After speaking with you, my suspicion is that she possessed all of these powers, and allows her children to govern over their gifts. I believe she granted you access to all of her power. We just don't know why yet."

"So, everyone in the village worships a different god?"

"Some choose to do so. Others worship them collectively. The gods are not jealous beings—they share the attention. Except for the Nameless Goddess. She demands respect from all."

"And the other gods, Raphael and Bridget and the other two—they are her children?"

"Yes. She gave them the ability to govern the different powers, and they are allowed to choose who will receive their gifts."

"How do you know which gift you have been given?" Megara asked. "What does that look like in the children?"

"It takes years for power to present itself," he explained. "Most children show no power until they are six or seven. You have been one of the rare exceptions."

"But not the only one? There have been others?"

"Adina was another one," Zaccharia said. "It has been accepted that the earlier a child presents their powers, the more powerful they will be. Both you and Adina presented abilities from birth."

"What does that look like?" Megara whispered in awe.

Zaccharia chuckled. "Adina grew tired of the mobile her mother had placed above her cradle. She changed the carvings above her. Her father watched her. I'm sure you have noticed that Adina's creation power presents as orange. It was quite a surprise to her father to see orange animals prancing in the air above his infant."

"And . . . me?"

Zaccharia's smile dimmed as he remembered. "You healed your mother the night you were born," he said. "The nursemaids weren't able to stop the bleeding, so they called on Katherine. The nursemaids had placed you upon your mother's breast, thinking it would be the only time she would be able to hold you. When Katherine arrived the nursemaids observed the hemorrhaging stop. They believed it was Katherine who had saved her, but when they removed you, the bleeding began again. Katherine couldn't stop it and demanded that you be brought forward as a final goodbye once more. It stopped again when you touched her."

Megara stilled, her heartbeat even seeming to stop. She remembered the night Adina and Leopold had allowed her to go hunt for them before they reached Domum. She had shifted into her stoat form and listened to their conversation for a few moments. Adina told Leopold she had been watching from the window as her mother saved Margaret.

"So everyone thought I was a healer, then," Megara breathed.

Zaccharia nodded. "One to rival Katherine and her husband. They were the two most powerful healers in the village—Uther being more powerful than Katherine, which was why he maintained his position on the council when she was dismissed."

"Why was she dismissed?"

"The council cannot have a married couple within their ranks, the village decision-making doesn't rely on one family. That same rule prevented Adina from joining the council when she was twelve, and instead she was sent to border patrol training.

"Had healing been your only gift—which I believe it could have been, had you not been taken—you would have taken Katherine's vacant position instead. As it was, Stace was born shortly afterward and demonstrated strong healing capabilities in her youth. She was granted the position a few years ago."

"There wasn't a female healer between Stace and Katherine?"

Zaccharia shook his head. "No one was able to outshine Katherine's skill, so the position remained empty."

"Does Stace has more healing skill than Katherine?"

"They have the same," Zaccharia corrected. "However, when the trial was completed, Uther was still on the council, so it restricted Katherine."

"Now that Uther is gone, can Katherine challenge Stace?"

"She could, I suppose. I don't see her doing that, though."

"Why not?"

"I believe the reminder of her late husband would be too painful," he explained.

"Could Adina join the council now?"

Zaccharia smiled. "If she chose to go through the trial, yes. Though she told the council this morning that she respects Edith too much to do so."

"You asked her?"

"I was not present for the conversation, but I heard about it after. I was the one to suggest they mention it to her while they spoke with her. She turned it down."

Megara didn't say anything for several moments. "Do you think Merlin took me because he saw how powerful I was when I was that little?"

"We don't know what he saw in you I wouldn't even know where to begin to guess. And here you are, eighteen years later, proficient in so much more than healing."

Megara studied the sketch of the Nameless Goddess, then at each of the seats in the council room. She could shape shift. She could use her words to translate her speech. She had never tried to heal with Merlin but she had healed Leopold during the battle with Camelot. She had tried to move things with her mind a few times, but it was not as easy as the other magic was to her. She could use the power of creation. And she remembered with a jolt the terrible night she had shifted herself into a mouse with Merlin. She had fallen asleep and had a dream about Arthur.

"I can have prophecies," she whispered, her words running together as she explained the dream to Zaccharia. He sat with no expression on his face as he listened to her ramble about her abilities. "I have them all."

Zaccharia nodded and tapped the sketch. "Like I said, I believe the Nameless Goddess allows you access to all of her powers."

"But why?" Megara demanded. "Why me?"

"I do not believe the why matters," he told her. "I believe what matters is how you choose to honor her gift." He leaned forward once more. "We need you to protect Domum. Though you do not like it,

258

until we can learn more about magic and what Merlin saw in you, you are the only one who can do it."

Megara turned toward the fire and thought about all she had learned. "All right," she sighed, turning to him. "I understand."

"I have faith in the Nameless One that she knew what she was doing," Zaccharia said. "You're meant for wonderful things."

"Will you teach me how to heal?" Megara asked. "I healed Leo but I don't know how. Merlin never taught me that kind of magic."

Zaccharia stood and gestured to the open space in the room. "I believe that is what we are here for."

CHAPTER
TWENTY-FOUR

L EOPOLD STOOD AT MARGARET'S door and took a breath. It had been a long day of absorbing what the council had told him that morning. He had spent most of the time staring at the wall of the attic without realizing what he was doing. He wanted to make a plan and decide what their next steps should be, but he had no idea where they would be going or when.

As the sun began to set, he knew he should get himself put together for the dance. He hadn't planned to go, but when he saw Megara walking back to the shop, it was all he wanted to do. He wanted her to have the experience of a village dance, and more importantly he wanted to be the one to accompany her.

He donned a pair of his nicer trousers and a warm shirt and cloak. Then he rambled to Margaret's house. He knew he had passed several couples on the bridge but couldn't remember who any of them were. And then he arrived. He had no idea what to say to Megara or Margaret. His brain had been so preoccupied all day he hadn't prepped for this moment.

He swallowed and knocked on the heavy door and listened for a response. The windows were lit up, and he was glad to see the women had enough wood for now. He looked at the meager pile beside the house and decided he would ask Jasper to assist him with gathering wood for them in the morning.

His head swiveled as the door opened and he smiled at Margaret. She invited him in with a wave of her arm. "She's almost ready," Margaret said. She swatted his shoulder. "That's for telling her she could wear her dirty street clothes tonight."

"It's just a midwinter dance, Margaret." Leopold chuckled. "It's nothing fancy."

Margaret made a face at him. "A dance of any kind is the perfect chance for a young woman to get dressed up and be treated like a princess for a night."

Leopold saw the sparkle of amusement in her eye and smiled. "I'll remember that for next time."

Margaret watched him for a moment before pulling him in for a hug. "You're a good man, Leo," she whispered. "Thank you for taking care of my Meggy."

"She's special," Leo whispered. "How could I not?"

Margaret pulled away and nodded. "Good. Enjoy the dance. I am going to have dinner next door with Widow Jane." Margaret pulled a cloak from a hook beside the door. "I'll see you this evening, Meggy!" she called before she left.

Leopold turned to the fireplace in the quiet. He let the warmth and the light soothe his mind. He heard her step into the room and turned to see her standing awkwardly in the doorway. Her hands fluttered around her as if she didn't know what to do with them. "I suppose your mother knew best," he said with a smile. Her hair was braided with multiple braids crisscrossing around her head. Her dress was pale blue and tied at the waist with a brown cord. It was simple, but she made it elegant. He could also tell she had dressed in layers for the cold.

Megara smiled and spun in a circle for him to see. "Appropriate for a dance?"

"Of course. We could never doubt Margaret on fashion, can we?"

Megara grinned at him. "Absolutely not."

He helped her don a cloak then returned to the hearth and scraped ashes onto the coals to keep them warm but to extinguish the fire. When he was finished he returned to the door and opened it for Megara. He held his arm out for her and she slipped her hand around it and stepped closer to him. She was already shivering.

"Thank you for inviting me," she said. "I wouldn't have thought to come."

"I thought so. I want you to be able to enjoy all that Domum has to offer a young lady."

"Before we have to leave it again." She sighed.

He thought through his response. "I don't know how long we will be gone," he said. "But I will make sure you come home as soon as I can. I promise."

"You make an awful lot of promises."

"You deserve promises," he said. "You have missed out on so much because of the greed of one man. You deserve the world being handed to you."

Megara was quiet for several moments until they crossed the bridge to the old town. "Have you ever felt jealous of those with magic?"

He was surprised by the change of subject. "What? Why?"

"I was wondering if you ever felt bitter about it."

"Not at all," Leopold said with confidence.

"Why not?"

"It's never bothered me."

"Do you still worship the gods?"

Leopold hesitated, not sure what she was thinking. "Not as devotedly as I should. Where is this coming from, Meggy?"

"Zaccharia told me about the gods today."

"Oh!" Leopold searched for more to say. They were nearing the large meeting hall, which was mostly used for small winter gatherings. He didn't want to delve too deeply into such a big conversation right before they entered the crowded space. "I was angry with the gods when Merlin killed my father, but I have never been bitter about not having magic. That is something for others to study. It just doesn't affect me."

Megara was quiet as they reached the doors of the meeting hall. They could hear that the small group of village musicians inside had already begun. "I don't want you to resent me," Megara said as she pulled Leopold to a stop. "I don't want magic to come between us."

Leopold looked down at her. "Meggy, magic is a part of who you are. It could never come between us because it isn't a separate matter. Do you understand?"

Megara studied his eyes in the fading light. "I think so."

"Come on," he said as he held the door open. "Let us celebrate before we begin our next journey."

As Leopold showed Megara the village dances, he marveled at the way her smile made his heart beat faster. He watched as she twirled with Emaline and Adina. Other young men from the village took her hand in turn as well. Leopold wasn't prepared to admit to anyone that he loved this woman. He didn't want to trap her into anything she wasn't ready for, and he knew she wasn't ready for the kind of love he had to offer. As much as his mother or Emaline or anyone else may cajole him about getting married or even badger him about Megara herself, he was not going to be the one to divert her happiness. For now, he was content to let her smile light up the room. He was gratified by the blue skies that were so similar to the color of her eyes. He was satisfied by existing in the same space as her. One day, when he felt ready, he would tell her. Until then, these quiet conversations with her were enough.

Leopold thought about the journey he was about to lead. He knew waiting for instruction would feel as though the council was torturing him. He knew it was going to be difficult for all of them to leave Domum. Though he acknowledged all of this, he had a small voice in his mind telling him this was his path. He was meant for this journey, meant to take his loved ones and bring them home safely. He still felt rolling in his stomach from the nerves, but he could handle that as long as the little voice remained. They would go on the journey, they would return, and then he could enjoy some peace.

Leopold took Megara's last dance that evening. As he held her hands and swayed with her, he saw his future tying itself to hers. He had promised to stay with her and protect her, and he would honor that promise.

As the last song came to a close, Megara's expression changed. She stumbled as her gaze locked onto the entrance doors. One of them was wide open, the wind pushing it back and forth.

Leopold attempted to move her out of the way of oncoming dancers. "What is it?" he asked.

Megara blinked rapidly. "Don't you see it?" He could barely hear her over the music. He ducked his head closer to her.

"The door?"

Her face paled. The now constant creature of anxiety within him paused and seemed to lift its head. As he watched, her eyes rolled to the back of her head. He caught her as she fell—just as the fires around the room were extinguished and screams filled the air.

BONUS CONTENT

MARGARET

This chapter takes place concurrently with chapters six through ten.

Opening the door with her back, Margaret carried the tray of food out. The platter was meant for the festival. Though she hadn't prepared the meat herself she was happy to assist in the staging. It brought her great pleasure to see lovely things. Fine clothing, mostly, but there was beauty in so much around her. She made it her goal to find something beautiful everyday. It was easy today, the day of the harvest festival. The decorations were full of bright colors and the food smelled delicious, but the smiles upon her neighbors' faces were the best part.

Margaret set her load on the table and when she straightened she saw a green butterfly float past her ear. She watched as it floated toward Adina. The woman noticed the insect and looked for the source. It was clearly a creation of magic, it was getting too late in the season for such a creature to still be flying around. Margaret followed Adina's gaze as she smiled at a young girl and then knelt down to speak with her.

Margaret admired Adina. She had grown into such a beautiful woman. She possessed the kind leadership skills her father, Uther. She inherited her mother's beauty and wit. At twenty-six years old she was more accomplished than most other women her age in the village. Her priorities had always been different, though. Where other girls had grown up dreaming of charming princes rescuing them from dragons, Adina was practicing to take the dragon on all by herself.

She knew, though, that same stubbornness often got Adina into disagreements with her parents. For as big as the village had grown, rumors were still festering and cruel. Margaret could never be certain if the stories were based on facts or the imaginings of bored women, so she tried to steer away from them, but the sheer number which inferred trouble in the home was hard to ignore.

Margaret's eyes were caught by the council pageboy passing her, heading toward the crouched woman and her loyal companion. Margaret observed the messenger speak with Leopold before scurrying away. Leopold caught Adina's attention and they left the festival.

Margaret didn't know much about Leopold. She knew his mother very well and had watched the boy grow into a hard working man. He was known to help the farmers in the old town when he wasn't training with the knights. He was quieter than his brothers, that much Margaret had no doubt of. Aldus, the eldest, was soft spoken, but Margaret knew him to talk one's ear off once he spoke of his hobbies. Jasper was wild and unpredictable, but so very kind. If he stopped moving long enough to catch his breath, he always spoke sweetly. This knowledge was from nearly fifteen years ago, of course. She hadn't had much interaction with them recently. Which was why she wasn't very familiar with Leopold. He wasn't around often enough to make himself known.

Their mother and sister were frequent guests in Margaret's home for tea. Anora had always been supportive and had the right things to say. And Emaline was the ideal daughter. She was courteous and willing to put her hands to good use, and always polite. Margaret had been there when Emaline was born and though it had been one of the most emotionally draining days, (though, in that time what day wasn't emotionally draining?) it had also been one of the most beautiful. And watching her grow and mature had been one of the greatest joys of her life.

Margaret caught herself in her musings and hurried to return to the kitchens for another plate of food. The sun was reaching the highest point which meant the festival would be starting soon. As soon as the food was placed Uther would begin the celebrations. Margaret had once considered entering the world of baking. She'd been offered an apprenticeship before she was married, and was ready to accept it when the council had approached her and suggested a courtship between herself and her husband. All thoughts of baking had left her mind. After her darkest days, the apprenticeship had been offered to her again. She couldn't imagine following that path anymore and instead found herself spending time with Widow Jane, the dressmaker. Of course, Widow Jane hadn't been a widow when Margaret had started the journey. It had been something they commiserated over years later.

Widow Jane was gifted with creation magic. Margaret was not. She could not learn to use magic because she possessed none of it. She could, however, study Jane's work and create templates and learn from

Jane's skill. If Jane could think it, she could make it. And she taught Margaret how to have the same ability, minus the magic involvement. But that was just fine with Margaret. The pin pricks served to wake up or distract her mind. The mathematics and measurements provided a stimulation to organize her own thoughts. The beauty of new pieces gave her peace.

Once upon a time, she'd been surrounded by magic. Her boys had run around on four feet more often than two. And her husband's foresight often saved their crops without the help from the council prophets. Her young daughter had always made Margaret's life easier, and that was magic enough in itself. Having several years go by after her sons were born, she wasn't sure she'd ever be granted another child. When she was blessed with a daughter, she thought the bliss would kill her.

The bliss may not have, but she came close to surrendering to the pain just a few years later.

Margaret sat at the table with her hands in her lap. Her fingers twirled the smooth stone in her hand over and over as she waited for the rest of the crowd to take their seats. The anxiety within her bloomed bigger with every passing moment. She didn't like change, and this was new. Uther had not arrived. In fact, she could look around the tables and know not one of the council members had graced them with their presence yet. How many of these festivals had Margaret attended? And not once had they been tardy like this before.

She jumped when a hand touched her shoulder. She looked over and saw the council's messenger at her side. His eyes were sparkling with excitement. "Widow Margaret," he panted. "The council would like to speak with you."

Margaret immediately stood and followed the boy. Why would they wish to speak with her? She hadn't been in their presence as a whole in years. Almost two decades. The memory made her stomach rise in her throat.

Once they reached the council building she paused at the door. The boy ran ahead but she stayed. She brushed her hair behind her ears and ran her hands down her skirts to straighten them. She noticed with a pang of regret a bright red stain on the fabric against her thigh, likely from one of the dishes she had transported.

Margaret took a deep breath and blew it out slowly before she pushed the wooden door open and entered the meeting room. The air was stuffy. It took her eyes a moment to adjust to the torchlight within the room. The council rarely opened the windows, especially during the daylight. If the torches were to go out, she knew the space would be pitched so dark she'd have to feel her way to the rug.

Margaret hadn't been here frequently. Looking around she observed nothing had changed despite the years. The artwork was still the same. The rug on the floor was still a faded red. The chairs creaked as council members situated themselves. "Welcome, Margaret," Uther greeted with a smile.

Margaret nodded her head and tried to smile. "I must say I'm surprised by the summons," she told him. "I thought the festival would be starting soon."

"We'll go to that right after this," Uther chuckled. "I am very excited for the meal. I could almost smell it from here."

"It looks wonderful," Margaret agreed, uncertain.

Olympia cleared her throat and shot Uther a meaningful look. Uther nodded at her and looked at Margaret with a serious expression. "Margaret, we have some news for you. We wanted you to hear it first from us."

Margaret tried to understand what he was saying. What news could there be that she would need to know? "Is it something I will be able to assist with?" she asked. "I'm no magic user, but I'll do my best."

"It's more what we can do for you," Valeriana said gently. She was a tall and slender woman and often reminded Margaret of wheat with her blond hair plaited in many braids.

"I am not understanding," Margaret said.

Judd addressed her. His voice was softer and kinder than she had heard it before. The contrast shocked her.

"We have sent Adina and Leopold on a quest. The gods have told us how we can finally accomplish your desires. We're bringing Megara home."

The world stood still.

How many times had she stood in this exact spot and begged the council, begged Uther, to send someone for Megara?

How many times had she cried herself to sleep with her failing as a mother to keep her children safe?

She had given up hope years ago of her daughter's return to her.

"How is that possible?" Margaret breathed, tears filling her eyes.

"The gods have always been aware of her," Gavin said. Her eyes slid to him. The man wasn't much older than her. They had been acquaintances and courted for company several years ago, but it never amounted to anything. She had told him things she had never put words to before. He, above all people, knew what this would mean to her. "They have been waiting for the right moment to bring her home. We may never know what their purposes were, but they've decided it's time for Meggy to come home."

A sob broke from Margaret. She felt weak. Gloriana rushed from her seat and grasped Margaret about the waist, holding her steady and ordering the messenger boy to bring forth a stool. When he produced one, Gloriana helped her sit. She knelt at her side and held her hand. "Tell me more," Margaret begged. "Tell me everything."

"The gods came to Ibb and Judd," Uther told her. "They said it was time to bring her home. They sent a warning, though. Megara has experienced great tribulations in her life. She will need sufficient time to heal. She's desperate for family, Margaret, desperate for you. But by the time Adina and Leopold reach her she will have suffered a loss of her own—her identity. She won't know where she belongs. And, there's one more thing you should be aware of."

Olympia squeezed Margaret's hand who spared her a quick glance before looking back to Uther with baited breath.

Edith spoke instead. "Merlin is dead, dear," she said with great kindness. "At Megara's hand."

Margaret felt her heart could not handle any more. Her only daughter was coming home, after eighteen long years she would see her baby again. But she had been mistreated those many long years by Merlin. The monster who stole her in the first place. It hadn't been enough to separate her from her mother, to kill her father and brothers, the brute had tortured her daughter to the point where she had to retaliate in the darkest manner.

"What do the gods say I should do?" Margaret asked, her spine straightening.

"Just love her," Gavin told her. "Be her mother. The gods will work on her soul, you need to heal her heart."

"You have the council's support," Edith said. "We will be here for you the whole way. Please do not hesitate to ask for help."

"I don't have the power to demand answers of the gods," Judd told her. "But I can take any question you may have to them and we can pray they will respond."

Margaret took a deep breath, squeezed Olympia's hand, and stood. "When will they be returning?" she asked.

"Only the gods know," Ibb said in her childish voice. "But, we believe about a week. That will give them time to travel to Camelot, find her, and bring her home."

Camelot. This whole time, Megara had been only days away from her in *Camelot*.

Margaret nodded. "I cannot thank you enough," she said with tears in her voice. "Thank you for bringing my baby home."

"May the gods prepare you," Uther said. "We wish you comfort."

Margaret nodded and accepted her dismissal.

She was still standing on the bridge when the council members left their building and headed across the river to the festival. She couldn't make her feet move. Her eyes stared at the mouth of the river which led to the sea. So much time had passed. Margaret had not been a mother in eighteen years. She didn't know where to begin in her attempt to make up for that. What would she say? What would they do?

I wonder what she looks like.

When Megara had been born she had been very attentive. Her eyes were always wide open and she'd giggle when she watched her brothers. She had barely begun to toddle around town when she was stolen. Even at that age, Margaret knew her daughter would be special. It sounded as though she'd been in the gods' sights all this time. What sort of things did they permit her to experience? Margaret feared the worst. All in the guise of preparation, or to make her stronger. She was not one to question the gods, but in this she would never be able to understand.

Margaret heard someone approaching across the bridge. The sun was setting and Margaret realized she was very hungry. "Hello, my friend," Anora greeted cheerfully. She and Emaline were walking arm in arm back across the bridge to the old town where they lived. "I didn't see you at the festival."

"Is it over already?" Margaret mused, not realizing how much time had passed while she stood frozen on the bridge.

"What's wrong?" Anora's forehead creased in concern. Emaline's expression was as perplexed as her mother's.

Margaret reached her hand forward and took her friend's. "Nothing, and everything," Margaret shook her head and huffed a sigh. "May we go to your house to speak?"

"Of course." Anora let go of her daughter and instead placed Margaret's arm through her own, keeping their hands together. Emaline took up Margaret's other side as they walked quickly along the paths. Once they reached the home Emaline rushed forward and lit a candle for the dining table. Anora helped Margaret to a seat and sat beside her. "Now, tell me what has happened."

Margaret's eyes filled with tears again as she smiled at her friend. "The council sent Leo and Adina on a quest."

"Yes, he told me," Anora nodded. "I helped him gather provisions before he left. Did the council tell you where they were going?" Her voice sounded confused, leaning toward envious.

Margaret took her hands again. "They've been sent for my Meggy," Margaret breathed. The tears fell freely. Anora's eyes widened and her jaw dropped. "The council is finally bringing Megara home to me."

"They've found her?" Emaline demanded. Margaret jumped and looked at the young woman. She had forgotten Emaline was present.

Margaret nodded with a grin. "They found her, and they're bringing her home."

Anora sat back in her chair, her eyes gazing off into the distance. "Meggy," she breathed. She shook her head. "What else did they say? Did they tell you why they sent my son?"

"I don't know why they sent who they did," Margaret sighed. "I wish they would have told me sooner so I could accompany them."

"I understand that," Anora nodded. She waited for Margaret to speak more.

"They . . . the council also told me something else. Something about Merlin."

Anora's expression changed to ice. "Merlin?" she asked in a monotone voice.

"Meggy killed him," Margaret said, easing the words out of her lips. Anora blinked several times and shook her head.

"What?"

"The council said Megara killed Merlin."

The silence in the room was thick.

"Merlin is dead?" Emaline asked. Margaret nodded. Emaline stood from the table and left the room. Margaret traced her movement then addressed her friend, still staring at the door closing behind the girl.

"Should I not have said that?" Margaret asked.

"Emaline has only heard stories," Anora reminded her. "She was born after Merlin left. I will check in with her later on how she's feeling about it. But I want to know about how you are right now. Meggy coming home. I can't even imagine what you're thinking."

Margaret wiped the tears from her eyes and smiled. "I feel like pieces are fitting together," she said. "The pain has eased over time, but now the hole is prepared to be filled. I wish the rest of my family could return to me as well, of course, but my baby girl . . ." Margaret swallowed and her eyebrows pulled together as she looked at her friend, desperate. "I don't know how to be a mother anymore," she said. "It's been so long . . . and she's not a baby now. I don't know how to parent her. The gods said I just have to love her, and of course I will, but how do I be a mother?"

Anora smiled and wiped tears from Margaret's cheeks. "You'll be a natural," she whispered. "As soon as she's in your arms you'll know what to do. It will take time to get to know each other, but you can do it."

"What do you do?" she asked.

"There's no training for it," Anora sighed. "What works for me won't work for you. I don't have a twenty year old daughter. My boys are grown, but they're a whole other experience."

"How do you feel about Leo going?"

"Now that I know where he's off to, much better. I don't like him being so far from me, but I know he's doing a good thing. So that makes it easier."

"I wouldn't have chosen anyone else," Margaret said with confidence. "There is no one better. It has come full circle."

The next morning Uther called a village meeting and informed them Megara would be coming home. He left out the details but instructed the village to welcome her with open arms. He advised them that she would have a hard time adjusting to village life and to be patient. Some rumors began to fly about her and how she spent her life. Margaret spent a lot of her time telling people the same answers.

"Yes, of course, I'm very excited."

"I'm a little nervous, but I am so happy she's coming home."

"No, there's nothing you can do for me right now."

"I don't know what strength of healing magic she possesses."

"Only the gods will know."

Margaret had spoken with the map maker Gaius and asked him for his best estimate of travel time. He had assured her it would be around a week for them to return. "My calculations tell me it will take them four days to travel to Camelot. Adina made it sound as though they wouldn't be in Camelot very long before making the return journey."

As the days passed Margaret spent her free time preparing her home. It started when she woke the morning of the third day to see her bedroom had become cluttered with clothing needing to be washed and projects sitting unfinished. She tidied her room and realized her entertaining area was covered in dust and dirt. After work she returned home and began conquering that room.

On the morning of the fourth day Margaret left her home for work and realized how overrun her garden had become. She vowed to care for it on the days she wasn't in the shop, which would be a couple days before Megara's return. *It will look fresh and clean for her when she arrives,* she decided. That whole day her mind played through variations of possibility. *They should be finding her today. How will that look? How will they find her? Will they go to the home she's been living in? Will they find her working in fields or in a trade? Will she have lots of friends she needs to say goodbye to? Will she be hesitant to return?*

Does she even know her own history?

Widow Jane had to ease Margaret to a chair when she began to hyperventilate. She sent one of the younger girls to bring Margaret a cup of water. "Good gracious," Jane griped. "What's gotten into you, girl?" They did not have a large age difference between them, but Jane insisted Margaret was still worthy of the moniker.

"What if she doesn't want to come home?" Margaret gasped. She began to rock back and forth on her seat. "What if they find her and she says she doesn't want to return with them? What will they do? What if they leave her there and give up?"

"This is Adina you're talking about," Jane reassured her. "That girl doesn't know what it means to give up."

"What if Megara is too stubborn and refuses?"

"The council said the gods are involved in this quest. Do you believe they will bring her home if that's what they promised? That's what this comes down to, girl. Do you trust the gods?"

Margaret twisted her smooth stone in her fingers and bit her lip as she considered the question. It had been years since she had prayed to the gods. Years since she offered them any worship. Would they punish her for that by getting her hopes up and letting her fall?

Jane patted Margaret's hand as if she could read her mind. "I have enough faith for the both of us," she assured her. "Why don't you take the afternoon off? Go visit your husband and boys. You deserve a break. In fact, I don't want to see you back in my shop until after Megara is home. Do you understand, girl? Do not come back here."

Margaret took a deep breath. "I understand."

"If you need me, send a message. But don't come back."

Margaret stood and hugged her oldest friend. "Thank you."

"Get out of here, girl."

Margaret took the trek into the old town. Across the river was the part of the village which had originally been settled. The water had acted as a barrier originally, so the first pioneers had built their home on the other side. As the community grew, eventually land was cleared on the north side of the river because they could only go so far south.

At the center of the old town was the original meeting hall. The company had used it to conduct official business before the population had grown too much to do so. The council then got their own building, but most village gatherings took place in the new part of town, in the town square. To the west of the meeting hall was the cemetery. Trees had been cleared every fifty years or so since then to accommodate more space. It was what had forced homes to be built north of the river, no one wanted to run out of space for the cemetery.

Margaret paused at the edge of the trees and took a breath. She could see through the few trunks which served as a boundary to the cemetery, to the large clearing behind. She closed her eyes. It had been months since she had come here. She used to be much better about it. Shortly after they had been buried, Margaret had been stopping by to see her family every morning. Anora and Jane intervened until Margaret agreed to spend only one evening a week there, to allow herself time to live her new life and find healing. As she found distance it did give her a chance to heal and her weekly visits turned to every two weeks, then three, then monthly. Then only on the special anniversaries and birthdays.

She had intended to visit and tell them the news, but guilt held her back. Could she tell her dead husband and sons that she was excited her living daughter was returning to her? Could she tell them how relieved she was to have family again?

Passing through the tree line was like entering a new world. The sounds quieted and the air became peaceful. Even the birds quieted and calmed. She made her way to their graves. Her eyes clung to familiar names on the newer headstones almost as if it were a distraction meant to make this visit easier. When she finally reached the three slim stones marking their final resting places she kissed her fingertips and touched each plaque before kneeling in front of the one on the farthest edge.

CLARENCE ADAMS

She let out a shaky breath and traced her fingers over his name.

"She's coming home, my love. Our Meggy. The gods have told the council at last how to find her. They've sent two of the most dedicated soldiers to get her. Adina Hawkins–Uther's eldest–and Leopold Sanders. You remember him, I'm sure. They're well known in the town for their services. The council sent them to bring her home.

"I'm worried, love. I'm worried about so much. What if I can't be her mother? What if she doesn't come home? What if she comes home and hates it here, hates me? I feel as though I can't sit still. I keep finding things to clean or things to repair before Meggy could see how disorganized I have become.

"I'm truly a mess," Margaret chuckled. "You wouldn't recognize our home. Although . . . I guess you never saw this home. I live alone now so I moved into a smaller one a few years ago. I don't remember if I told you that. I'm sure I did, it was a hard decision and very scary to move to a new home by myself. I had been hoping it would be a fresh start. Sometimes the house feels empty though.

"But now Megara is coming, maybe it won't feel so lonely." She sighed. "I miss you, love. And the boys. I wish you could be welcoming her home with me. I wish our lives had not been so uprooted. I wish you were here. I am always thinking of you, in everything I do. Every second of every day I am thinking of you and our boys." She looked at the other two stones. "I hope you boys are keeping your father on his toes. I hope you know I miss you, too, and your silly pranks. I miss your smile, Colin. It brought sunshine to my life. And Conor, your laugh was sweeter than birdsong." Tears filled her eyes. She could barely remember either of those qualities. But she knew from her journals how precious they had been to her.

"I'll try to be the best mom I can be," she promised her family. "But if you know of any way to help me, I would appreciate all the assistance you can give me."

Margaret stood after several minutes of imagining their responses. She sat with her face tilted to the sun and her eyes closed, appreciating the warmth on her skin and peacefulness of the grove. She pushed herself to her feet. "I suppose I should use this break from Jane to prepare the home some more. I need to finish the garden. Maybe I'll sew her a new dress. Though, I don't know what she will look like or her sizes so I suppose that wouldn't work. I'll think of something, though. Goodbye, my love. Boys, know that I love all of you." She kissed her fingertips once more and touched them each before leaving the grove.

They were late.

Margaret had a hard time going to sleep on the evening of the eighth day. She paced anxiously long after the fire had died. She knew Gaius and the council could be wrong about the dates, but she couldn't sleep all the same. The anxiety ate her alive. She was wearing a path in her floor by the time the sun rose the next morning.

She rushed to the door the moment she heard a knock. She felt as though she would be sick. She pulled it open with bated breath before letting it out in a huff. Widow Jane stood on the stoop with a basket. "Good morning to you, too, girl," she said as she pushed her way past Margaret. "Did you get any sleep at all?"

"None. Why aren't they here yet?"

"Travel can be unpredictable," Jane reminded her. She was pulling various baked goods from her basket. "Sit, girl. It's time to break your fast."

"I don't think I can eat," Margaret argued.

Jane glared at her and pointed to the chair. "You will if I have to push it down your pretty throat myself."

Margaret knew it was no idle threat.

The moment the flaky crust touched her tongue, though, Margaret's stomach rumbled angrily. She couldn't remember eating the day before at all. She inhaled the pastries without any more argument.

Hours after Jane had left, Anora arrived to check on her. Margaret had a sneaky suspicion she'd be receiving a lot of visits as the days moved on. After her visit with Jane Margaret had felt much calmer about the tardiness of the party. After Anora left, Margaret felt more like herself. She was able to hum again. She was able to breathe without the paralyzing fear.

Anora had brought some tea with her, and Margaret had counted that as her midday meal. She stood next to her hearth and stirred the stew she was preparing for dinner. She would not allow herself to go hungry this night. She knew it had been foolish to forgo the sustenance the day before. If she was going to be prepared for Megara's return, she would have to take better care of herself.

Her shutters were open to allow for fresh air through the house, the air moving the curtains slightly. She listened to the laughter of the children outside as they played. She tasted the stew, ensuring no more herbs would need to be added when she heard his voice.

"This is it. This is Margaret's house. She moved into a smaller one after . . . well, when she was alone."

Margaret froze with the spoon inches from her lips. Her heart began to thud in her ribs. She nearly knocked her pot in her hurry to place the spoon inside and remove her apron. She rushed to the door and threw it open, her excitement making her head feel fuzzy. She blinked several times at the couple before her.

There Leopold stood, his chin high and a soft smile on his face. And behind him Margaret could see a blond head hiding in his shadow. A tear slipped down Margaret's cheek. "Meggy?" she croaked.

Leopold turned his back to Margaret. There were several heartbeats of hesitation before he began walking backwards toward the door, toward Margaret. Margaret pulled her stone from her pocket and began twisting it quickly, gnawing on her lip. *She's really here.*

They reached the stoop and Leopold stepped to the side, allowing Margaret a full view of her daughter.

Her breath caught in her throat as she stared. She hadn't come to a clear conclusion on her guess for what her child would look like, but this was nothing like she imagined.

Margaret felt as though she were looking into a cracked mirror. She saw herself, but the image was wrong. Megara looked as though the breeze would knock her down, she was so frail. Her hair was limp and matted. Her eyes were dull. Her cheeks sallow.

Megara stretched thin fingers toward her mother, hesitating in uncertainty.

Margaret closed the distance between their fingers, a sob making its way out of her throat. Megara's eyes widened and she stepped forward and enveloped her mother in a hug. She was so thin Margaret could touch opposing elbows with her hands while her arms were around her daughter.

"Hello, mother," Megara whispered in her ear.

Margaret inhaled for what seemed like the first time in eighteen years. She pulled her daughter into her home and closed the door securely behind them.

References

Council

Creation - Edith and Leif

   Prophecy - Ibb and Judd

   Healing - Stace and (Uther) Zaccharia

   Psychokinesis - Valeriana and Roland

   Language - Olympia and Gavin

   Shapeshifting - Glorianna and Henry

Gods

The Nameless Goddess - Goddess of creation and shapeshifting

   Raphael - God of healing

   Bridget - Goddess of time

   Prudentia - Goddess of guidance

   Ohad - God of skills and language

Translations

Pulchra Arcanum - Beautiful Secrets

   Lingua Mortuorum - Tongue of the Dead

   Movere triticum - Move wheat

   Mutare ad mus - Change to mouse

   Redi ad me - Return to myself

   Superus - Otherworldly

   Intellege - Understand

   Ignis flammans - Flaming fire

   Febricitantem - Relieve the fever

   Pulchra papilio - Beautiful butterfly

   Mihi nomen est Olympia. Verba tua magica non sunt. Expediam. -
My name is Olympia. Your words are not magic. I will explain.

Acknowledgements

I have so many people from this journey to thank. From the very beginning, thank you to Cameron, my wonderful husband. I wrote the first draft two months after we were married. This was the first time you had seen my completely insane writing process. You read every day's progress. You supported the work with so much chocolate and love. Thank you for seeing me at my lowest and encouraging me forward.

At the same time, I'd like to thank my alpha readers, Samantha, Krystel, and Emery. You read the first draft as it was born, and I am grateful for your encouragement and the questions that helped this story come into the world. And thank you for the many beta readers who shared their opinions—whether I appreciated them at the time or not.

Thank you to the woman I have looked up to since middle school: Karen Hoover. You were my introduction to the publishing world. You have been so excited for me every step of the way. Thank you for always being willing to share your knowledge and resources. I will never stop being grateful for your existence in my life.

Sabrina! My husband's best friend's wife. My daughter's godmother. My best friend. We met through mere happenstance, and you chose to love me where I am. Your friendship has been the purest I have ever experienced. Your excitement after you read the abandoned first draft is what convinced me to finish the story. It's always uncomfortable to read things from friends, especially the ugly beginnings. I am so grateful you took the chance and fell in love with this story and then decided to celebrate my works so much. Thank you for helping me find joy again in writing.

I also need to thank Jessica Guernsey. I felt so immature when I met you. Half the time, I still do. I admire the confidence and courage you have in your life, specifically your teaching and writing. I have appreciated your mentorship and your natural means of supporting new (and experienced) authors reach their goals. Thank you for putting up with my hounding and relentless questions. I owe so much to your continued support and motivation.

Lastly and certainly not least, I need to sincerely and gratefully acknowledge my editor Tristi Pinkston for her consistently gentle and thoughtful guidance. She worked tirelessly and kindly to ensure this book was polished with care as quickly as possible. Her insightful suggestions were delivered gently, always encouragingly, and skillfully, making this process more enjoyable and rewarding than I ever thought possible. I truly appreciate her endlessly dedicated patience and expertise which contributed so greatly to this work.

When I began my writing journey I never realized how many people touch an author's work before it reaches the readers. I am blessed beyond measure to have supporters like all of you. Thank you.

About the author

Mandy resides in Northern Utah with her husband, their daughter, and their two dogs. She holds a degree in social work which compliments her degree in criminal justice. She has dedicated her career to child welfare, a field she is deeply passionate about.

In her literary pursuits, Mandy has made a mark with her debut novel, My World of Glass, published in 2018, with the audiobook version released in 2023. Additionally, she authored two novellas during her high school years, both of which garnered local recognition and acclaim.

As a writer, Many finds that the realm of fiction serves as a powerful outlet for processing her experiences and emotions, allowing her to weave intricate narratives that resonate with her readers. She supports the claim that anyone can be an author—you just have to start.

Connect with Mandy online at
www.mandytremelling.com and social media.